NEW TOEIC

特蒐！ 新多益聽力、閱讀模擬試題，
累積實力，邁向「金色證書」殿堂

關鍵 金色 字彙1200

書林編輯部/著

國家圖書館出版品預行編目資料

NEW TOEIC 關鍵金色字彙1200 / 書林編輯部 編著.－－
　一版－－臺北市：書林，2011.11
　面；　公分－－（應試高手；14）
　ISBN　978-957-445-432-7（平裝附光碟片）

　1. 多益測驗　　2. 詞彙

805.1895　　　　　　　　　　　　　　　100019852

應試高手 14
NEW TOEIC 關鍵金色字彙 1200

編　　　　著　書林編輯部
執 行 編 輯　劉怡君
校　　　對　王建文・李虹慧
英 文 顧 問　Lynn Sauvé
出 版 者　書林出版有限公司
地　　　址　100台北市羅斯福路四段60號三樓
　　　　　　Tel: (02) 2368-4938　2365-8617　Fax: (02) 2368-8929　2363-6630
台北書林書店　106台北市新生南路三段88號2樓之5　　Tel (02)2365-8617
學 校 業 務 部　Tel (02) 2368-7226・(04) 2376-3799・(07) 229-0300
經 銷 業 務 部　Tel (02) 2368-4938
發 行 人　蘇正隆
郵　　　撥　15743873・書林出版有限公司
登 記 證　局版臺業字第一八三一號
出 版 日 期　2011年11月一版初刷，2018年7月七刷
定　　　價　280元
I　S　B　N　978-957-445-432-7

NEW TOEIC

關鍵金色 字彙1200

書林編輯部/著

Table of Contents

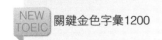

認識多益測驗

什麼是多益測驗？

　　TOEIC 代表 Test of English for International Communication（國際溝通英語測驗）。多益測驗乃針對英語非母語人士所設計之英語能力測驗，測驗分數反映受測者在國際職場環境中與他人以英語溝通的熟稔程度。參加本測驗毋需具備專業的知識或字彙，因為測驗內容以日常使用之英語為主。多益測驗是以職場為基準點的英語能力測驗中，世界最頂級的考試。在 2010 年全球有超過六百萬人報考多益測驗，並在 120 個國家中有超過 10,000 家的企業、學校或政府機構採用多益測驗，同時在全球超過 165 個國家是最廣為接受且最方便報考的英語測驗之一。

多益測驗的內容

　　多益的設計，以職場的需要為主。測驗題的內容，從全世界各地職場的英文資料中蒐集而來，題材多元化，包含各種地點與狀況。

一般商務	契約、談判、行銷、銷售、商業企劃、會議
製造業	工廠管理、生產線、品管
金融／預算	銀行業務、投資、稅務、會計、帳單
企業發展	研究、產品研發
辦公室	董事會、委員會、信件、備忘錄、電話、傳真、電子郵件、辦公室器材與傢俱、辦公室流程
人事	招考、雇用、退休、薪資、升遷、應徵與廣告
採購	比價、訂貨、送貨、發票
技術層面	電子、科技、電腦、實驗室與相關器材、技術規格
房屋／公司地產	建築、規格、購買租賃、電力瓦斯服務
旅遊	火車、飛機、計程車、巴士、船隻、渡輪、票務、時刻表、車站、機場廣播、租車、飯店、預訂、脫班與取消
外食	商務／非正式午餐、宴會、招待會、餐廳訂位
娛樂	電影、劇場、音樂、藝術、媒體
保健	醫藥保險、看醫生、牙醫、診所、醫院

多益測驗方式

第一大類：聽力

總共有一百題，共有四大題。考生會聽到各種各類英語的直述句、問句、短對話以及短獨白，然後根據所聽到的內容回答問題。聽力的考試時間大約為四十五分鐘。

- ✍ 第一大題：照片描述　十題（四選一）
- ✍ 第二大題：應答問題　三十題（三選一）
- ✍ 第三大題：簡短對話　三十題（四選一）
- ✍ 第四大題：簡短獨白　三十題（四選一）

第二大類：閱讀

總共有一百題，題目及選項都印在題本上。考生須閱讀多種題材的文章，然後回答相關問題。考試時間為七十五分鐘，考生可在時限內依自己能力調配閱讀及答題速度。

- ✍ 第五大題：單句填空　四十題（四選一）
- ✍ 第六大題：短文填空　十二題（四選一）
- ✍ 第七大題：單篇文章理解　二十八題（四選一）
  　　　　　　雙篇文章理解　　二十題（四選一）

考生選好答案後，要在與題目卷分開的答案卷上劃卡。雖然答題時間約為兩小時，但考試時考生尚須在答案卷上填寫個人資料，並簡短的回答關於教育與工作經歷的問卷，因此真正待在考場內時間會較長。

多益測驗計分方式

考生用鉛筆在電腦答案卷上作答。考試分數由答對題數決定，再將每一大類（聽力類、閱讀類）答對題數轉換成分數，範圍在 5 到 495 分之間。兩大類加起來即為總分，範圍在 10 到 990 分之間。答錯不倒扣。

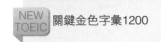

多益成績與英語能力參照

TOEIC 成績	語言能力	證照顏色
905~990	英文能力十分近似於英語母語人士，能夠流暢有條理表達意見、參與談話，主持英文會議、調和衝突並做出結論，語言使用上即使有瑕疵，亦不會造成理解上的困擾。	金色 (860~990)
785~900	可有效地運用英文滿足社交及工作上所需，措辭恰當、表達流暢；但在某些等定情形下，如：面臨緊張壓力、討論話題過於冷僻艱澀時，仍會顯現出語言能力不足的情況。	藍色 (730~855)
605~780	可以英語進行一般社交場會的談話，能夠應付例行性的業務需求，參加英文會議，聽取大部份要點；但無法流利的以英語發表意見、作辯論，使用的字彙、句型也以一般常見為主。	綠色 (470~725)
405~600	英文文字溝通能力尚可，會話方面稍嫌辭彙不足、語句簡單，但已能掌握少量相關語言，可以從事英語相關程度較低的工作。	棕色 (220~465)
255~400	語言能力僅僅侷限在簡單的一般日常生活對話，同時無法做連續性交談，亦無法用英文工作。	橘色 (10~215)
10~250	只能以背誦的句子進行問答而不能自行造句，尚無法將英文當作溝通工具來使用。	

NEW TOEIC 關鍵金色字彙 1200 使用說明

1 英文字彙通常有多個意思，本書採用該字於多益考試中最常測驗的意思及用法，幫助集中學習，節省準備多益測驗時間。

2 本書每頁均有此虛線，其作用在於方便讀者複習字彙，沿著虛線向外摺頁，可立即小試身手，檢測學習效果。

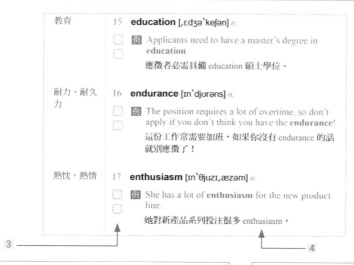

3 當您做完第一次測驗時，可在第一個方塊中註記測試結果（如沒有問題，可於方塊上✔；還需要再加強，就在方塊上打✘，您可以依照自己的習慣加上符號或日期，記錄學習成果）。第二個方塊的使用方式同上。

4 本書中的中文例句保留該字的英文，此一編排方式可讓您於中文例句中再次記憶該字的用法及意思，學習效果加乘。

考前 30 天衝刺計畫

☐ **Day 1** ■ 1.1 Recruitment ability~switch 實力累積： 49 words	☐ **Day 2** ■ 1.2 Employment accurately~workplace ■ 1.3 Promotion assignment~respect 實力累積： 118 words	☐ **Day 3** ■ 1.4 Salaries & Benefits allowance~welfare 實力累積： 153 words + 20 questions
☐ **Day 4** ■ 2.1 Enterprise access~vote 實力累積： 203 words	☐ **Day 5** ■ 2.2 Company Ranking administrator~worker ■ 3.1 Supplies & Equipment acquainted~documentary 實力累積： 251 words + 40 questions + 1 Mini Toeic	☐ **Day 6** ■ 3.1 Supplies & Equipment email~whiteboard 實力累積： 296 words
☐ **Day 7** ■ 3.2 At the Office appointment~post 實力累積： 352 words	☐ **Day 8** ■ 3.2 At the Office print~website ■ 3.3 Meeting & Presentation advance~inquire 實力累積： 400 words	☐ **Day 9** ■ 3.3 Meeting & Presentation interrupt~workshop 實力累積： 438 words
☐ **Day 10** ■ 3.4 Building architecture~utility 實力累積： 478 words + 60 questions	☐ **Day 11** ■ 4.1 Advertising absorb~potential 實力累積： 525 words	☐ **Day 12** ■ 4.1 Advertising preliminary~trend ■ 4.2 Marketing aggressive~management 實力累積： 577 words
☐ **Day 13** ■ 4.2 Marketing market~wealthy 實力累積： 612 words + 80 questions + 2 Mini Toeic	☐ **Day 14** ■ 5.1 Air Travel am~landing 實力累積： 660 words	☐ **Day 15** ■ 5.1 Air Travel Lost and Found~turbulence ■ 5.2 Accommodation accomodation~voucher 實力累積： 709 words

Day 16	Day 17	Day 18
■ 5.3 Schedule Arrangement accelerate~visit	■ 5.4 Transportation avenue~wheel	■ 6.1 Dining attend~tray
實力累積： 746 words	實力累積： 774 words + 100 questions	實力累積： 814 words
Day 19	Day 20	Day 21
■ 6.2 Art & Music antique~violinist ■ 6.3 Plays & Movies attractive~theater	■ 6.4 Leisure & Hobbies acquaintance~vegetarian	■ 7.1 Accounting accountant~yearly
實力累積： 858 words	實力累積： 884 words + 120 questions + 3 Mini Toeic	實力累積： 928 words
Day 22	Day 23	Day 24
■ 7.2 Assets afford~tenant ■ 8.1 Purchasing approve~rebate	■ 8.1 Purchasing receipt~vend ■ 8.2 Logistics airmail~X-ray	■ 8.2 Logistics
實力累積： 980 words + 140 questions	實力累積： 1037 words	實力累積： 1037 words + 160 questions + 4 Mini Toeic
Day 25	Day 26	Day 27
■ 9.1 Equipment advanced~wire ■ 9.2 Production amazing~industrial	■ 9.2 Production invention~technician	■ 10.1 Contract agreement~term ■ 10.2 Legal Affairs accumulate~stressful
實力累積： 1099 words	實力累積： 1147 words + 180 questions	實力累積： 1198 words
Day 28	Day 29	Day 30
■ 10.3 Tax advantage~violation	■ Review 1.1~5.4	■ Review 6.1-10.3
實力累積： 1227 words + 200 questions + 5 Mini Toeic	實力累積： 1227 words + 200 questions + 5 Mini Toeic	實力累積： 1227 words + 200 questions + 5 Mini Toeic

Chapter 1
Personnel 人事

At the beginning of the employment process, a company matches an open position with someone who is looking for a job. A successful candidate must have the education and skills that the company needs. After being hired, an employee may stay in the same job, or get promoted to a higher position. Company policies control the employee's benefits and working hours.

Personnel
人事

1 Recruitment 徵聘人員 ①

能力

1 **ability** [əˈbɪlətɪ] *n.*

☐ 例 This job requires the **ability** to speak both English and French.

這份工作需要英法語 ability。

學術的

2 **academic** [ˌækəˈdɛmɪk] *adj.*

☐ 例 We are looking for an office administrator with a solid **academic** background.

我們正在找具有紮實 academic 背景的行政人員。

口音，腔調

3 **accent** [ˈæksɛnt] *n.*

☐ 例 Our company is looking for native English speakers with a British **accent**.

本公司徵求母語為英語，且具英國 accent 的人士。

成就；專長

4 **accomplishment** [əˈkɑmplɪʃmənt] *n.*

☐ 例 Being able to speak English fluently is one of Amy's many **accomplishments**.

會說一口流利的英文是艾美的許多 accomplishments 之一。

適用於

5 **applicable** [ˈæplɪkəb!] *adj.*

☐ 例 This training is **applicable** to new employees.

這項訓練 applicable 新進員工。

6 application [ˌæpləˈkeʃən] *n.*　　申請表

例 If you want to work here, you need to fill out this **application**.

如果你想要在這工作，必須填寫這份 application。

7 apply for [əˈplaɪˈfɔr] *phr.*　　申請

例 Many graduates **apply for** internships at big corporations.

許多畢業生會 apply for 到大公司實習。

8 attachment [əˈtætʃmənt] *n.*　　附件

例 I emailed my resume as an **attachment**.

我以 attachment 形式寄出履歷表。

9 background [ˈbækˌɡraʊnd] *n.*　　背景，學經歷

例 Candidates need to have a **background** in law to be considered for the position.

應徵該職位的人必須有法律 background。

10 candidate [ˈkændəˌdet] *n.*　　（競選或求職的）候選人

例 Over one thousand **candidates** are competing for the position.

超過一千名 candidates 在競爭這個職位。

11 capable [ˈkepəbl̩] *adj.*　　有能力，能夠

例 Jack is **capable** of juggling many tasks at the same time.

傑克 capable 同時處理多件工作。

證書	12	**certificate** [sə`tɪfəkɪt] *n.*

例 A **certificate** in English will help you find a better job.

擁有英文 certificate 可以幫你找到較好的工作。

首要的	13	**chief** [tʃif] *adj.*

例 Betty always considers her multicultural background her **chief** asset.

貝蒂一直認為多元文化背景是她最 chief 本錢。

勝任	14	**competent** [`kɑmpətənt] *adj.*

例 It's too early to say if he is **competent** enough to do this job.

要說他是否能 competent 這份工作還言之過早。

教育	15	**education** [ˌɛdʒə`keʃən] *n.*

例 Applicants need to have a master's degree in **education**.

應徵者必需具備 education 碩士學位。

耐力，耐久力	16	**endurance** [ɪn`djʊrəns] *n.*

例 The position requires a lot of overtime, so don't apply if you don't think you have the **endurance**!

這份工作常需要加班，如果你沒有 endurance 的話就別應徵了！

熱忱，熱情	17	**enthusiasm** [ɪn`θjuzɪˌæzəm] *n.*

例 She has a lot of **enthusiasm** for the new product line.

她對新產品系列投注很多 enthusiasm。

18 **experience** [ɪkˈspɪrɪəns] *n.*　　　　經驗

例 You need to have enough work **experience** to get the job.

你需要足夠的工作 experience 才能獲該職位。

19 **expert** [ˈɛkspɝt] *n.*　　　　專家，行家

例 Tina is the **expert** when it comes to accounting.

蒂娜是會計 expert。

✦ 20 **expertise** [ˌɛkspɝˈtiz] *n.*　　　　專長，技能

例 David's **expertise** is in computer programming.

寫電腦程式是大衛的 expertise。

21 **fit** [fɪt] *v.*　　　　適合

例 This candidate's qualifications **fit** the position perfectly.

這位應徵者的資格非常 fit 這個職位。

22 **hire** [haɪr] *v.*　　　　聘僱，雇用

例 The company has stopped **hiring** people due to their tight budget.

這家公司因為預算緊縮而不再 hiring 人了。

23 **impressive** [ɪmˈprɛsɪv] *adj.*　　　　令人印象深刻的

例 In order to get a job interview, you need to have an **impressive** resume.

為了能有面試的機會，你必須寫份 impressive 履歷。

代替，取代	**24**	**instead** [ɪnˋstɛd] *adv.*
	例	More and more companies prefer outsourcing work **instead** of hiring new people.
		越來越多的公司傾向工作外包 instead 雇用新人。
求職者	**25**	**job hunter** [ˋjɑbˋhʌntɚ] *n.*
	例	Many **job hunters** have difficulty finding a job they like.
		許多 job hunters 很難找到他們喜歡的工作。
…活，勞動	**26**	**labor** [ˋlebɚ] *n.*
	例	The warehouse position isn't suitable for applicants who can't endure hard **labor**.
		倉庫的工作不適合做不了粗 labor 的人。
執照，許可證	**27**	**license** [ˋlaɪsn̩s] *n.*
	例	You need to have a special **license** to drive the truck.
		你要有特別的 license 才能駕駛卡車。
獲得	**28**	**obtain** [əbˋten] *v.*
	例	You need to obtain a certified copy of your diploma to complete your application.
		你需要 obtain 一份合格的學位副本才能完成申請。
職缺	**29**	**opening** [ˋopənɪŋ] *n.*
	例	We have several **openings** in the HR division.
		我們人資部門有一些 openings。

6

30 **panel** [ˋpænl̩] n.　　　　專門的小組，評判的小組

例 The **panel** of interviewers decided that none of the candidates were qualified for the position.

面試官 panel 決定，應試者中無人能勝任此職位。

31 **portfolio** [pɔrtˋfolɪ͵o] n.　　　　作品集

例 When applying for a graphic designer position, a well-organized **portfolio** is essential.

應徵美術設計時，一定要備好完整的 portfolio。

32 **postpone** [postˋpon] v.　　　　延遲，延緩

例 We can't **postpone** the deadline any longer.

我們無法再 postpone 截止期限了。

33 **prerequisite** [priˋrɛkwəzɪt] n.　　　　必要條件；前提

例 Previous experience in sales is a **prerequisite** for this job.

具備銷售相關經驗是這項工作的 prerequisite。

34 **profession** [prəˋfɛʃən] n.　　　　（需專門技能的）行業，職業

例 Sally has made up her mind to go into the teaching **profession**.

莎莉決定要從事教書的 profession。

35 **profile** [ˋprofaɪl] n.　　　　概述

例 This applicant's resume matches the **profile** for a position in accounting, not sales.

該名應徵者的資歷適合會計部門的職務 profile，而非業務部門。

資格，限定條件	36	**qualification** [ˌkwɑləfəˈkeʃən] *n.*
	☐ ☐	**例** If you don't meet the **qualifications**, don't apply for the position. 如果不符合該工作的 qualifications，就別應徵了。
合格的	37	**qualified** [ˈkwɑləˌfaɪd] *adj.*
	☐ ☐	**例** After years of training, Holly is finally a **qualified** doctor. 經過多年的訓練，荷莉終於成為 qualified 醫生。
辭職，辭掉	38	**quit** [kwɪt] *v.*
	☐ ☐	**例** It isn't wise to **quit** your job with the economy (being) so unstable. 現在經濟不穩定，quit 你的工作是很不明智的。
推薦	39	**recommend** [ˌrɛkəˈmɛnd] *v.*
	☐ ☐	**例** Fred is highly **recommended** as a good assistant. 佛瑞德極受 recommended，說他是稱職的助理。
招募，招聘	40	**recruit** [rɪˈkrut] *v.*
	☐ ☐	**例** The company is **recruiting** new people. 這家公司在 recruiting 新人。
招聘人員	41	**recruiter** [rɪˈkrutɚ] *n.*
	☐ ☐	**例** Karen is the **recruiter** you should talk to if you are looking for a job. 如果你要找工作，凱倫是 recruiter 可以找她談談。

42　reference [ˈrɛfərəns] *n.*　推薦，介紹

例 Some companies ask applicants for a **reference** letter.

有些公司會要求應徵者提供 reference 信。

43　reject [rɪˈdʒɛkt] *v.*　拒絕

例 Greg's application was **rejected**.

克雷格的申請遭到 rejected 了。

44　require [rɪˈkwaɪr] *v.*　需要

例 This job **requires** knowledge of various computer programs.

這份工作 requires 瞭解各種電腦程式。

45　requirement [rɪˈkwaɪrmənt] *n.*　必要條件

例 You won't be considered for the position if you don't meet the **requirements**.

若你不具備 requirements，是不會列入考慮的。

46　resume [ˌrɛzjʊˈme] *n.*　履歷表

例 You should always keep your **resume** updated in case you decide to look for a new job.

你的 resume 要常更新，以備決定要找新工作。

47　seek [sik] *v.*　尋找，尋求

例 The company is **seeking** someone who can handle customers overseas.

這家公司在 seeking 能處理海外客戶的人員。

技巧，技藝 | 48 **skill** [skɪl] *n.*

☐ 例 Driving a bulldozer takes special **skills**.
☐ 駕駛推土機需要特殊的 skills。

改變，轉換 | 49 **switch** [swɪtʃ] *v.*

☐ 例 It's hard to **switch** career paths when you reach
☐ middle age.
當你到了中年就很難 switch 職業跑道了。

２ Employment 就業 ②

正確無誤 | 50 **accurately** [ˋækjərɪtlɪ] *adv.*

☐ 例 Be sure you write the names **accurately** on each
☐ envelope.
確定每個信封上姓名的書寫 accurately.

有野心的，| 51 **ambitious** [æmˋbɪʃəs] *adj.*
有雄心的

☐ 例 Jerry is very **ambitious** in his career.
☐ 傑瑞對他的事業非常 ambitious。

職業，生涯 | 52 **career** [kəˋrɪr] *n.*

☐ 例 It took my younger sister a long time to choose a
☐ **career**.
我妹妹花了很長的時間才決定她的 career。

挑戰，艱鉅 | 53 **challenge** [ˋtʃæləndʒ] *n.*
任務

☐ 例 It will be a **challenge** to have the task completed
☐ in two days.
要在兩天內完成這項工作是個艱難的 challenge。

54 communication [kə͵mjunəˈkeʃən] *n.*　溝通

例 Make sure all **communication** with our clients is accurate.

要確認我們與客戶的 communication 無誤。

55 database [ˈdetə͵bes] *n.*　資料庫

例 All employee information is stored in a **database**.

所有的員工個資皆儲存於 database 中。

56 description [dɪˈskrɪpʃən] *n.*　說明，描述

例 Job **descriptions** provide information about employee responsibilities.

工作內容 descriptions 記載員工的職務責任。

57 devote [dɪˈvot] *v.*　獻身，致力

例 Mr. Lin has **devoted** ten years to the company as a forklift operator.

林先生 devoted 於這家公司擔任堆高機操作員已有十年的時間。

58 duty [ˈdjutɪ] *n.*　責任

例 The company has a **duty** to the shareholders.

該公司對股東負有 duty。

59 duties [ˈdjutɪz] *n.*　職責

例 Fulfilling guest needs is one of the concierge's **duties**.

滿足顧客需求是旅館服務台人員的 duties 之一。

• duty 當職責的意思時，需為複數

雇用

60 **employ** [ɪmˋplɔɪ] *n.*

例 That international airline **employed** over a hundred people this year.

那家國際航空公司去年 employed 超過一百位員工。

受雇者，員工

61 **employee** [͵ɛmplɔɪˋi] *n.*

例 Due to the economic recession, many **employees** have been let go.

因為經濟衰退，許多 employees 都給辭退了。

雇主，老闆

62 **employer** [ɪmˋplɔɪɚ] *n.*

例 Maria's **employer** rejected her request for additional vacation time.

瑪麗亞的 employer 拒絕她增加休假時間的要求。

受雇，就業

63 **employment** [ɪmˋplɔɪmənt] *n.*

例 The **employment** rate has increased by two percent since last year.

自去年起，employment 率已增加兩個百分點。

全部，整個

64 **entire** [ɪnˋtaɪr] *adj.*

例 The **entire** staff has gone on strike due to unfair treatment.

entire 員工為不平等待遇而集體罷工。

開除，解雇

65 **fire** [faɪr] *v.*

例 Due to David's poor work performance, he was **fired** last week.

大衛因為工作表現不佳，所以上週給 fired。

66　**flexible** [ˈflɛksəbl̩] *adj.*　　　　　　有彈性

☐　例　My working hours are pretty **flexible**.

☐　　　我的工作時間非常 flexible。

67　**freelance** [ˈfri͵læns] *n. adj.*　　　　自由業者
（的）

☐　例　We hired a **freelance** photographer for the photo

☐　　　shoot.

　　　　我們聘雇了一名 freelance 攝影師來拍攝照片。

68　**handbook** [ˈhænd͵bʊk] *n.*　　　　　　手冊

☐　例　Please check the employee **handbook** for

☐　　　information about extending business trips for

　　　　vacation.

　　　　有關將商務旅行延長為休假之事宜，請查閱員工
　　　　handbook。

69　**in charge** [ɪnˈtʃɑrdʒ] *phr.*　　　　　　負責

☐　例　Katie is **in charge** of the Editing Department.

☐　　　凱蒂 in charge 編輯部門。

70　**income** [ˈɪn͵kʌm] *n.*　　　　　　　　收入，所得

☐　例　With two **incomes**, the couple can easily

☐　　　purchase a large home.

　　　　因為有兩份 incomes，這對夫妻才能輕鬆購買一
　　　　間大房子。

71　**interview** [ˈɪntɚ͵vju] *n.*　　　　　　面試，面談

☐　例　I have a job **interview** tomorrow afternoon.

☐　　　我明天下午有一個工作 interview。

參加面試者　72 **interviewee** [ˌɪntə·vjuˈi] *n.*

例 Most **interviewees** are nervous during interviews.

許多 interviewees 在面試過程中都會緊張。

主持面試者　73 **interviewer** [ˈɪntə·ˌvjuə·] *n.*

例 The **interviewer** asked some difficult questions during the job interview.

那位 interviewer 在面試時問了許多刁鑽的問題。

使用，佔據　74 **occupy** [ˈɑkjəˌpaɪ] *v.*

例 Robert's volunteer work at the hospital **occupies** most of his spare time.

羅伯特當醫院義工的工作 occupies 了他大部分的閒暇時間。

職前講習　75 **orientation** [ˌɔrɪɛnˈteʃən] *n.*

例 All new employees must attend an **orientation** session.

所有的新進員工都必須參加 orientation 會。

全體人員，職員　76 **personnel** [ˌpɝˈsn̩ˈɛl] *n.*

例 We should ask **personnel** from both departments to attend the meeting.

我們應該找那兩個部門的 personnel 參加此會議。

精確的，明確的　77 **precise** [prɪˈsaɪs] *adj.*

例 It is important to be very **precise** when communicating instructions to employees.

給員工 precise 指示很重要。

14

78 probation [proˈbeʃən] *n.*

試用期，考察期

例 In Taiwan, new employees must go through a three-month **probation** period before being officially hired.

在台灣，新進員工在正式任用前必需通過三個月的 probation。

79 resign [rɪˈzaɪn] *v.*

辭職

例 The general manager was forced to **resign** from his position.

那位總經理被迫 resign。

80 resignation [ˌrɛzɪgˈneʃən] *n.*

辭職

例 Joshua put his **resignation** letter on the manager's desk last night before he left the office.

喬舒亞昨晚下班前，將他的 resignation 信放在經理辦公桌上。

81 retire [rɪˈtaɪr] *v.*

退休

例 Most people **retire** at 65.

大部分的人都在六十五歲的時候 retire。

82 satisfy [ˈsætɪsˌfaɪ] *v.*

滿意

例 I have to make sure that my boss is **satisfied** with my work before I leave the office.

我必須在下班前確定老闆 satisfied 我的工作。

83 sufficient [səˈfɪʃənt] *adj.*

足夠的，充足的

例 Our team doesn't have **sufficient** support to finish the project.

我們的團隊沒有 sufficient 支援以完成這項計畫。

任務，工作　84　**task** [tæsk] *n.*

☐
☐
例 Monica can handle multiple **tasks** at the same time.

莫妮卡能夠同時處理好幾件 tasks。

受訓者　85　**trainee** [tren`i] *n.*

☐
☐
例 I helped show the **trainees** how to use the photocopier.

我幫忙向 trainees 展示如何使用影印機。

訓練人員　86　**trainer** [`trenɚ] *n.*

☐
☐
例 A **trainer** in each department is responsible for getting new employees ready for the job.

一個部門裡的 trainer 要負責帶新人熟悉工作。

訓練，培訓　87　**training** [`trenɪŋ] *n.*

☐
☐
例 It takes years of **training** to be a good doctor.

要成為一位醫師得花上多年的 training。

調動　88　**transfer** [træns`fɚ] *v.*

☐
☐
例 Patricia wants to **transfer** to another department.

派翠西亞想 transfer 到另一個部門。

拒絕　89　**turn down** [`tɝn `daʊn] *v. phr.*

☐
☐
例 I **turned down** a job offer to go work for another company yesterday.

我昨天 turn down 跳槽到別家公司的工作機會。

90 **workforce** [ˈwɝk͵fɔrs] *n.*   職場

☐ 例 After graduation from high school, some people
☐ join the **workforce** rather than attend college.

有些人高中畢業後，沒繼續升學就進入
workforce。

91 **workload** [ˈwɝk͵lod] *n.*   工作量

☐ 例 Employees in the factory are unhappy with their
☐ current **workload**.

工廠員工對他們目前的 workload 不滿意。

92 **workplace** [ˈwɝk͵ples] *n.*   工作場所

☐ 例 It is important to dress professionally in the
☐ **workplace**.

在 workplace 穿著符合專業是很重要的。

3 Promotion 升遷 ③

93 **assignment** [əˈsaɪnmənt] *n.*   工作，任務

☐ 例 Jennifer always completes her **assignments** by
☐ the deadline.

珍妮佛總是能在期限內完成 assignments。

94 **celebrate** [ˈsɛlə͵bret] *v.*   慶祝

☐ 例 We are going out tonight to **celebrate** Tina's
☐ promotion.

我們今晚要去 celebrate 蒂娜獲得升遷。

恭喜　95 **congratulation** [kən͵grætʃə`leʃən] *n.*

☐
☐ 例 **Congratulations**! Our boss really liked your ideas on how to boost sales.

Congratulations! 老闆很喜歡你增加銷售的辦法。

● 當恭喜或祝賀時，需為複數

☆ 任命，指定　96 **designate** [`dɛzɪg͵net] *v.*

☐
☐ 例 Jason was **designated** the leader of the production team.

傑森受 designated 為該生產團隊的主管。

選舉，推選　97 **elect** [ɪ`lɛkt] *v.*

☐
☐ 例 The board of directors **elected** Johnson as the new CEO.

董事會已決定 elected 強森擔任執行長一職。

☆ 評估　98 **evaluate** [ɪ`væljʊ͵et] *v.*

☐
☐ 例 The factory manager is **evaluating** staff performance this month.

工廠經理會在這個月 evaluating 員工的工作績效。

傑出，優異　99 **excellent** [`ɛksḷənt] *adj.*

☐
☐ 例 Mary does an **excellent** job organizing staff events.

瑪麗對於處理員工的事務非常 excellent。

☆ 執行，主管　100 **executive** [ɪg`zɛkjʊtɪv] *adj.*

☐
☐ 例 Kate is the **executive** editor in this publishing company.

凱特是這家出版社的 executive 編輯。

18

101 **feedback** [ˈfid͵bæk] *n.*　　　　　　回饋

例 Martin asked his boss for **feedback** on his performance.

馬丁請他老闆就他的工作表現給予 feedback。

102 **hard-working** [ˈhardˈwɝkɪŋ] *adj.*　　努力工作的

例 Bella is a **hard-working** employee. It's no wonder (that) she got a raise so soon.

貝拉是個 hard-working 的員工。難怪她很快就加薪了。

103 **incompetent** [ɪnˈkampətənt] *adj.*　　無能，不勝任

例 Missing deadlines all the time makes Dave look **incompetent**.

戴夫老是無法按時完成工作，顯得他很 incompetent。

104 **leader** [ˈlidɚ] *n.*　　　　　　　領導者

例 As the **leader** of this project, you have to assign each of us our tasks.

作為這個專案的 leader，你必須指派工作給我們。

105 **leadership** [ˈlidɚ͵ʃɪp] *n.*　　　　領導才能

例 Strong **leadership** skills will help you move ahead in this company.

擁有強大的 leadership 能讓你在公司有出頭天。

106 **nominate** [ˈnamə͵net] *v.*　　　　　提名，推薦

例 Ms. Jackson has been **nominated** for Manager of the Year.

傑克森太太被 nominated 為年度最佳經理。

傑出的，出色的	107	**outstanding** [ˋaʊtˋstændɪŋ] *adj.*
	☐ ☐	例 Among all the resumes, Heather's was the most **outstanding**.
		在所有的履歷表中，海瑟的是最 outstanding。
表現；績效	108	**performance** [pɚˋfɔrməns] *n.*
	☐ ☐	例 Our boss was disappointed with our team's **performance**.
		老闆對我們這個團隊的 performance 感到失望。
職位，職務	109	**position** [pəˋzɪʃən] *n.*
	☐ ☐	例 What **position** do you hold in the company you are currently working for?
		你在目前任職的公司擔任何種 position？
進展	110	**progress** [ˋprɑgrɛs] *n.*
	☐ ☐	例 Please give me regular updates on the **progress** of the project.
		請告訴我這項計畫的定期的最近 progress。
有希望	111	**promising** [ˋprɑmɪsɪŋ] *adj.*
	☐ ☐	例 The business relationship between those two companies looks **promising**.
		那兩家公司間的合作關係看來很 promising。
晉升	112	**promote** [prəˋmot] *v.*
	☐ ☐	例 After the annual evaluation, the CEO will announce who will be **promoted** to production manager.
		在年度考核後，執行長將宣布誰會 promoted 為生產部經理。

113 **promotion** [prəˈmoʃən] *n.*   晉升

☐ 例 Larry has been waiting for a **promotion** for years.

☐ 賴瑞等 promotion 等很久了。

114 **prosperity** [prɑsˈpɛrətɪ] *n.*   興旺

☐ 例 I wish your company success and **prosperity**.

☐ 祝你的公司成功與 prosperity。

115 **pursue** [pəˈsu] *v.*   追求，致力於

☐ 例 John has decided to **pursue** a singing career after high school.

☐ 約翰決定在高中畢業之後 pursue 歌唱生涯。

116 **reliable** [rɪˈlaɪəbl̩] *adj.*   可靠的

☐ 例 William is considered the most **reliable** employee in the company.

☐ 威廉應算是公司裡最 reliable 員工。

117 **reputation** [ˌrɛpjəˈteʃən] *n.*   名譽，名聲

☐ 例 You may ruin your **reputation** if you are always behind schedule.

☐ 你會因為老是無法趕上期限而壞了自己的 reputation。

118 **respect** [rɪˈspɛkt] *n.*   尊敬，敬重

☐ 例 Good leaders are able to earn the **respect** of the staff.

☐ 好的主管要能贏得下屬的 respect。

津貼，補助 | 119 **allowance** [əˋlʊəns] *n.*

☐
☐
例 Our company offers each division an **allowance** for stationery.
公司配給各部門購買文具的 allowance。

協助，支援 | 120 **assistance** [əˋsɪstəns] *n.*

☐
☐
例 Without your **assistance**, I never would've finished the job on time.
若沒你的 assistance，我不可能準時完成工作的。

福利 | 121 **benefit** [ˋbɛnəfɪt] *n.*

☐
☐
例 That law firm provides very good employee **benefits**.
那家律師事務所提供非常好的員工 benefits。

獎金，紅利 | 122 **bonus** [ˋbonəs] *n.*

☐
☐
例 In Taiwan, employees receive an annual **bonus** before Chinese New Year.
在台灣，員工會在農曆年前收到年終 bonus。

賠償；補償 | 123 **compensate** [ˋkɑmpənˏset] *v.*

☐
☐
例 The injured construction worker will be **compensated** by the insurance company.
保險公司會 compensated 那位受傷的建築工人。

賠償，賠償金 | 124 **compensation** [ˏkɑmpənˋseʃən] *n.*

☐
☐
例 Victims of the industrial accident will be paid at least three million dollars in **compensation**.
工業事故的受害者將至少獲得三百萬的 compensation。

125 concern [kənˋsɝn] *n.*   關心的事

例 Having our products delivered on time is one of our biggest **concerns**.

將貨品準時送達是我們最 concerns。

126 contest [ˋkɑntɛst] *n.*   比賽，競賽

例 The two sales teams are working day and night to win the **contest**.

這兩個行銷團隊拼命要贏得 contest。

127 data [ˋdetə] *n.*   資料，數據

例 The **data** from the employee survey showed that most staff members would prefer a longer lunch break.

員工調查報告的 data 顯示，大多數的職員寧可午餐休息時間長一點。

128 deadline [ˋdɛd,laɪn] *n.*   期限，截止期限

例 The project has to be completed by the **deadline**.

這個專案一定要在 deadline 內完成。

129 deal with [ˋdil`wɪθ] *v. phr.*   應付，處理

例 Receptionists often need to **deal with** customer complaints.

接待員常常要 deal with 客人的抱怨。

130 earn [ɝn] *v.*   賺

例 Tom **earned** a lot of money by selling clothing online.

湯姆靠在網路上賣衣服 earned 了不少錢。

☆ 利潤，收益　131 **earnings** [ˈɝnɪŋz] *n.*

　例 The biotechnology company just detailed its first fiscal quarter **earnings**.

　這家生技公司剛公佈了他們的會計年度第一季 earnings。

☆ 效率　132 **efficiency** [əˈfɪʃənsɪ] *n.*

　例 Mark's **efficiency** at work allows him to complete many tasks in a short amount of time.

　馬克的 efficiency 讓他可以在短時間內完成多項工作。

☆ 有效率　133 **efficient** [əˈfɪʃənt] *adj.*

　例 It would be a more **efficient** use of time to have the photocopier staple the papers together rather than do it yourself.

　用影印機裝訂紙張要比你自己做來得 efficient 多了。

努力　134 **effort** [ˈɛfɚt] *n.*

　例 Nick has put a lot of **effort** into the project since he started it last year.

　這項計畫從去年開始到現在，尼克投注了不少 effort。

☆ 差事　135 **errand** [ˈɛrənd] *n.*

　例 Our manager's assistant is always running personal **errands** for her.

　我們經理的助理老是幫他處理私人 errands。

24

136 pass [pæs] *n.*

通行證，入場證

例 Our company will issue you a **pass** for the fitness room.

公司將會發給你健身房的 pass。

137 pay [pe] *v.*

支付

例 This job doesn't **pay** much, so I have to find a part-time job.

這份工作 pay 的薪水不高，所以我必需再找一個兼職的工作。

138 pension [ˈpɛnʃən] *n.*

退休金，養老金

例 When I retire, I will have to survive on a small **pension**.

我退休之後，只能靠著微薄的 pension 度日。

139 permission [pɚˈmɪʃən] *n.*

許可

例 I asked my boss for **permission** to take a vacation day next week.

我向老闆要求下週休假的 permission。

140 productive [prəˈdʌktɪv] *adj.*

多產

例 Some people are more **productive** in the morning.

有些人在早上工作比較 productive。

141 raise [rez] *n.*

加薪

例 After working a year for the company, Fran asked her boss for a **raise**.

法蘭在公司工作滿一年之後，跟老闆要求 raise。

減少，降低

142 **reduce** [rɪˋdjus] *v.*

例 My company is planning to **reduce** the number of staff members.

公司計畫 reduce 職員人數。

減少，降低

143 **reduction** [rɪˋdʌkʃən] *n.*

例 There was a dramatic **reduction** in profits for many companies last year.

許多公司的收益在去年大幅 reduction。

退還，償還

144 **refund** [rɪˋfʌnd] *v.*

例 My company will **refund** all food purchases made on the trip.

我公司將會 refund 我在出差時花在購買食物的錢。

補償

145 **reimburse** [ˌrimˋbɝs] *v.*

例 I don't think the company will **reimburse** me for any alcoholic beverages consumed on the trip.

我不認為公司會 reimburse 給我出差時飲酒的花費。

度假勝地

146 **resort** [rɪˋzɔrt] *n.*

例 The conference is being held at a four-star **resort**.

會議在四星級的 resort 舉行。

責任

147 **responsibility** [rɪˌspɑnsəˋbɪlətɪ] *n.*

例 It's my **responsibility** to go through every detail of this project.

為這個計畫的每個環節把關是我的 responsibility。

148 **reward** [rɪˋwɔrd] *v.*

獎勵，獎賞

例 The company **rewarded** Tom's good work performance by giving him a bonus.

公司發獎金給湯姆以 rewarded 他的優異表現。

149 **salary** [ˋsælərɪ] *n.*

薪水，薪資

例 The **salary** they offered for the position was much lower than I thought it would be.

他們對這職位提出的 salary 比我預期的低很多。

150 **wages** [ˋwedʒɪz] *n.*

工資，薪水

例 Jane's **wages** aren't high enough to support her lifestyle.

珍的 wages 無法負擔她的生活方式。

151 **weekday** [ˋwik͵de] *n.*

平日（週一至週五）

例 The office is only open on **weekdays**.

這間辦事處只有 weekdays 上班。

152 **weekend** [ˋwik͵ɛnd] *n.*

週末

例 Most employees have **weekends** off.

大部分工作者 weekends 都不用上班。

153 **welfare** [ˋwɛl͵fɛr] *n.*

福利

例 We need to cut costs for the **welfare** of the company.

我們必需刪減公司的 welfare 費用。

Exercises

請從選項中，選出最適當的答案完成句子。

1. Being able to speak a foreign language well is quite a(n) _____. It takes a long time and it takes hard work.

   (A) requirement (B) employment (C) compliment (D) accomplishment

2. We are glad to inform you that your _____ for the job vacancy has been accepted.

   (A) education (B) indication (C) implication (D) application

3. Human beings are _____ of jealousy at birth; in other words, jealousy is inborn.

   (A) capable (B) dependable (C) susceptible (D) reliable

4. This car sells well because of its _____ and reliability; it lasts a long time and has few mechanical problems.

   (A) endurance (B) persistence (C) insistence (D) resistance

5. Her male colleagues were eager to help Lisa repaint her apartment, but their _____ waned when they were told Lisa wouldn't be home during the repaint.

   (A) suspension (B) intension (C) enthusiasm (D) patience

6. Employ and _____ are synonyms; they mean the same thing.

   (A) hint (B) clue (C) hire (D) hide

7. If you are applying for a job, you need to send your _____ and autobiography.

   (A) realization (B) repentance (C) resume (D) requirement

8. Jim decided to join the _____ after high school rather than going to college.

   (A) market (B) workforce (C) fair (D) exhibition

9. A _____ force was assigned to rescue the victims in the war zone.

   (A) work (B) task (C) job (D) business

10. To know more about the candidate, the ＿＿＿＿＿＿＿ asked him a few personal questions.

    (A) interviewer (B) supplier (C) buyer (D) performer

11. You can call on me on either Friday or Saturday; I'm ＿＿＿＿＿＿＿.

    (A) deductible (B) flexible (C) determinable (D) indispensable

12. An employer has the right to dismiss an employee during ＿＿＿＿＿＿＿ for unsuitability.

    (A) interview (B) employment (C) probation (D) suspension

13. Email is the most popular form of office ＿＿＿＿＿＿＿ today.

    (A) skill (B) challenge (C) experience (D) communication

14. The secretary was fired; the manager considered her ＿＿＿＿＿＿＿.

    (A) extraordinary (B) extra (C) insufficient (D) incompetent

15. Alan has worked here for five years. He wants to ask his manager for a ＿＿＿＿＿＿＿ next month.

    (A) promotion (B) respect (C) resignation (D) leadership

16. You take up a(n) ＿＿＿＿＿＿＿ with a certain organization when you start a job there.

    (A) celebration (B) election (C) position (D) application

17. Make no more complaints. All the losses you suffered have been ＿＿＿＿＿＿＿ for.

    (A) depended (B) compensated (C) recommended (D) suspended

18. The government's new housing project will ＿＿＿＿＿＿＿ a lot of people.

    (A) attempt (B) accept (C) perform (D) benefit

19. The hourly ＿＿＿＿＿＿＿ working at a convenience store is around NT$ 100.

    (A) wage (B) increase (C) decrease (D) bill

20. You can improve your ＿＿＿＿＿＿＿ by planning in advance and by doing important things first.

    (A) adequacy (B) sufficiency (C) efficiency (D) fluency

Chapter 2
Organization 組織

An organization is made up of many people. Each person has their function and rank within the organization according to their skills and experience.

2 Organization
組織

1 Enterprise 企業 ⑤

使用權　154 **access** [ˈæksɛs] *n.*

例 Temporary employees do not have **access** to building security codes.

臨時雇員沒有大樓安全碼的 access。

稱呼　155 **address** [əˈdrɛs] *v.*

例 Our boss insists that we **address** him by his first name.

我們老闆堅持要我們直接 address 他的名字。

行政　156 **administration** [ədˌmɪnəˈstreʃən] *n.*

例 The **administration** in the company is disorganized.

這家公司的 administration 一蹋糊塗。

採取，接納　157 **adopt** [əˈdɑpt] *v.*

例 If we **adopt** a positive attitude, we may be more productive at work.

如果我們 adopt 樂觀的態度，在工作上也許會更具生產力。

建議，忠告　158 **advice** [ədˈvaɪs] *n.*

例 Could you give me some **advice** on how to prepare for my interview?

您可以給我一些如何準備面試的 advice 嗎？

159 against [əˈgɛnst] *prep.*   反對

☐
☐ 例 There were many employees who were **against** the parking increase.

有許多員工 against 停車費漲價。

160 allocate [ˈæləˌket] *v.*   分配；分派

☐
☐ 例 Each employee is **allocated** a certain number of photocopies.

每個員工都 allocated 一定數量的影印本。

161 allow [əˈlaʊ] *v.*   允許，許可

☐
☐ 例 The office employees are **allowed** to smoke on the balcony.

辦公室的員工 allowed 到陽台抽菸。

162 apprentice [əˈprɛntɪs] *n.*   學徒，見習生

☐
☐ 例 Our company is open to hiring **apprentices**.

我們公司在徵求 apprentices。

163 branch [bræntʃ] *n.*   分公司

☐
☐ 例 The other **branch** has more employees.

本公司其他的 branch 有更多員工。

164 build [bɪld] *v.*   建立；發展

☐
☐ 例 Over the past few years, we have **built** up our clientele.

過去幾年來，我們已經 built 自己的客戶。

生意；營業；公司	165	**business** [ˋbɪznɪs] *n.*
	☐	例 I heard the **business** was in trouble.
	☐	我聽說 business 出了問題。

生意人，商人	166	**businessperson** [ˋbɪznɪsˏpɝsn̩] *n.*
	☐	例 He wants to be a **businessperson**, just like his father.
	☐	他想要成為 businessperson，一如他的父親。

中心，中心點	167	**center** [ˋsɛntɚ] *n.*
	☐	例 My desk is in the **center** of the office.
	☐	我的辦公桌就在辦公室的 center。

打卡上班	168	**clock in** [ˋklɑk ˋɪn] *v. phr.*
	☐	例 What time do you usually **clock in**?
	☐	你通常幾點 clock in？

打卡下班	169	**clock out** [ˋklɑk ˋaʊt] *v. phr.*
	☐	例 I **clocked out** a little early today.
	☐	我今天有點提早 clocked out。

委員會	170	**committee** [kəˋmɪtɪ] *n.*
	☐	例 The **committee** will be meeting after work to discuss the staff party.
	☐	Committee 下班後要開會討論職員派對。

公司	171	**company** [ˋkʌmpənɪ] *n.*
	☐	例 The **company** has been in business for over twenty years.
	☐	這家 company 已經營業二十幾年了。

172 **competitor** [kəmˋpɛtətə] *n.*

☐
☐ 例 I heard our biggest **competitor** is going out of business.

我聽說我們最大的 competitor 即將要結束營業。

競爭者，對手

173 **compliance** [kəmˋplaɪəns] *n.*

☐
☐ 例 We need your company's **compliance** in order for us to continue with the deal.

我們需要貴公司的 compliance，以便能繼續這項交易。

遵守

174 **comprehensive** [ˌkɑmprɪˋhɛnsɪv] *adj.*

☐
☐ 例 The document gave new employees a **comprehensive** overview of the company.

這份文件讓新員工對公司有 comprehensive 概觀。

廣泛的，全面的

175 **consider** [kənˋsɪdə] *v.*

☐
☐ 例 The owner of the shop is **considering** whether or not to close his business.

這家店的老闆正 considering 要不要結束營業。

考慮

176 **contact** [ˋkɑntækt] *n.*

☐
☐ 例 Peter has a lot of **contacts** within the industry.

彼得在業界有許多 contacts。

人脈

177 **council** [ˋkaʊnsl] *n.*

☐
☐ 例 The **council** decided against the plans to expand the office.

council 決定駁回擴建辦公室的計劃。

議會；委員會

部門	**178 department** [dɪˈpɑrtmənt] *n.*

例 The entire **department** was asked to begin dressing more professionally at work.

整個 department 員工在職場上要開始穿得更專業些。

部門，科，課	**179 division** [dəˈvɪʒən] *n.*

例 Tracy works for a small **division** within the company.

崔西在公司裡一個小小的 division 裡工作。

企業；公司	**180 enterprise** [ˈɛntəˌpraɪz] *n.*

例 The product will contribute greatly to the success of our **enterprise**.

我們 enterprise 能成功，這項產品將厥功尤偉。

建立，確定	**181 establish** [əˈstæblɪʃ] *v.*

例 We need to **establish** the qualities we are looking for in an employee before conducting interviews.

在舉行面試之前，我們需要先 establish 想找何種特質的員工。

執行者，主管	**182 executive** [ɪgˈzɛkjʊtɪv] *n.*

例 The **executives** are having a lunch meeting.

Executives 正舉行午餐會議。

擴展，擴張	**183 expansion** [ɪkˈspænʃən] *n.*

例 There are rumors of company **expansion** floating around the office.

辦公室裡流傳著公司 expansion 的謠言。

184 **founder** [ˈfaʊndɚ] *n.*   創辦人

例 The **founder** of the company gave a speech at the business dinner.

公司 founder 在商業晚宴上發表演說。

185 **franchise** [ˈfræntʃaɪz] *n.*   加盟店；加盟權

例 They are opening a new **franchise** in Miami.

他們在邁阿密要開一家新的 franchise。

186 **headquarters** [ˈhɛdˈkwɔrtɚz] *n. pl.*   總部；總公司

例 Our **headquarters** are downtown.

我們的 headquarters 位於市中心。

187 **in-house** [ˈɪnˌhaʊs] *adj.*   內部的

例 We will use our **in-house** editor to look over the document.

我們將會請公司 in-house 編輯來檢閱文件。

188 **initiate** [ɪˈnɪʃɪˌet] *v.*   開始（一項計畫等）

例 The company decided to **initiate** a new project last month.

這家公司在上個月決定 initiate 一項新的計畫。

189 **operation** [ˌɑpəˈreʃən] *n.*   經營，營運

例 The company has only been in **operation** for about five years.

這公司目前只 operation 了五年。

機構；組織	**190 organization** [ˌɔrgənaɪˈzeʃən] *n.*
	☐ 例 The **organization** was established over three decades ago.
	☐ 該 organization 已經成立三十多年之久。
人員配置	**191 placement** [ˈplesmənt] *n.*
	☐ 例 The **placement** of the intern in our division was a bad decision.
	☐ 我們部門的實習生 placement 是糟糕的決定。
政策	**192 policy** [ˈpɑləsɪ] *n.*
	☐ 例 The **policy** is being revised by the supervisors.
	☐ Policy 正在主管的手上進行修改。
基本信條，原則	**193 principle** [ˈprɪsəpl] *n.*
	☐ 例 You can be creative as long as you follow company **principles**.
	☐ 只要遵循公司的 principles，你可以很有創意。
☆改革，改良	**194 reform** [rɪˈfɔrm] *v.*
	☐ 例 We have to **reform** the filing system to help us save time.
	☐ 我們必須 reform 檔案管理系統來幫我們節省時間。
資源；資產	**195 resource** [rɪˈsɔrs] *n.*
	☐ 例 Employees are the most important **resource** at this company.
	☐ 我們的員工是公司最重要的 resource。

196 **significant** [sɪgˈnɪfəkənt] *adj.* 重大的

例 The people who broke into the office did **significant** damage to the staff room.

闖入公司的人給員工休息室帶來 significant 破壞。

197 **stockholder** [ˈstɑkˌholdɚ] *n.* 股東

例 **Stockholders** share in the profits of the company.

Stockholders 可以共享公司所獲的盈餘。

198 **staff** [stæf] *n.* 職員

例 Our company has a **staff** of forty-five people.

本公司有四十五位 staff。

199 **subsidiary** [səbˈsɪdɪˌɛrɪ] *n.* 子公司

例 That company is a **subsidiary** of our competitor.

那家公司是競爭對手的 subsidiary。

200 **system** [ˈsɪstəm] *n.* 系統；制度

例 The **system** in place isn't as effective as it could be.

現行的 system 未若預期的有效。

201 **team** [tim] *n.* 團隊

例 Employees should treat each other like members of a **team**.

員工應對待彼此有如一個 team 的成員。

各式各樣的　202 **various** [ˈvɛrɪəs] *adj.*

例 There are **various** ways we can improve organization in the office.

我們有 various 方式可改善公司的組織。

投票，表決　203 **vote** [vot] *v.*

例 Everyone **voted** to go to that restaurant for the annual staff party.

大家 voted 決定員工年度聚餐要去那家餐廳。

2 Company Structure 公司架構 ⑥

主管，（機構的）管理人　204 **administrator** [ədˈmɪnə,stretɚ] *n.*

例 Ms Bailey is the **administrator** in our office.

貝立小姐是我們辦公室的 administrator。

助理，助手　205 **assistant** [əˈsɪstant] *n.*

例 Mr. Roberts is looking for an **assistant** to help him with the administrative work.

羅伯茲先生在找 assistant 幫他處理行政事物。

查帳員，稽核員　206 **auditor** [ˈɔdɪtɚ] *n.*

例 An **auditor** is coming to examine the company financial records.

一位 auditor 要來查公司的財務紀錄。

老闆，上司　207 **boss** [ˈbɔs] *n.*

例 Our **boss** is in San Francisco on business till next Wednesday.

我們 boss 到舊金山出差了，下星期三才回來。

208 CEO [ˈsiˈiˈo] *n.*　　　　　執行長

例 The new **CEO** from England is ready to make big changes in the company.

來自英國的 CEO 準備在公司做出重大改革。

209 chairperson [ˈtʃɛrˌpɜˈsn̩] *n.*　　（會議或委員會的）主席

例 The **chairperson** asked for everyone's attention.

Chairperson 要大家專心注意聽。

210 code [kod] *n.*　　　　密碼

例 Only permanent employees have the security **code** to enter the building.

只有固定員工有進入大樓的安全 code。

211 colleague [ˈkɑlig] *n.*　　　　同事

例 My **colleagues** invited me out for a drink after work.

我的 colleagues 請我下班後喝一杯。

212 consultant [kənˈsʌltənt] *n.*　　　　顧問

例 Nick works in our office as an English **consultant**.

尼克在我們公司擔任英文 consultant。

213 coworker [ˈkoˌwɜˈkə] *n.*　　　　同事

例 I usually go for a drink with my **coworkers** on Fridays.

我通常會在週五跟 coworkers 小酌一番。

減少，降低　　214 **decrease** [dɪˋkris] *v.*

例 In order to make more profit, we have to **decrease** costs.

為了要增加利潤，我們必需 decrease 成本。

副經理　　215 **deputy manager** [ˋdɛpjətɪˋmænɪdʒɚ] *n.*

例 Janet has a great chance at being promoted to **deputy manager**.

珍娜很有機會升為 deputy manager。

工程師，技師　　216 **engineer** [͵ɛndʒəˋnɪr] *n.*

例 The **engineers** work in a separate office from administration.

Engineers 的工作地點與行政管理部門分開。

全體教師　　217 **faculty** [ˋfæk!tɪ] *n.*

例 The entire **faculty** will have to attend the meeting this afternoon.

Faculty 都要出席今天下午的會議。

前任的，以前的　　218 **former** [ˋfɔrmɚ] *adj.*

例 The **former** president contributed a lot to the company.

那位 former 總經理對公司貢獻良多。

總經理　　219 **general manager** [ˋdʒɛnərəl ˋmænɪdʒɚ] *n.*

例 Ellen hopes to be promoted to **general manager** one day.

艾倫希望有天能當上 general manager。

220　**government** [ˈɡʌvɚnmənt] *n.*　政府

例 It is said the **government** will increase the tax rate for foreign companies.

聽說 government 將調升外資公司的稅率。

221　**increase** [ɪnˈkris] *v.*　增加

例 Sales have **increased** a lot since last quarter.

銷售量自上一季以來已 increased 不少。

222　**manager** [ˈmænɪdʒɚ] *n.*　經理

例 Being a **manager** is not as easy as people think.

當 manager 不是大家想的那麼簡單。

223　**newcomer** [ˈnjuˌkʌmɚ] *n.*　新來者，新人

例 Please welcome company **newcomer** Alison to our team.

請大家歡迎公司的 newcomer 愛麗森加入團隊。

224　**peer** [pɪr] *n.*　同儕

例 I find it uncomfortable when I'm asked to evaluate the performance of my **peers**.

評比 peers 的工作表現讓我很不自在。

225　**position** [pəˈzɪʃən] *n.*　職位，職務

例 What **position** do you hold in the company you are currently working for?

你在目前的公司擔任何種 position？

總經理

226 **president** [ˈprɛzədənt] *n.*

例 **Presidents** in large corporations make important decisions on a daily basis.

大企業的 presidents 每天都要裁定重大決策。

程式設計師

227 **programmer** [ˈprogræmɚ] *n.*

例 A computer **programmer** will be at the office this morning to help employees who are experiencing difficulty.

電腦 programmer 今天早上會到公司協助有困難的員工。

業務人員

228 **salesperson** [ˈselzˌpɝsn̩] *n.*

例 If you decide to become a **salesperson**, be prepared to work long hours.

如果你要當 salesperson，要有工作超時的心理準備。

秘書

229 **secretary** [ˈsɛkrəˌtɛrɪ] *n.*

例 Ms. Jones has been Mr. Smith's **secretary** for years.

瓊斯小姐擔任史密斯先生的 secretary 已經許多年了。

（級別或地位）高的，資深的

230 **senior** [ˈsinjɚ] *adj.*

例 Nicole is the most **senior** employee in her company.

妮可是她公司裡最 senior 員工。

231 **supervisor** [ˈsupɚˌvaɪzɚ] *n.*

主管；監督者

☐
☐ 例 Nina's **supervisor** doesn't mind when she's late for work.

妮娜的 supervisor 不介意她上班遲到。

232 **typist** [ˈtaɪpɪst] *n.*

打字員

☐
☐ 例 Renee was a **typist** before she went back to college.

瑞妮回到校園前的工作是 typist。

233 **vice president** [ˈvaɪsˈprɛzədənt] *n.*

副總經理

☐
☐ 例 Everyone is wondering who is going to be promoted to **vice president** of the company.

大家都在猜誰會升到 vice president 的職位。

234 **worker** [ˈwɝkɚ] *n.*

工作者，工人

☐
☐ 例 Many **workers** have left the factory since it went under new ownership.

自從這間工廠換東家之後，許多的 workers 都離開了。

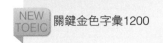

Exercises

請將符合字義的單字填入空格。

executive	staff	division	position
secretary	advice	branch	founder

1. related to managing businesses and making decisions ___executive___.

2. a suggestion about what someone should do ___advice___.

3. a job in a company or organization ___position___.

4. a group of people who work for an organization ___staff___.

5. someone who establishes a business or organization ___founder___.

6. a smaller office of a company in a different location ___division___.

7. an assistant who schedules appointments for a boss ___secretary___.

8. a department ___branch___.

I Photographs (30)

Look at the pictures below and listen to the statements. Then choose the statement that best describes what you see in the picture.

1. (A) (B) (C) (D)

2. (A) (B) (C) (D)

II Conversations (31)

You will hear some conversations between two people. Listen to the conversations and answer the questions below.

Questions 3-5

3. Where is this conversation most likely taking place?
   (A) At a job interview.
   (B) At a resume writing class.
   (C) At Sunray Industries.
   (D) At a print shop.

4. Where does the man learn about the woman's former employer?
   (A) From Sunray Industries.
   (B) From her resume.
   (C) From her project manager.
   (D) From her friends.

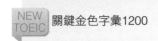
5. What was the woman's last job about?

    (A) Taking calls from customers.

    (B) Managing office resources.

    (C) Managing new projects.

    (D) Interviewing new workers.

Questions 6-7

6. What does the man suggest to avoid the traffic jam?

    (A) Leaving at night.

    (B) Being late for the concert.

    (C) Taking a two-week vacation.

    (D) Leaving earlier than planned.

7. Why is it hard for the woman to take Friday off?

    (A) She is about to quit her job.

    (B) Her boss is on vacation.

    (C) Her boss expects everyone to follow the rules for taking leave.

    (D) She has too much work to do.

Ⅲ Short Talks (32)

You will hear some short talks given by a single speaker. Listen to the short talks and answer the questions below.

Questions 8-9

8. According to the talk, what should one plan for before an interview?

    (A) Adding experience to your resume.

    (B) Getting the result you want.

    (C) Becoming a better person.

    (D) Being talkative at the interview.

9. According to this talk, how should one answer questions?

    (A) With only the truth.

    (B) However you want.

    (C) With what they want to hear.

    (D) With a "yes" or a "no."

Questions 10-11

10. Which of these statements is NOT true?

    (A) The club only interviewed one candidate.

    (B) Michael used to play baseball for the Bears.

    (C) Michael starts his new job today.

    (D) Everyone in the organization likes Michael.

11. What is said about Michael?

    (A) He has been the manager of the club for the last two years.

    (B) He has a lot of experience.

    (C) He is president of the team.

    (D) He managed another team.

Ⅳ Incomplete Sentences

A word or phrase is missing in each of the sentences below. Four answer choices are given below each sentence. Select the best answer to complete the sentence.

12. This parking lot is for _____ of this building only!

    (A) candidates   (B) opportunities (C) products   (D) employees

13. Thousands of cancer patients have _____ from the new drug.

    (A) overcame   (B) benefited   (C) interviewed (D) fulfilled

14. Mr. Parker quit his job and started his own company after his request for a _____ and a pay raise was rejected by his employer.

    (A) promotion   (B) career   (C) resume   (D) performance

15. Thank you for your _____ in this matter.

    (A) career   (B) cooperation (C) culture   (D) vacation

16. Smith _____ in Singapore two years ago.

    (A) live   (B) lives   (C) lived   (D) living

17. The sunny weather we have been enjoying _____ to stay around for a few more days.

    (A) will   (B) shall   (C) does   (D) is going

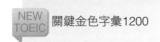

18. Mr. Flake bought _____.

    (A) his son a toy car   (B) a toy car his son

    (C) a toy car to his son   (D) a toy car at his son

19. I left my glasses in the office _____ I was here earlier.

    (A) or   (B) when   (C) and   (D) which

V Reading Comprehension

In this part you will read a selection of texts. Each text is followed by several questions. Select the best answer for each question and circle the letter (A), (B), (C), or (D).

Questions 20-21 refer to the following memo.

July 4, 2010
Memo
To: All Employees of State Bank, Downtown Branch

Susan Newman has been promoted to Secretary of the Board of Directors of State Bank. Ms. Newman has been with the bank for more than 10 years. She always exceeds the expectations of her co-workers and managers. Today's promotion is a result of her excellent performance. Please join me in congratulating Ms. Newman.

Matt Weinstein
Manager, Human Resources

20. What is the purpose of this memo?

    (A) To let Susan Newman know that she was promoted.

    (B) To let the Board of Directors know that Susan Newman was promoted.

    (C) To let the employees of the bank know that Susan Newman was promoted.

    (D) To let the employees know that the bank just hired a new secretary.

21. Why was Ms. Newman promoted?

    (A) She has worked for the bank for many years.

    (B) Her managers are very happy with her performance.

    (C) She worked in her last position for ten years.

    (D) The bank wanted to hire a newcomer.

Questions 22-23 refer to the following memo.

Memo: To all department managers

Re: Overtime costs

Because we are trying to keep costs down in the coming winter, all managers need to keep overtime under 70 hours per week. Last winter, our overtime costs were more than we had planned. If overtime hours are more than 70 hours in your department, contact HR immediately and we will give you more staff to help with the work.

If this winter is as busy as last winter, and we can keep costs down, we will all enjoy another successful year!

Thanks,

Don

22. What is the purpose of this memo?

    (A) To hire new employees.

    (B) To work 70 hours a week.

    (C) To thank managers for their hard work.

    (D) To keep overtime costs down.

23. hat can you say about this company?

    (A) It is a hotel.

    (B) It is losing money.

    (C) Winter is a busy time of the year.

    (D) It has more than 70 employees.

VI Text Completion

Read the text that follows. A word or phrase is missing in some of the sentences. For each blank, four answer choices are given. Select the best answer to complete the text.

The Daily Gregorian is (24)_____ hard-working, high-energy people to sell subscriptions to our newspaper. The Daily Gregorian has been reporting the news to this area for over 60 years, as well as providing a place for community announcements and advertisements from local businesses.

(25)_____ you have a good personality, you can make money merely by speaking with people about our newspaper. There are two types of (26)_____ – telephone sales and door-to-door sales.

Most people in this community who are not current subscribers have simply let their subscriptions end and are waiting for someone to (27)_____ them and help them to re-subscribe. You could be that person! Send your (28)_____ to **jobs@dailygregorian.com** today!

24. (A) reducing   (B) enriching   (C) hiring   (D) notifying
25. (A) If   (B) Yet   (C) But   (D) And
26. (A) requests   (B) positions   (C) advancement (D) resources
27. (A) enrich   (B) respect   (C) attach   (D) contact
28. (A) memo   (B) resume   (C) candidate   (D) attachment

Office Life 辦公室生活

The office is the place where daily business activities are conducted. Office procedures include dealing with documents, contacting customers and interacting with co-workers, holding meetings, giving presentations, and promoting company products or services.

Office Life
辦公室生活

1 Supplies & Equipment 用品設備 ⑦

熟悉 | **235 acquainted** [əˈkwentɪd] *adj.*

例 I'm sure the computer program will be easy once I get **acquainted** with it.

我相信一旦我對電腦程式 acquainted 後，它也就不難了。

冷氣機 | **236 air conditioner** [ˈɛr kənˈdɪʃənɚ] *n. phr.*

例 The **air conditioner** runs all day in hot weather.

天氣炎熱時，air conditioner 整天開著。

佈告欄 | **237 bulletin board** [ˈbʊlətn̩ ˌbɔrd] *n. phr.*

例 Please put the information about the parking fee increase on the **bulletin board**.

請在 bulletin board 上張貼停車費漲價的消息。

名片 | **238 business card** [ˈbɪznɪs ˌkɑrd] *n.*

例 Every employee in the office is provided with **business cards** to give to clients.

公司提供每名員工 business cards，以便能發給客戶。

櫥，櫃 | **239 cabinet** [ˈkæbənɪt] *n.*

例 There is no more room in the **cabinet** to store office supplies.

Cabinet 裡已經沒有多餘的空間存放辦公用品。

240 **calculator** [ˈkælkjəˌletɚ] *n.*　　計算機

　例 Could I borrow your **calculator** to add up these totals?

　我可以借你的 calculator 好合計總數嗎？

241 **cart** [kɑrt] *n.*　　手推車，購物車

　例 Sheila filled her **cart** with supplies for the office.

　席拉在 cart 裡裝滿了辦公用品。

242 **carton** [ˈkɑrtn̩] *n.*　　紙箱

　例 The **carton** contained damaged merchandise.

　Carton 裡放了損壞的商品。

243 **cartridge** [ˈkɑrtrɪdʒ] *n.*　　（墨水）匣

　例 Could you please order a new ink **cartridge** for the printer?

　能請您訂購新的列表機墨水 cartridge 嗎？

244 **clipboard** [ˈklɪpˌbɔrd] *n.*　　帶夾筆記板

　例 Judy attached her paper to a **clipboard** so she could write while standing.

　茱蒂把紙夾在 clipboard 上，這樣她才能站著寫字。

245 **computer** [kəmˈpjutɚ] *n.*　　電腦

　例 My **computer** is too slow to go on the Internet.

　我的 computer 上網速度太慢。

會議室

246 **conference room** [ˈkɑnfərəns ˌrum] *n. phr.*

☐ 例 The **conference room** can seat up to sixteen
☐ people.

這間 conference room 能容納十六個人。

影印機

247 **copier** [ˈkɑpɪɚ] *n.*

☐ 例 Jeffery jammed the **copier** about an hour ago.
☐ 傑佛瑞一小時前把 copier 卡紙了。

電線

248 **cord** [kɔrd] *n.*

☐ 例 The printer stopped working because the **cord**
☐ was unplugged.

因為拔掉 cord，所以印表機無法運作。

工商名錄

249 **directory** [dəˈrɛktərɪ] *n.*

☐ 例 The office name could not be located in the
☐ **directory**.

Directory 中找不到該公司的名字。

光碟

250 **disk** [dɪsk] *n.*

☐ 例 Robert backed-up his files on a **disk**.
☐ 羅伯特把檔案備份在 disk 上。

紀錄片

251 **documentary** [ˌdɑkjəˈmɛntərɪ] *n.*

☐ 例 That **documentary** was shown at the last
☐ conference I attended.

我上次參加的會議播放了那部 documentary。

252 **e-mail** [ˋi͵mel] *n.* 電子郵件

例 Please be sure to keep your **e-mails** professional.

請務必讓您的 e-mails 顯示專業性。

253 **envelope** [ˋɛnvə͵lop] *n.* 信封

例 Don't forget to seal the **envelopes** before you mail them.

把信寄出前，別忘了封 envelopes。

254 **environment** [ɪnˋvaɪrənmənt] *n.* 環境

例 We are using recycled paper to help save the **environment**.

我們使用回收紙來幫忙拯救 environment。

255 **equipment** [ɪˋkwɪpmənt] *n.* 設備

例 The **equipment** in the factory is really old.

這家工廠的 equipment 非常老舊。

256 **eraser** [ɪˋresɚ] *n.* 橡皮擦

例 Could I borrow your **eraser**?

能借我你的 eraser 嗎？

257 **extension number** [ɪkˋstɛnʃən ͵nʌmbɚ] *n. phr.* 分機號碼

例 Could you please give me Robert Smith's **extension number**?

您能給我羅伯特・史密斯的 extension number 嗎？

設施，設備　258 **facility** [fəˈsɪlətɪ] *n.*

　　例 The building's **facilities** include underground parking and a fitness room.

　　這大樓的 facilities 包括地下停車場以及一間健身房。

傳真　259 **fax** [fæks] *v.*

　　例 The secretary **faxed** the receipt to the client.

　　該秘書將收據 faxed 給客戶。

檔案　260 **file** [faɪl] *n.*

　　例 The **files** are located in the cabinet behind the water cooler.

　　Files 就放在飲水機後面的櫃子裡。

檔案夾，資料夾　261 **folder** [ˈfoldɚ] *n.*

　　例 I put the information for each client in a separate **folder**.

　　我把要給每位客戶的資料放在不同的 folder 裡。

家具　262 **furniture** [ˈfɝnɪtʃɚ] *n.*

　　例 The **furniture** in the office is a little outdated.

　　辦公室裡的 furniture 有些過時了。

硬體　263 **hardware** [ˈhɑrdˌwɛr] *n.*

　　例 My computer **hardware** is a little outdated.

　　我電腦的 hardware 有些老舊。

264 headphone [ˈhɛdˌfon] *n.*

☐
☐　例 If you need to listen to audio files in the office, please use **headphones**.

如果您需要在辦公室裡聽有聲檔案，請使用 headphones。

耳機

265 instruction [ɪnˈstrʌkʃən] *n.*

☐
☐　例 The **instructions** were not included in the box.

Instructions 並未附在箱子裡。

操作指南，使用說明

266 internal [ɪnˈtɜ·nl] *adj.*

☐
☐　例 How much **internal** memory does your computer have?

你電腦的 internal 記憶容量為何？

內部的

267 internet [ˈɪntɚˌnɛt] *n.*

☐
☐　例 Employees are prohibited from surfing the **Internet** at work.

員工不得在公司裡隨意瀏覽 Internet。

網際網路

268 laptop [ˈlæpˌtɑp] *n.*

☐
☐　例 I left my **laptop** on the bus.

我把 laptop 忘在公車上了。

筆記型電腦

269 letter [ˈlɛtɚ] *n.*

☐
☐　例 It is faster to send a **letter** by air than by land.

空運 letter 比寄陸運還要迅速。

信，函件

印有箋頭
（公司行號
名稱地址）
之信紙

270 letterhead [ˋlɛtɚˌhɛd] *n.*

例 Employees are asked to write all letters to clients on company **letterhead**.

公司要求員工一律使用公司的 letterhead 寫信給客戶。

清單，目錄

271 list [lɪst] *n.*

例 Please make a **list** of the office supplies you need.

請將您所需的辦公用品列在 list 上。

標誌

272 logo [ˋlogo] *n.*

例 Our company **logo** is green and black.

本公司的 logo 是綠黑兩色。

郵件

273 mail [mel] *n.*

例 Jason's nephew sorts **mail** in the mail room.

傑森的姪子在郵務室分發 mail。

手冊，指南

274 manual [ˋmænjʊəl] *n.*

例 The **manual** said to let the laptop battery drain completely before recharging.

Manual 說要讓筆記型電腦的電池完全耗盡後，才可再充電。

會議室

275 meeting room [ˋmitɪŋ ˌrum] *n. phr.*

例 Unfortunately, the **meeting room** is already booked.

很遺憾地，meeting room 已經有人預約了。

276 memo [ˈmɛmo] *n.*

☐
☐ 例 The **memo** was sent out to all supervisors and managers within the company.

Memo 已送到公司內部所有主管與經理的手上。

備忘錄

277 notice [ˈnotɪs] *v.*

☐
☐ 例 If you **notice** me leaving a little early today, it is because I have a doctor's appointment.

如果你 notice 我今天有點早退,那是因為我有預約看醫生。

注意到

278 office [ˈɔfɪs] *n.*

☐
☐ 例 The **office** is moving to a larger space on another floor of the building.

Office 將搬遷至同棟大樓裡空間較大的樓層。

公司,辦公室

279 office supplies [ˈɔfɪs səˈplaɪz] *n. phr.*

☐
☐ 例 Please let me know what **office supplies** you need and I will order them for you.

請告知我您所需的 office supplies,我將會為您訂購。

辦公用品

280 paperwork [ˈpepɚˌwɝk] *n.*

☐
☐ 例 Christine's position requires a lot of **paperwork**.

克莉絲汀的職位需要做很多的 paperwork。

文書工作,書面作業

281 partition [parˈtɪʃən] *n.*

☐
☐ 例 Employee desks are separated by **partitions**.

員工的座位都是用 partitions 隔開的。

隔板,分隔物

電話號碼　282　**phone number** [ˈfon ˌnʌmbɚ] *n. phr.*

例 My **phone number** is on my business card.
我的名片上面有我的 phone number。

影印本　283　**photocopy** [ˈfotoˌkɑpɪ] *n.*

例 How many **photocopies** do you want me to make?
你要我影印幾份 photocopies？

記事本　284　**planner** [ˈplænɚ] *n.*

例 I'm not sure when I'm available because I left my **planner** at home.
我不知道我什麼時候有空，因為我把 planner 忘在家裡了。

印表機　285　**printer** [ˈprɪntɚ] *n.*

例 The printer only **prints** in black and white.
這台 printer 只能列印出黑白兩色。

處理器　286　**processor** [ˈprɑsɛsɚ] *n.*

例 This computer **processor** is slow and needs to be updated.
這台電腦 processor 太慢了，需要更新。

投影機　287　**projector** [prəˈdʒɛktɚ] *n.*

例 The **projector** is often used to present data during meetings.
Projector 經常在會議時用來呈現數據資料。

288 **report** [rɪˋpɔrt] *n.*　　　　　　　　　　報告

　例 The year-end **report** will be available next week.

　　下星期年終 report 將會出爐。

289 **scanner** [ˋskænɚ] *n.*　　　　　　　　　掃描機

　例 We only have one **scanner** in the office.

　　我們辦公室裡只有一台 scanner。

290 **screen** [skrin] *n.*　　　　　　　　　　螢幕

　例 Please turn off your computer **screen** when you are not sitting at your desk.

　　如果你沒坐在桌前，請關閉電腦的 screen。

291 **stamp** [stæmp] *n.*　　　　　　　　　　郵票

　例 Don't forget to put a **stamp** on each envelope.

　　別忘了在每個信封上貼上 stamp。

292 **stationery** [ˋsteʃənˌɛrɪ] *n.*　　　　　　文具

　例 Please only use the **stationary** with the new logo.

　　請只使用有新標誌的 stationary。

293 **substitute** [ˋsʌbstəˌtjut] *n.*　　　　　　替代品

　例 We don't have any sugar **substitute** for the coffee in the staff room.

　　我們的員工休息室裡沒有任何咖啡用的糖 substitute（代糖）。

打卡鐘，計
時鐘

294 **time clock** [ˈtaɪm ˌklɑk] *n. phr.*

☐
☐ 例 Companies depend on the **time clock** to keep track of the hours their employees work.

公司依靠 time clock 來查看職員的上班時間。

語音信箱

295 **voicemail** [ˈvɔɪsˌmel] *n.*

☐
☐ 例 I have six messages in my **voicemail** that I haven't listened to yet.

我的 voicemail 裡有六通尚未聽取的留言。

白板

296 **whiteboard** [ˈhwaɪtˌbɔrd] *n.*

☐
☐ 例 You can use the **whiteboard** in the conference room during your presentation.

你可使用會議室裡的 whiteboard 進行簡報。

2 At the Office 辦公室 ⑧

預約，見面
的約定

297 **appointment** [əˈpɔɪntmənt] *n.*

☐
☐ 例 Marianne asked her manager if she could leave a few minutes early so she could attend a doctor's **appointment**.

瑪莉安娜向她的經理要求早退，以便能赴上醫師的 appointment。

安排，整理

298 **arrange** [əˈrendʒ] *v.*

☐
☐ 例 Please **arrange** the files alphabetically.

請將檔案按照英文字母的順序來 arrange。

299 **arrangement** [əˈrendʒmənt] *n.*　佈置，整理

☐ 例 The **arrangement** of these files is confusing.

☐ 這些檔案的 arrangement 令人混淆。

300 **aspect** [ˈæspɛkt] *n.*　面向

☐ 例 There are a few **aspects** about my position that I
☐ like and a few I don't.

我喜歡我這職位的一些 aspects，但也有一些是我
不喜歡的。

301 **assemble** [əˈsɛmbḷ] *v.*　收集，彙集

☐ 例 Can you help me **assemble** these handouts?

☐ 你能幫我 assemble 這些傳單嗎？

302 **attach** [əˈtætʃ] *v.*　附上，加上

☐ 例 Don't forget to **attach** your resume to the email.

☐ 請別忘了隨電子郵件 attach 您的履歷表。

303 **categorize** [ˈkætəgəˌraɪz] *v.*　分類

☐ 例 Please **categorize** the files according to purpose.

☐ 請將檔案按其目的 categorize。

304 **available** [əˈveləbḷ] *adj.*　有空

☐ 例 Are you **available** to meet after lunch?

☐ 午餐後你 available 碰個面嗎？

瀏覽，隨便翻閱	305	**browse** [braʊz] *v.*
	例	I've been **browsing** the classified section for new job opportunities.
		我一直以來都在 browsing 分類廣告，找新的工作機會。
打電話	306	**call** [kɔl] *v.*
	例	I took a message and told the client you would **call** her back.
		我記下客戶的留言並說你會回 call 給她。
來電者	307	**caller** [ˈkɔlɚ] *n.*
	例	An unknown **caller** left a disrespectful message on the company answering machine.
		有個不知名的 caller 在公司的電話答錄機上留下無禮的留言。
小心，謹慎	308	**caution** [ˈkɔʃən] *n.*
	例	Walk with **caution**, the floors have just been mopped.
		走路要 caution，地板才剛擦過。
手機	309	**cell phone** [ˈsɛl ˌfon] *n. phr.*
	例	We have a strict no-**cell-phone** policy in the office.
		我們公司有個「禁止使用 cell phone」的規定。
拿走	310	**collect** [kəˈlɛkt] *v.*
	例	Please be sure to **collect** all your belongings before leaving the conference room.
		離開會議室前，請記得 collect 您所有的隨身物品。

311 **connection** [kəˈnɛkʃən] *n.*　連接

例 Our office internet **connection** is not working today.

今天我們公司網路的 connection 壞掉了。

312 **consecutive** [kənˈsɛkjətɪv] *adj.*　連續的，不斷的

例 Julia has been absent for five **consecutive** days.

茱莉亞已經 consecutive 五天缺席了。

313 **conservative** [kənˈsɝvətɪv] *adj.*　保守的

例 Our boss tends to be very **conservative** with his investments.

我們老闆對於他的投資持非常 conservative 態度。

314 **constructive** [kənˈstrʌktɪv] *adj.*　有建設性的

例 I don't want to hear what you think about my presentation unless it is **constructive**.

我不想聽你對我報告的看法，除非是 constructive。

315 **control** [kənˈtrol] *v.*　控制

例 If you are not in a good mood, it is important to try to **control** yourself at work.

在職場上，心煩時能 control 你的脾氣很重要。

316 **convince** [kənˈvɪns] *v.*　說服

例 Margret is trying to **convince** me to go to the two-day conference with her.

瑪格麗特正試著 convince 我跟她一起參加為期兩日的會議。

副本

317 copy [ˈkɑpɪ] *n.*

例 Could you please make me twenty **copies** of this document?

能請你幫我把這份文件印二十份 copies 嗎？

通信，通信聯繫

318 correspondence [ˌkɔrəˈspɑndəns] *n.*

例 I have been maintaining **correspondence** with the CEO since we were introduced years ago.

自從幾年前我與執行長經人介紹認識後，我們就一直維持 correspondence。

辯論，討論

319 debate [dɪˈbet] *v.*

例 The manager and supervisor **debated** over the length of employee break times.

經理與主管 debated 關於員工休息時間的長短。

決定

320 decision [dɪˈsɪʒən] *n.*

例 The final **decision** on the project has not yet been made.

這計畫尚未定下最後的 decision。

宣佈，聲明

321 declaration [ˌdɛkləˈreʃən] *n.*

例 My boss made a **declaration** that she would retire by the end of the year.

我老闆做了個 declaration，她會在年底退休。

授權，委託

322 delegate [ˈdɛləˌget] *v.*

例 I **delegated** part of my work to Judy.

我 delegated 茱蒂我的部分工作。

323 detach [dɪˋtætʃ] *v.*　分開，分離

例 It is important to **detach** yourself from work related stress when you go home.

回家後，能把自己從工作壓力中 detach 很重要。

324 dial [ˋdaɪəl] *v.*　撥（號）

例 I accidentally **dialed** the wrong number.

我不小心 dialed 錯誤的號碼。

325 digital [ˋdɪdʒɪtl] *adj.*　數位（的）

例 I left my new **digital** camera on the bus.

我把 digital 相機遺留在公車上了。

326 disposal [dɪˋspozl] *n.*　丟棄；處置

例 Please only use the garbage can for **disposal** of items that cannot be recycled.

此垃圾桶只用於 disposal 不能回收的垃圾。

327 download [ˋdaʊn͵lod] *v.*　下載

例 My manager asked me to **download** this program onto her computer.

我的經理要我 download 這程式到她的電腦裡。

328 election [ɪˋlɛkʃən] *n.*　選舉

例 An **election** will be held next month.

下個月將舉行 election。

装進，（隨函）附寄

329 enclose [ɪnˋkloz] *v.*

例 Don't forget to **enclose** a copy of the invoice in the envelope for the customer.

別忘了在信封裡 enclose 要給客戶的發票。

執行，實施

330 enforce [ɪnˋfɔrs] *v.*

例 We have many rules in the office, but they are rarely **enforced**.

我們公司有許多規定，卻很少 enforced。

提高

331 enhance [ɪnˋhæns] *v.*

例 Could you help me **enhance** the clarity of this image?

您能幫我 enhance 影像的清晰度嗎？

登記，報名

332 enroll [ɪnˋrol] *v.*

例 I **enrolled** in a yoga class to help me de-stress after work.

下班後，我 enrolled 瑜珈課來抒解壓力。

註冊／報名人數

333 enrollment [ɪnˋrolmənt] *n.*

例 **Enrollment** in the adult swimming class is much higher than last year.

成人游泳班的 enrollment 比去年成長很多。

外部的，外接的

334 external [ɪkˋstɝnl̩] *adj.*

例 You should back up your files on an **external** hard drive.

你應該把檔案備份到 external 硬碟。

335 **focus** [ˈfokəs] *v.*　　　　　　　　　　　集中於，專注於

☐　例 There is too much talking in the office for me to
☐　**focus** on my work.

　　辦公室裡人聲嘈雜，我沒辦法 focus 在工作上。

336 **forward** [ˈfɔrwɚd] *v.*　　　　　　　　　轉寄；發送

☐　例 Could you please **forward** me the email the
☐　manager sent to staff?

　　能請您將經理發給員工的電子郵件 forward 給我
　　嗎？

337 **highlight** [ˈhaɪˌlaɪt] *v.*　　　　　　　　強調

☐　例 Our boss **highlighted** a few important ideas we
☐　learned at the conference.

　　我們老闆 highlighted 一些我們在會議上學到的重
　　要概念。

338 **implement** [ˈɪmpləˌmɛnt] *v.*　　　　　執行，實施

☐　例 Employees were asked to **implement** the new
☐　process immediately.

　　員工被要求立刻 implement 幾個新步驟。

339 **incoming** [ˈɪnˌkʌmɪŋ] *adj.*　　　　　　新來的

☐　例 The **incoming** manager has a lot of experience.
☐　Incoming 經理閱歷豐富。

340 **in regard to** [ɪn rɪˈgɑrd tu] *phr.*　　　關於

☐　例 I would like to speak with you **in regard to**
☐　your frequent absences from work.

　　我想跟你談談 in regard to 你時常請假的事。

安裝

341 **install** [ɪnˈstɔl] *v.*

例 Could you help me to **install** this software on my computer?

能請您幫我把這軟體 install 到我的電腦上嗎？

留言

342 **leave a message** [ˈliv ə ˈmɛsɪdʒ] *v. phr.*

例 If I don't answer my phone, please **leave a message**.

如果我沒有接電話，就請你 leave a message。

提到，提及

343 **mention** [ˈmɛnʃən] *v.*

例 Don't forget to **mention** the boss when you thank the staff for their hard work.

當你感謝辛勤的工作人員時，別忘了 mention 我們的老闆。

留言

344 **message** [ˈmɛsɪdʒ] *n.*

例 I had five **messages** waiting for me on my answering machine.

我的電話答錄機裡有五通未聽的 messages。

監控，監督

345 **monitor** [ˈmɑnətɚ] *v.*

例 Our supervisor **monitors** the work of employees very closely.

我們的主管密切 monitors 員工工作。

建立人脈，互相交往

346 **network** [ˈnɛtˌwɝk] *v.*

例 Conferences offer working professionals a great opportunity to **network**.

研討會提供在職的專業人員 network 的絕佳機會。

347 **note** [not] *n.*

☐
☐ 例 Please take **note** of anything you think should be shared at the next meeting.

請寫 note 記下任何你覺得應該在下次會議裡分享的事情。

348 **online** [ˌɑnˈlaɪn] *adv.*

☐
☐ 例 Employees should not chat with their friends **online** during work hours.

員工不應在工作時間 online 跟朋友聊天。

349 **opinion** [əˈpɪnjən] *n.*

☐
☐ 例 What is your **opinion** of the new company logo?

你對公司的新標誌有何 opinion？

350 **path** [pæθ] *n.*

☐
☐ 例 My supervisor told me I was on the right **path** with my work.

我的主管跟我說我工作的 path 是正確的。

351 **plug** [plʌg] *v.*

☐
☐ 例 Could you help me **plug** my computer in?

您能幫我把電腦 plug 嗎？

352 **post** [post] *v.*

☐
☐ 例 Could you please **post** the details of the workshop on the bulletin board?

能麻煩您在佈告欄上 post 研討會的細節嗎？

列印 | 353 **print** [prɪnt] *v.*

例 I **printed** two copies of the document.

我 printed 了兩份文件。

確認；重申 | 354 **reaffirm** [ˌriəˈfɝm] *v.*

例 I called the client back to **reaffirm** the details.

我回電給客戶，reaffirm 細節部分。

收到 | 355 **receive** [rɪˈsiv] *v.*

例 I haven't **received** the parcel you sent last week.

我還沒 received 你上星期寄出的包裹。

認可，認出 | 356 **recognize** [ˈrɛkəɡˌnaɪz] *v.*

例 I hope that people **recognize** our involvement in this charity.

我希望人們能 recognize 我們在這場賑濟上的貢獻。

回收利用 | 357 **recycle** [riˈsaɪkl] *v.*

例 Please **recycle** all scrap paper in the office.

請將辦公室裡的廢紙 recycle。

參考，參照 | 358 **refer to** [rɪˈfɝ tu] *v.*

例 If you aren't sure how to assemble the shelf, **refer to** the manual.

如果你不確定要怎麼組裝架子，那就 refer to 說明書吧。

359 reminder [rɪˈmaɪndɚ] *n.*   提醒函

☐
☐ 例 Employees were sent a **reminder** to turn off their computers at night.

員工們都收到 reminder，提醒晚上電腦都要關機。

360 replace [rɪˈples] *v.*   更換

☐
☐ 例 The batteries in my camera need to be **replaced**.

我相機裡的電池需要 replaced。

361 reply [rɪˈplaɪ] *n.*   回覆

☐
☐ 例 I am waiting for the client's **reply** to my email.

我在等客戶對我電子郵件的 reply。

362 response [rɪˈspɑns] *n.*   回覆

☐
☐ 例 I accepted the proposal in my email **response**.

我在電子郵件的 response 裡接受了提議。

363 restriction [rɪˈstrɪkʃən] *n.*   限制，約束

☐
☐ 例 Staff members are under many **restrictions** while in the office.

在公司裡，職員受到許多 restrictions。

364 rule [rul] *n.*   規定，章程

☐
☐ 例 There are no official **rules** in the office.

辦公室裡沒有正式的 rules。

（傳）送

365 **run** [rʌn] *v.*

☐ 例 Could you please **run** these papers to the human resources department?

能麻煩您把這些文件 run 到人力資源部門嗎？

掃描

366 **scan** [skæn] *v.*

☐ 例 My client asked me to **scan** the receipt and email it to him.

我的客戶要求我 scan 收據並以電子郵件寄給他。

監督，管理

367 **supervisory** [ˌsupɚˈvaɪzəri] *adj.*

☐ 例 Employees in **supervisory** positions need to go through extensive training.

在 supervisory 職位的員工需要經過充份的訓練。

發生，舉行

368 **take place** [ˈtekˈples] *v. phr.*

☐ 例 When will the next meeting **take place**?

下次會議將於何時 take place？

內文，文字

369 **text** [tɛkst] *n.*

☐ 例 Please read the **text** carefully before sending.

在寄出前，請仔細閱讀 text。

解決（問題）

370 **troubleshoot** [ˈtrʌblˌʃut] *v.*

☐ 例 After **troubleshooting** the problem, Jim gave up trying to find a solution.

Troubleshooting 後，吉姆放棄找解決辦法。

371 **update** [ˈʌpdet] *n.*

例 My manager likes to receive regular **updates** on the progress of the project.

我的經理喜歡按時收到案子進度的 updates。

更新；最新訊息

372 **website** [ˈwɛbˌsaɪt] *n.*

例 The company **website** was designed by the boss's son.

公司的 website 是老闆的兒子所設計的。

網站，網頁

3 Meeting & Presentation 會議與簡報 (9)

373 **advance** [ədˈvæns] *adj.*

例 We always have meetings without **advance** notice.

我們每次開會都不會收到 advance 通知。

預先的

374 **afterward** [ˈæftəwəd] *adv.*

例 We are planning on going to the conference and then going for dinner **afterward**.

我們計畫出席會議，afterward 再去吃晚餐。

之後，後來

375 **agenda** [əˈdʒɛndə] *n.*

例 Patricia wrote the meeting time in her **agenda**.

派翠西亞在 agenda 上寫下開會的時間。

記事簿；議程

376 **agreement** [əˈgrimənt] *n.*

例 Henry signed the **agreement** after the meeting.

亨利在會議後簽下了 agreement。

同意書，協議書

替代的，可供選擇的

377 **alternative** [ɔlˋtɝnətɪv] *adj.*

例 Maybe there is an **alternative** solution to the problem.

也許會有解決這問題的 alternative 方案。

宣佈，發表

378 **announce** [əˋnaʊns] *v.*

例 My boss **announced** his plans to retire this afternoon.

今天下午，我老闆 announced 他的退休計畫。

宣佈，通知

379 **announcement** [əˋnaʊnsmənt] *n.*

例 An emergency **announcement** was made over the speaker system.

透過廣播系統發佈了一項緊急的 announcement。

掌聲

380 **applause** [əˋplɔz] *n.*

例 Please hold your **applause** until the end of the speech.

請將你們的 applause 留待至演說的尾聲。

爭吵，爭論

381 **argue** [ˋɑrgjʊ] *v.*

例 It is rude to **argue** in front of guests.

在賓客面前 argue 是沒禮貌的。

注意

382 **attention** [əˋtɛnʃən] *n.*

例 It was brought to my **attention** that you have been late 3 days this week.

你這星期已經遲到三天，引起了我的 attention。

383 **attn** *n.*

☐
☐ 例 The fax that came in this morning read, "**attn**: all staff members."

今天早上進來的傳真上面寫著：「attn：所有職員」。

attention 的縮寫

384 **brief** [brif] *adj.*

☐
☐ 例 I hope the staff meeting is **brief**.

我希望員工會議 brief 就好。

短暫的；簡短的

385 **briefing** [ˈbrifɪŋ] *n.*

☐
☐ 例 The manager gave us a **briefing** on our new clients before the meeting began.

在會議開始前，經理就為我們做了新客戶的 briefing。

簡報

386 **chart** [tʃɑrt] *n.*

☐
☐ 例 The manager used many **charts** throughout his presentation.

經理在整個報告中大量使用 charts。

圖表

387 **comment** [ˈkɑmənt] *v.*

☐
☐ 例 Frank asked us to **comment** on the quality of his presentation.

法蘭克請我們 comment 他簡報的品質。

評論，發表意見

388 **conclusion** [kənˈkluʒən] *n.*

☐
☐ 例 I've come to the **conclusion** that I am not suited for this position.

我下了一個 conclusion，我不適合這個工作。

結論，決定

同意，贊成	**389 concur** [kənˈkɝ] *v.*	

例 James **concurred** with the boss's opinion.

詹姆士 concurred 他老闆的意見。

主持；帶領	**390 conduct** [kənˈdʌkt] *v.*	

例 Sarah is not comfortable **conducting** meetings.

莎拉對於要 conducting 會議感到不自在。

商談，協商	**391 confer** [kənˈfɝ] *v.*	

例 The manager needed to **confer** with the CEO before making a decision.

經理需要先與執行長 confer，才能做出決定。

（正式）會議	**392 conference** [ˈkɑnfərəns] *n.*	

例 The **conference** is held at the same location every year.

每年的 conference 都在相同的地點舉行。

有信心	**393 confident** [ˈkɑnfədənt] *adj.*	

例 Michelle is **confident** about the proposal she will be presenting at tomorrow's meeting.

蜜雪兒對於要在明天會議中提出的提案很 confident。

集會，代表大會	**394 congress** [ˈkɑŋgrəs] *n.*	

例 I'm going to attend the **congress** of our representatives from across the country this afternoon.

今天下午我將出席一場全國公司代表 congress。

395 consensus [kən'sɛnsəs] *n.*

共識

例 We have come to a **consensus** that the department needs to be reorganized.

我們已達成 consensus，要重新打理那個部門。

396 convention [kən'vɛnʃən] *n.*

會議，大會

例 The **convention** was cancelled this year.

今年的 convention 取消了。

397 disapproval [ˌdɪsə'pruvl] *n.*

不贊成

例 Our boss expressed her **disapproval** of the project at the last meeting.

我們老闆在上回會議中對這企劃案表示 disapproval。

398 discipline ['dɪsəplɪn] *n.*

紀律

例 If you are going to work from home, you have to have a lot of **discipline**.

如果你打算在家工作，你就必須建立許多 discipline。

399 discuss [dɪ'skʌs] *v.*

討論

例 My supervisor told me that she had some items she wanted to **discuss** with me.

我主管說她要跟我 discuss 一些事項。

400 inquire [ɪn'kwaɪr] *v.*

詢問

例 I will contact the hotel to **inquire** about the fees for booking the conference room.

我會聯絡飯店 inquire 預定會議室的費用。

中斷，打斷　　401　**interrupt** [ˌɪntəˈrʌpt] *v.*

☐　例 The meeting was **interrupted** by the fire alarm.
☐　會議因火災警報而 interrupted。

介紹　　402　**introduction** [ˌɪntrəˈdʌkʃən] *n.*

☐　例 We will begin the meeting by making some
☐　**introductions**.
　　我們的會議將由一些 introductions 開啟序幕。

議題　　403　**issue** [ˈɪʃʊ] *n.*

☐　例 The most important **issues** should be discussed
☐　first.
　　應該優先討論最重要的 issues。

項目　　404　**item** [ˈaɪtəm] *n.*

☐　例 We have six important **items** on the agenda for
☐　the staff meeting.
　　我們議程上有六項重要的 items 要在員工會議上進
　　行討論。

演講，講課　　405　**lecture** [ˈlɛktʃɚ] *n.*

☐　例 The **lecture** was very informative.
☐　這堂 lecture 讓人增廣見聞。

演講者；講　　406　**lecturer** [ˈlɛktʃərɚ] *n.*
師

☐　例 The **lecturer** spoke for almost two hours straight.
☐　Lecturer 講了幾乎整整兩小時。

407 lunch meeting [ˈlʌntʃ ˌmitɪŋ] *n. phr.*

午餐會議

☐
☐ 例 The **lunch meeting** will be held in the restaurant downstairs.

Lunch meeting 將在樓下的餐廳舉行。

408 marker [ˈmɑrkɚ] *n.*

標記;馬克筆

☐
☐ 例 Jill drew on the graph with a green **marker** to indicate the rise in sales.

吉兒在圖表上以綠色 marker 表示銷售量的上升。

409 material [məˈtɪrɪəl] *n.*

素材,資料

☐
☐ 例 The **materials** used in the presentation held the interest of the people at the meeting.

報告中使用的 materials 抓住與會者的興趣。

410 meeting [ˈmitɪŋ] *n.*

會議

☐
☐ 例 The **meeting** will start at 2:30.

Meeting 將於兩點三十分開始。

411 minute [ˈmɪnɪt] *n.*

分鐘

☐
☐ 例 How many **minutes** do we have until we can leave the office?

我們還有多少 minutes 才能離開辦公室?

412 minutes [ˈmɪnɪts] *n.*

會議記錄

☐
☐ 例 Our boss was angry that no one took **minutes** at the meeting.

我們老闆對於會議中沒人寫 minutes 非常生氣。

☆ 反對，異議

413 **objection** [əbˈdʒɛkʃən] *n.*

例 Several staff members raised **objections** to the plan.

好幾個職員對此計畫提出 objections。

對手，對方隊

414 **opposition** [ˌɑpəˈzɪʃən] *n.*

例 The **opposition** leader at the debate spoke first.

辯論時，opposition 的領隊先發言。

部分

415 **part** [pɑrt] *n.*

例 Every employee has an important **part** to play in the company.

公司裡的每個員工都扮演很重要的 part。

☆ 參與者

416 **participant** [pɑrˈtɪsəpənt] *n.*

例 How many **participants** will be at the workshop tomorrow?

明天的專題研討會將會有多少 participants 出席？

出席，在場

417 **presence** [ˈprɛzns̩] *n.*

例 The manager's **presence** made everyone nervous.

經理的 presence 讓每個人都很緊張。

出席的，在場的

418 **present** [ˈprɛznt̩] *adj.*

例 How many people will be **present** at the meeting?

有多少人會 present 會議？

419 **presentation** [ˌprɛznˈteʃən] *n.*　　　報告，演示

- ☐ **例** The **presentation** lasted over two hours.
- ☐ Presentation 進行了兩個小時以上。

420 **proceed** [prəˈsid] *v.*　　　繼續進行

- ☐ **例** Does anyone have any questions before we **proceed**?
- ☐ 在我們 proceed 之前，有任何人要提出問題嗎？

421 **propose** [prəˈpoz] *v.*　　　提議，建議

- ☐ **例** I have an idea I would like to **propose** to the boss.
- ☐ 我想向老闆 propose 一個想法。

422 **purpose** [ˈpɝpəs] *n.*　　　目的

- ☐ **例** The **purpose** of this meeting is to discuss upcoming employee evaluations.
- ☐ 此次會議的 purpose 是要討論即將來臨的員工評鑑。

423 **rearrange** [ˌriəˈrendʒ] *v.*　　　重新安排

- ☐ **例** Suzanne had to **rearrange** her schedule so she could attend the workshop.
- ☐ 蘇珊必須 rearrange 她的時間表，以便能參加研討會。

424 **reschedule** [riˈskɛdʒʊl] *v.*　　　重新安排（時間表）

- ☐ **例** I might have to **reschedule** our meeting on Friday to Monday.
- ☐ 我可能必須將我們這週五的會議 reschedule 到下週一。

Chapter
3
辦公室生活

研討會；研討班	425	**seminar** [ˈsɛməˌnɑr] *n.*

☆

☐ ☐ 例 The **seminar** may be of interest to employees who want a promotion.

想升職的員工可能會對這 seminar 感興趣。

會議，集會	426	**session** [ˈsɛʃən] *n.*

☐ ☐ 例 The **session** will last four to five hours.

這個 session 將會持續四至五小時。

解決（辦法）	427	**solution** [səˈluʃən] *n.*

☐ ☐ 例 Let's have a quick meeting to think of some **solutions** to the problem.

讓我們簡短開會一下，想想問題的 solutions。

演講者	428	**speaker** [ˈspikɚ] *n.*

☐ ☐ 例 One of the **speakers** at the conference is an old classmate of mine.

會議裡有個 speaker 是我的老同學。

演講	429	**speech** [spitʃ] *n.*

☐ ☐ 例 The **speech** given by the speaker was boring.

這演說者的 speech 著實無趣。

陳述，聲明	430	**statement** [ˈstetmənt] *n.*

☐ ☐ 例 Our boss made some rude **statements** at our last meeting.

我們老闆在上次會議裡說了些不禮貌的 statements。

431 subject [ˈsʌbdʒɪkt] *n.*　　主題

☐
☐　例 What is the **subject** of debate between John and Maria?

約翰與瑪麗亞在辯論什麼 subject？

432 subscribe [səbˈskraɪb] *v.*　　同意

☐
☐　例 I don't **subscribe** to the same beliefs as the boss.

我不 subscribe 跟老闆相同的信念。

433 summary [ˈsʌmərɪ] *n.*　　概要，概述

☐
☐　例 Could you please give me a **summary** of what happened at the meeting I missed yesterday?

我錯過了昨天的會議，能麻煩您提供我一份會議 summary 嗎？

434 teleconference [ˈtɛləˌkɑnfərəns] *n.*　　遠距會議

☐
☐　例 I was asked to join the **teleconference** with our overseas clients this morning.

我們海外客戶要求我加入今早的 teleconference。

435 topic [ˈtɑpɪk] *n.*　　主題

☐
☐　例 The main **topic** of the meeting was the new parking fees.

會議的首要 topic 是新的停車費率。

436 videoconference [ˈvɪdɪoˌkɑnfərəns] *n.*　　視訊會議

☐
☐　例 We have regular **videoconferences** with our overseas clients.

我們與海外客戶平常會進行 videoconferences。

觀點，見解 | 437 **viewpoint** [ˈvjuˌpɔɪnt] *n.*

例 You have to see the details in the document from different **viewpoints**.

你必須從不同的 viewpoints 看文件裡的細節。

研討會 | 438 **workshop** [ˈwɝkˌʃɑp] *n.*

例 Are you attending the **workshop** next week?

你會參加下星期舉辦的 workshop 嗎？

4 Building 建築物 (10)

建築 | 439 **architecture** [ˈɑrkɪˌtɛktʃɚ] *n.*

例 The firm is looking to move to an office building with a more modern style of **architecture**.

該公司等著搬到較現代 architecture 的辦公室。

檔案室 | 440 **archives** [ˈɑrkaɪvz] *n.*

例 All the old issues of our catalog are stored in the **archives**.

所有過季的目錄都存放在 archives 裡。

街區 | 441 **block** [blɑk] *n.*

例 The company headquarters is only two **blocks** from the train station.

公司總部離火車站只有兩個 blocks。

建築（業）者，營造商 | 442 **builder** [ˈbɪldɚ] *n.*

例 Our boss is disappointed with the **builder** because the project is two months behind schedule.

我們老闆對 builder 不滿，因為工程落後兩個月。

443 capacity [kəˈpæsətɪ] *n.*

例 Please do not exceed the elevator **capacity**.

請勿超過電梯所能負載的 capacity。

容量

444 centimeter [ˈsɛntəˌmitɚ] *n.*

例 The doorways were built two **centimeters** lower than the original plans.

這門口做得比原施工圖低了兩 centimeters。

公分，厘米

445 chamber [ˈtʃembɚ] *n.*

例 The formula for our company's best selling product is stored in a secret **chamber** in the office.

我們公司最暢銷產品的配方就放在公司某個祕密的 chamber 裡。

室，房間

446 construction [kənˈstrʌkʃən] *n.*

例 If the **construction** on the new building doesn't speed up, we won't be able to move until the spring.

假如新大樓的 construction 速度再不加快些，我們將無法在來年春天前搬遷。

建築，建造，工程

447 contractor [ˈkɑntræktɚ] *n.*

例 The **contractor** told us the job would be done ahead of schedule.

Contractor 告訴我們工程將會提前完工。

（工程）承包人

448 corridor [ˈkɔrɪdɚ] *n.*

例 We decided on an open-concept office space, and eliminated the need for **corridors**.

我們決定採用開放的辦公空間，排除 corridors 的需求。

走廊，迴廊

窗簾	**449 curtain** [ˈkɝtn̩] *n.*
	例 Employees were asked to close the **curtains** in the summer to keep the office space cool.
	夏季時，公司要求員工緊閉 curtains，以便維持涼爽的辦公空間。

訂金	**450 deposit** [dɪˈpɑzɪt] *n.*
	例 The real estate agent advised us to enclose a ten percent **deposit** with our offer.
	房仲建議我們在開價外附上百分之十的 deposit。

拆毀	**451 destroy** [dɪˈstrɔɪ] *v.*
	例 The company plans to **destroy** the building that is currently on the property they purchased.
	公司計畫 destroy 矗立在所購入那塊土地上的建物。

不利，缺點	**452 disadvantage** [ˌdɪsədˈvæntɪdʒ] *n.*
	例 It would be a huge **disadvantage** to our clients if we cannot find a more convenient location.
	如我們無法找到更便利的地點，將會對我們的客戶非常 disadvantage。

電扶梯	**453 escalator** [ˈɛskəˌletɚ] *n.*
	例 The **escalator** must be in good working order when the property is sold.
	房產出售時，escalator 必須運作良好。

出口	**454 exit** [ˈɛgzɪt] *n.*
	例 The **exits** are located at the end of the hallway.
	走道的盡頭就是 exits。

90

455 expand [ɪkˋspænd] *v.*

擴展，擴充

例 The office space is large enough to allow us to **expand** over the next few years.

這辦公室大到能容納我們往後數年 expand 之用。

456 floor plan [ˋflɔr ˏplæn] *n. phr.*

樓層平面圖

例 The **floor plan** will allow for every employee to have a view of the city from their desk.

Floor plan 將顧及到每位員工，從他們的位子就能看到外面市區的景色。

457 flooring [ˋflɔrɪŋ] *n.*

（總稱）室內地面／地板

例 Replacing the carpet **flooring** will be a big expense.

換掉鋪地毯的 flooring 將會是一大筆開銷。

458 furnish [ˋfɝnɪʃ] *v.*

給（房間）配置（家具等）

例 How much do you think it will cost to **furnish** the staff room with a sofa and table?

你覺得買張沙發跟桌子來 furnish 員工休息室要花多少錢？

459 gas [gæs] *n.*

瓦斯

例 The heating system of this building was recently changed from electric to **gas**.

這棟大樓最近才從電力暖氣換成 gas 暖氣。

460 heater [ˋhitɚ] *n.*

暖氣

例 There are **heaters** in every room of the office.

公司裡的每間辦公室都有 heaters。

高度

461 **height** [haɪt] *n.*

例 The **height** of the storage area is perfect for tall shelving units.

儲藏室的 height 正適合放高的層架。

高樓

462 **high-rise** [ˈhaɪˌraɪz] *n.*

例 The top floor of the **high-rise** went on the market today.

High-rise 的頂樓今天開始銷售。

室內

463 **interior** [ɪnˈtɪrɪɚ] *n.*

例 The outside of the building is in great condition, but the **interior** needs some work.

大樓的外觀狀況絕佳，但 interior 則需要整修。

室內設計

464 **interior design** [ɪnˈtɪrɪɚ dɪˌzaɪn] *n.*

例 I got some great ideas for our new office color scheme in an **interior design** magazine.

我從 interior design 雜誌中找新辦公室配色的靈感。

照明

465 **lighting** [ˈlaɪtɪŋ] *n.*

例 The **lighting** fixtures in the staff washroom will need to be replaced before this place is put on the market.

在公開銷售前，員工專用洗手間裡的 lighting 設備得換新。

地段，地點

466 **location** [loˈkeʃən] *n.*

例 If the **location** were more convenient, we would be interested in purchasing the property.

如果 location 可以更便利些，我們就會有興趣買這件房產。

467 **measurement** [ˈmɛʒɚmənt] *n.*

例 The total **measurement** of the floor space is 2000 square feet.

總樓層的 measurement 為 2000 平方英尺。

468 **neighborhood** [ˈnebɚ͵hʊd] *n.*

例 There are five comparable properties available in the same **neighborhood**.

這 neighborhood 就有五件條件差不多的房產待售中。

469 **next door** [ˈnɛkst ˈdɔr] *adv. phr.*

例 There is a great hotel right **next door** for clients visiting from out of town.

Next door 就有一家大飯店可供外地客戶拜訪時住宿。

470 **plumber** [ˈplʌmɚ] *n.*

例 I would like to have a qualified **plumber** do an inspection of the plumbing as a condition of the offer.

我想找個 plumber 來檢測房子的水管系統，作為出價的條件。

471 **quality** [ˈkwɑlətɪ] *n.*

例 The construction materials were all top **quality**.

用於工程的建材全都是頂級 quality 的建材。

472 **relocate** [riˈloket] *v.*

例 Our office is **relocating** at the end of the month.

我們辦公室月底即將要 relocating。

尺寸，大小

附近，鄰近地區

隔壁

水管工

品質

重新安置

樓梯

473 **staircase** [ˈstɛrˌkes] *n.*

☐ 例 We should take the **staircase** instead of the
☐ elevator.

我們應該不搭電梯，而是走 staircase。

（房屋的）
樓層

474 **story** [ˈstorɪ] *n.*

☐ 例 Our new client is looking for a two-**story** office
☐ space.

我們新客戶正在找兩層 story 的辦公室。

結構

475 **structure** [ˈstrʌktʃɚ] *n.*

☐ 例 The property inspector informed us that the
☐ **structure** of the building was weak.

房產的建築檢查員告知我們房子的 structure 有些
脆弱。

環境

476 **surroundings** [səˈraʊndɪŋz] *n.*

☐ 例 Mr. Henderson wants to move the office to a
☐ building with greener **surroundings**.

韓德森先生想將辦公室搬到 surroundings 比較綠化
的大樓裡。

地下的

477 **underground** [ˈʌndɚˈgraʊnd] *adj.*

☐ 例 The building offers **underground** parking.
☐ 大樓有提供 underground 停車場。

（電力、瓦
斯等）公用
事業設施

478 **utility** [juˈtɪlətɪ] *n.*

☐ 例 The fee includes all **utilities**.
☐ 費用包含所有的 utilities。

Exercises -3

請從選項中，選出最適當的答案完成句子。

1. The new regulation took effect after all the members _____;
from then on all the company employees had to observe it.

   (A) consented   (B) contended   (C) concerned   (D) concurred

2. This trail is the only _____ to the remote village in the mountains.

   (A) method   (B) access   (C) solution   (D) outcome

3. That man must be from Georgia; he speaks with a heavy southern _____.

   (A) pronunciation   (B) tone   (C) accent   (D) sound

4. Taiwan lacks natural _____; all the gasoline is imported.

   (A) coals   (B) surroundings   (C) resources   (D) sources

5. I'm not _____ with the man; he is a stranger to me.

   (A) accustomed   (B) acquainted   (C) acquired   (D) acknowledged

6. If I don't take the chance, what _____ do I have?

   (A) alternatives   (B) possibilities   (C) probabilities   (D) opportunities

7. When the performance was over, the dancers received loud _____ from the audience.

   (A) approval   (B) annoyance   (C) disturbance   (D) applause

8. After a lengthy discussion, they still couldn't reach a _____
whether to increase their investment or not.

   (A) notion   (B) destination   (C) conclusion   (D) portion

9. When I met my cousin at the airport, I could hardly _____
her because I hadn't seen her for years.

   (A) recognize   (B) distinguish   (C) paralyze   (D) analyze

10. The committee members were given a(n) _____ regarding
the financial status of the company.

   (A) abstract   (B) realization   (C) procrastination   (D) briefing

11. Give me some _____. Tell me what you think about my presentation.

    (A) establishments (B) comments (C) remarks (D) reminders

12. There was a message on my _____ telling me my rent was due in two days.

    (A) voicemail (B) vent (C) space (D) trade

13. There will be three candidates _____ for presidency this time.

    (A) accounting (B) campaigning (C) activating (D) stimulating

14. Please fill the tank to _____; we have a long way to go.

    (A) density (B) necessity (C) capacity (D) ability

15. If you deposit or withdraw money from a bank, you have a _____ with the bank.

    (A) transparency (B) transaction (C) transportation (D) interaction

16. Jason's hobby is music. He has _____ over ten thousand music CDs.

    (A) suspected (B) applied (C) assumed (D) collected

17. The roads are slippery due to the rain. Please drive with _____.

    (A) caution (B) tension (C) sensation (D) pretension

18. To use this computer, you have to enter a _____.

    (A) passport (B) password (C) puzzle (D) riddle

19. Just follow the _____ described in the manual, and you will be able to assemble the machine.

    (A) proposals (B) productions (C) procedures (D) purposes

20. In writing an essay, a(n) _____ is needed. But, make it brief, and present your main points right after that.

    (A) proportion (B) introduction (C) summarization (D) development

Chapter 4

Sales & Marketing 業務行銷

A company's main goal is to create value by offering products or services to consumers. Companies promote their products and services using a variety of marketing activities. These include marketing sales presentations, buying advertising space, and communicating a positive image of the company to the public via public relations.

Sales & Marketing
業務行銷

1 Advertising 廣告 ⑪

消耗，耗費 | 479 **absorb** [əbˋsɔrb] *v.*

例 Advertising will **absorb** a huge amount of the budget.

打廣告會 absorb 大筆預算。

登廣告 | 480 **advertise** [ˋædvɚˏtaɪz] *v.*

例 Available properties are **advertised** in the classified section of the newspaper.

待售的房地產會 advertised 在報紙的分類廣告上。

廣告 | 481 **advertisement** [ˏædvɚˋtaɪzmənt] *n.*

例 We should put an **advertisement** in the newspaper.

我們應該在報紙上登 advertisement。

廣告商 | 482 **advertiser** [ˏædvɚˋtaɪzɚ] *n.*

例 We hired an **advertiser** to promote our services.

公司聘請了 advertiser 來宣傳我們的服務。

分配額；配置 | 483 **allocation** [ˏæləˋkeʃən] *n.*

例 We only have an **allocation** of ten thousand dollars to spend on advertising.

我們只有十萬元的 allocation 可用在廣告上。

484 ambassador [æmˋbæsədɚ] *n.*   代表；大使

例 The company hired a celebrity to be an **ambassador** for their new line of make-up.

該公司聘請名人當 ambassador，為他們的新化妝品系列代言。

485 anticipate [ænˋtɪsə,pet] *v.*   預測；預料

例 The team can **anticipate** sales projections for next year based on this year's sales.

業務團隊能依據今年的銷售額 anticipate 明年度的銷售金額。

486 booklet [ˋbʊk,lɪt] *n.*   小冊子

例 People are handing out **booklets** about flu prevention on the street.

有人在街上發送預防感冒的 booklets。

487 boost [bust] *v.*   提高；促進

例 We may be able to **boost** sales if we put more money into advertising.

如果我們刊登更多廣告，或許可以 boost 銷售額。

488 brand [brænd] *n.*   商標，牌子

例 This **brand** is not as popular as it used to be.

這 brand 現在沒有以前那麼受歡迎了。

489 brochure [broˋʃʊr] *n.*   小冊子

例 We recently created a **brochure** to explain the benefits of this skin cream.

我們最近做了一本 brochure 說明這款護膚乳液的好處。

預算   490   **budget** [ˈbʌdʒɪt] *n.*

例 The marketing team was given a strict **budget** for the promotion of the new clothing line.

行銷團隊在促銷服飾新品上有嚴格的 budget 限制。

活動   491   **campaign** [kæmˈpen] *n.*

例 Our new **campaign** will attract more clients.

我們的新 campaign 將會吸引更多的客戶。

個案，案例   492   **case** [kes] *n.*

例 That marketing firm has some high-profile **cases**.

該行銷公司有一些高知名度的 cases。

名人   493   **celebrity** [səˈlɛbrətɪ] *n.*

例 We need to get a **celebrity** to be the face of our new product.

我們需要請 celebrity 來代言我們的新產品。

（報紙、雜誌的）專欄   494   **column** [ˈkaləm] *n.*

例 Our product was mentioned in a newspaper **column**.

報紙上的 column 裡有提到我們的產品。

專欄作家   495   **columnist** [ˈkaləmnɪst] *n.*

例 The **columnist** gave our product a great review.

Columnist 為我們的產品做了個很棒的評論。

496 commentary [ˈkɑmən‚tɛrɪ] *n.*

☆ 評論；實況報導

☑ The media **commentary** about our new perfume is very positive.

媒體對我們新款香水的 commentary 非常正面。

497 commercial [kəˈmɝˌʃəl] *n.*

（電視、廣播中的）商業廣告

☑ We finished filming the **commercial** yesterday.

我們昨天才剛拍完 commercial。

498 compose [kəmˈpoz] *v.*

創作（詩、樂曲等）

☑ We need to hire someone to **compose** a jingle for our new commercial.

我們需要聘人來為新廣告 compose 押韻動聽的廣告詞。

499 conduct [kənˈdʌkt] *v.*

實施

☑ After **conducting** the survey we realized there was no market for the product.

在 conducting 市調後，我們才發現這產品根本就沒有市場。

500 coordinator [koˈɔrdn̩‚etɚ] *n.*

協調員，企劃人員

☑ The marketing **coordinator** said we should launch the product before our competitors.

行銷 coordinator 說我們應該搶在對手之前讓產品上市。

501 develop [dɪˈvɛləp] *v.*

發展，開發

☑ We need to **develop** a new marketing strategy.

我們需要 develop 新的行銷策略。

有效的 | 502 **effective** [əˋfɛktɪv] *adj.*

☐ 例 We have to come up with an **effective** strategy to promote the product.

☐ 我們必須想個 effective 策略來推銷產品。

藝人，表演者 | 503 **entertainer** [ˌɛntəˋtenə] *n.*

☐ 例 It is important to secure a popular **entertainer** to help promote our product.

☐ 找到受歡迎的 entertainer 來幫忙促銷我們的產品很重要。

執行，實施 | 504 **execute** [ˋɛksɪˌkjut] *v.*

☐ 例 The sales team is **executing** their plan to attract more customers.

☐ 業務團隊正 executing 他們的計畫以求吸引更多的客戶。

（廣告）傳單 | 505 **flyer** [ˋflaɪə] *n.*

☐ 例 The advertisement is being printed on **flyers** and distributed this week.

☐ 廣告已刊登在 flyers 上，並於此週發派。

募款者；募款活動 | 506 **fundraiser** [ˋfʌndˌrezə] *n.*

☐ 例 The company donated some merchandise for the **fundraiser**.

☐ 公司為支持 fundraiser 而捐出一些商品。

募款的 | 507 **fundraising** [ˋfʌndˌrezɪŋ] *adj.*

☐ 例 The **fundraising** committee asked us for donations.

☐ Fundraising 委員會要求我們捐獻。

508 influential [ˌɪnfluˈɛnʃəl] *adj.*

發揮影響

☐
☐ 例 The marketing strategy must be **influential** enough to attract new customers.

行銷策略必須能夠 influential 才能吸引新顧客。

509 invest [ɪnˈvɛst] *v.*

投資

☐
☐ 例 Many people have **invested** in our new business.

許多人已經 invested 我們的新生意。

510 investigate [ɪnˈvɛstəˌget] *v.*

調查；研究

☐
☐ 例 We need to **investigate** why sales have suddenly dropped.

我們必須 investigate 為什麼銷售額突然下降。

511 investment [ɪnˈvɛstmənt] *n.*

投資

☐
☐ 例 Our **investment** in the new product has certainly paid off.

我們在新產品上的 investment 確實有獲利。

512 investor [ɪnˈvɛstə˞] *n.*

投資人

☐
☐ 例 We will have a meeting with **investors** tomorrow afternoon.

我們明天下午將與 investors 一起開會。

513 layout [ˈleˌaʊt] *n.*

版面設計，版面編排

☐
☐ 例 The **layout** for the new advertisement looks great.

新廣告的 layout 看起來很棒。

傳單

514 leaflet [ˈliflɪt] *n.*

例 This **leaflet** explains the benefits of using the product.

這份 leaflet 說明了使用本產品的好處。

連結

515 link [lɪŋk] *n.*

例 Click on the **link** in this email to visit our website.

點擊此電子郵件中的 link 便可參觀我們公司的網頁。

登入

516 login [ˈlɑɡˌɪn] *v.*

例 I forgot to **login** to the website.

我忘記 login 此網站。

媒體

517 media [ˈmidɪə] *n.*

例 We need to get the attention of the **media** to help boost sales.

我們需要得到 media 的關注，才能增加產品的銷售。

商品，貨品

518 merchandise [ˈmɝtʃənˌdaɪz] *n.*

例 The **merchandise** will be shipped from the factory in the morning.

早上有批 merchandise 會從工廠運送出去。

新聞播報員

519 newscaster [ˈnjuzˌkæstɚ] *n.*

例 The **newscaster** reported bad news for the economy.

Newscaster 報導經濟上的壞消息。

520 **newsletter** [ˈnjuzˌlɛtɚ] *n.*

例 Our sales team was highlighted in the company **newsletter**.

我們的銷售團隊在 newsletter 上成為焦點。

簡訊，內部公報

521 **outlet** [ˈaʊtˌlɛt] *n.*

例 Overstock of last year's merchandise is sold at factory **outlets**.

去年過剩的庫存商品在 outlets 販售。

暢貨中心；特賣會

522 **perspective** [pɚˈspɛktɪv] *n.*

例 The graphic designers had different **perspectives** on the layout for the book.

平面造型設計者對書的版面設計有不同的 perspectives。

看法，觀點

523 **poll** [pol] *n.*

例 **Polls** show that most women prefer fruity to floral scents.

Polls 顯示出大多數的女人比較喜歡水果香味，不是花香。

民調，民意測驗

524 **possibility** [ˌpɑsəˈbɪlətɪ] *n.*

例 There is a **possibility** that I may be promoted if this product line is successful.

如果此系列產品大賣，或許有 possibility 我會升職。

可能性

525 **potential** [pəˈtɛnʃəl] *n.*

例 I don't believe sales have reached their full **potential**.

我不相信銷售員已經完全發揮他們的 potential。

潛力，潛能

526 preliminary [prɪˈlɪməˌnɛrɪ] *adj.*

例 The **preliminary** feedback from clients suggests that we should offer a broader range of services.

客戶 preliminary 意見反映建議我們應該提供更加寬廣的服務範圍。

報刊

527 press [prɛs] *n.*

例 There hasn't been any mention of our new campaign in the **press**.

Press 上尚未有任何關於我們新活動的報導。

產品

528 product [ˈprɑdʌkt] *n.*

例 The **product** is sold at numerous locations across the city.

這款 product 的販售地點遍及本市。

問卷

529 questionnaire [ˌkwɛstʃənˈɛr] *n.*

例 In order to understand customer preferences, we should ask them to fill out a **questionnaire**.

為了解客戶的喜好，我們應該請客戶填寫 questionnaire。

代言人；發言人

530 spokesperson [ˈspoksˌpɝsn̩] *n.*

例 We need to find a celebrity to be a **spokesperson** for our new product.

我們需要找個名人來擔任 spokesperson，為我們的新產品代言。

資助，贊助

531 sponsor [ˈspɑnsɚ] *v.*

例 Our company **sponsors** two professional athletes.

我們公司 sponsors 兩名職業運動選手。

532 **strategy** [ˈstrætədʒɪ] *n.*   策略

例 The marketing team came up with a brilliant **strategy**.

行銷團隊想到了一個高明的 strategy。

533 **suggest** [səˈdʒɛst] *v.*   建議，提議

例 Our team leader **suggested** we start targeting a younger clientele.

我們團隊的領導者 suggested 我們開始把目標放在較年輕的顧客群。

534 **survey** [ˈsɝve] *n.*   調查

例 The customer **survey** showed that most women are willing to pay more for a high-quality product.

顧客 survey 顯示出，大多數的女性願意多付錢買高品質的產品。

535 **target** [ˈtɑrgɪt] *v.*   把…作為目標

例 We need to **target** single men in this campaign.

此次活動裡我們要 target 單身男人。

536 **trend** [trɛnd] *n.*   趨勢

例 It is important that all clothing manufactured is in line with current **trends**.

不論製作什麼樣的衣服，符合流行 trends 很重要。

積極的，果
敢的

537 **aggressive** [əˈgrɛsɪv] *adj.*

例 You need to be more **aggressive** with your sales
strategy.

你的銷售策略需更加 aggressive 一些。

大概的，大
約的

538 **approximate** [əˈprɑksəmɪt] *adj.*

例 We need an **approximate** arrival date for the
delivery.

我們需要到貨的 approximate 日期。

文章

539 **article** [ˈɑrtɪkl̩] *n.*

例 One of our products was mentioned in this
magazine **article**.

這雜誌裡有篇 article 提到我們其中的一個產品。

評估

540 **assessment** [əˈsɛsmənt] *n.*

例 Following our **assessment**, we decided to double
the production.

根據我們的 assessment，我們決定加倍生產。

作者

541 **author** [ˈɔθɚ] *n.*

例 The **author** will be signing copies of her newest
book this weekend.

這位 author 將在本周末舉辦新書發表簽名會。

平均

542 **average** [ˈævərɪdʒ] *n.*

例 We sell an **average** of five hundred bottles of
shampoo a month at that store.

我們在那間商店 average 一個月賣出五百瓶洗髮
精。

543 **circumstance** [ˋsɝkəm͵stæns] *n.*

□
□ 例 Under different **circumstances**, I think the product would have had better success.

在不同的 circumstances 下，我認為這項產品會更成功。

544 **close down** [ˋkloz ˋdaʊn] *v. phr.*

□
□ 例 If this product is not successful, we will have to **close down** the business.

如果這產品賣不好，我們公司將必須 close down。

545 **collaborate** [kəˋlæbə͵ret] *v.*

□
□ 例 The two teams stayed at the office until 10 pm **collaborating** on the new project.

直到晚上十點，兩團隊都還留在辦公室 collaborating 新的企劃案。

546 **commerce** [ˋkɑmɝs] *n.*

□
□ 例 International **commerce** is unstable at the moment.

國際 commerce 目前很不穩定。

547 **compete** [kəmˋpit] *v.*

□
□ 例 Our new product will have to **compete** with many other similar products.

我們的新產品將必須與許多其他類似的產品 compete。

情況，情勢，環境

停業

合作；共同工作

商業；貿易

競爭

競爭；比賽 | 548 **competition** [ˌkɑmpəˈtɪʃən] *n.*

☐
☐
例 Our product is in direct **competition** with a product from another company.
我們的產品與另一家公司所生產的產品面臨直接的 competition。

結果，因此 | 549 **consequently** [ˈkɑnsəˌkwɛntlɪ] *adv.*

☐
☐
例 The product was defective, and **consequently**, all boxes were removed from the shelves.
由於產品有瑕疵，consequently 全部產品都下架了。

相當大的；相當多的 | 550 **considerable** [kənˈsɪdərəbl] *adj.*

☐
☐
例 A **considerable** amount of money was spent on advertizing the product.
他們花了一筆 considerable 錢在產品廣告上。

消費者 | 551 **consumer** [kənˈsumɚ] *n.*

☐
☐
例 **Consumers** will appreciate the low cost of the merchandise.
Consumers 會喜歡低價的商品。

與…相比 | 552 **in contrast to** [ɪnˈkɑntræst tu] *phr.*

☐
☐
例 **In contrast to** our competitor's product, our product comes with a five-year warranty.
In contrast to 競爭對手的產品，我們的產品多加上五年的保固。

十年 | 553 **decade** [ˈdɛked] *n.*

☐
☐
例 Over the past **decade**, we have sold over a million units of this product.
過去 decade 來，這產品我們賣了超過上百萬組。

554 decline [dɪˋklaɪn] *v.*

☐ 例 Sales have **declined** since last quarter.

☐ 銷售額自上一季以來已經 declined。

555 devise [dɪˋvaɪz] *v.*

想出；設計

☐ 例 The sales team **devised** a new plan for the product.

☐ 銷售團隊為產品 devised 了一個新計畫。

556 double [ˋdʌbl] *adv.*

兩倍（地）

☐ 例 We have sold **double** the number of products this month.

☐ 我們這個月就已經賣了 double 多的產品。

557 drop off [ˋdrɑp ˋɔf] *v. phr.*

把…順便送過來

☐ 例 They said they would **drop off** the samples in the morning.

☐ 他們說早上會把樣品 drop off。

558 enlarge [ɪnˋlɑrdʒ] *v.*

擴大，擴展

☐ 例 If we **enlarge** the area of the promotion, we will be able to get more customers.

☐ 假如我們 enlarge 促銷的區域，我們將能找到更多的客戶。

559 estimate [ˏɛstəˋmet] *v.*

估計

☐ 例 The manufacturer **estimated** it would take three days before they would be ready to ship the product.

☐ 廠商 estimated 他們需要三天的時間才能把貨備好。

Chapter 04

業務行銷

發展；進化

560 **evolve** [ɪˈvɑlv] *v.*

例 The product has **evolved** a lot over the past two years.

這兩年來，產品已歷經 evolved 許多次。

獨家（地）

561 **exclusively** [ɪkˈsklusɪvlɪ] *adv.*

例 For the first two months, the product will be sold **exclusively** on-line.

前兩個月，這產品將會在線上 exclusively 販售。

解釋；說明

562 **explain** [ɪkˈsplen] *v.*

例 The instructions **explain** how to use the product.

說明書 explain 如何使用本產品。

爆炸

563 **explode** [ɪkˈsplod] *v.*

例 The product cannot be used close to open flames or it will **explode**.

不能在靠近開放式火焰處使用本產品，否則可能會 explode。

補救；修理

564 **fix** [fɪks] *v.*

例 If we don't **fix** this error, we may lose clients.

如果我們不 fix 錯誤，我們可能會失去客戶。

預測，預報

565 **forecast** [ˈfɔrˌkæst] *n.*

例 Our financial **forecast** doesn't look very good.

我們的財務 forecast 看起來不太樂觀。

566 **goal** [gol] *n.*

例 We haven't met our sales **goals** for this quarter.

我們尚未達到本季的銷售 goals。

目標

---

567 **guidance** [ˈgaɪdn̩s] *n.*

例 I look forward to your **guidance** on how to proceed with the project.

我期待接受您的 guidance 如何進行此企劃案。

指導，引導

---

568 **handle** [ˈhændl̩] *v.*

例 Jim is currently **handling** our most important clients.

吉姆目前 handle 我們最重要的客戶群。

負責，處理

---

569 **implement** [ˈɪmpləˌmɛnt] *v.*

例 We need to **implement** more effective sales strategies for this product.

我們需要 implement 更有效率的銷售策略來銷售產品。

實施；執行

---

570 **improve** [ɪmˈpruv] *v.*

例 If the sales don't **improve**, we will have to discontinue the product.

假如銷售額沒有 improve，我們將得中斷本產品的銷售。

改善，改進

---

571 **initial** [ɪˈnɪʃəl] *adj.*

例 The **initial** costs to manufacture the product are too high.

生產製造該產品的 initial 費用太高了。

初始的，最初的

創新的　572 **innovative** [`ɪnə,vetɪv] *adj.*

例 Our sales team has come up with an **innovative** idea to promote our products.

我們的銷售團隊提供一個 innovative 的想法來促銷產品。

新聞記者　573 **journalist** [`dʒɝ·nḷɪst] *n.*

例 The **journalist** wanted to do an article on our company.

Journalist 想要寫篇文章報導我們公司。

把（商品）投入市場；上市　574 **launch** [lɔntʃ] *v.*

例 The product will be **launched** in the fall.

產品將於秋季 launched。

當地的，本地的　575 **local** [`lokḷ] *adj.*

例 Our company is being featured on the **local** news tonight.

今晚 local 新聞將會特別報導我們公司。

損失；虧損　576 **loss** [lɔs] *n.*

例 We cannot afford to take any **losses** in sales.

我們無法承擔任何銷售上的 losses。

管理階層，資方　577 **management** [`mænɪdʒmənt] *n.*

例 **Management** will be meeting today to discuss productivity in the office.

Management 今天將要開會討論辦公室裡的生產力。

578 **market** [ˈmɑrkɪt] *n.*　　市場

□
□ 例 If we want to sell more merchandise, we need to target a younger **market**.

如果我們想要銷售更多的商品，就必須針對年輕族群的 market。

579 **marketing** [ˈmɑrkɪtɪŋ] *n.*　　行銷

□
□ 例 The **marketing** plan is going to cost the company a lot of money.

Marketing 計畫將會讓公司花掉一大筆錢。

✦ 580 **merger** [ˈmɝdʒɚ] *n.*　　（公司等的）合併

□
□ 例 News of the company **merger** has already hit the media.

公司 merger 的消息已經在媒體上披露。

581 **objective** [əbˈdʒɛktɪv] *n.*　　目標；目的

□
□ 例 Our main **objective** is to promote our services throughout a broader area.

我們的主要 objective 是將服務推廣至更為廣大的地區。

582 **opportunity** [ˌɑpɚˈtjunətɪ] *n.*　　機會

□
□ 例 James was offered an **opportunity** to join the marketing department.

詹姆士得到一個能加入行銷部門的 opportunity。

583 **outline** [ˈaʊtˌlaɪn] *n.*　　綱要，概要

□
□ 例 The **outline** of the project was missing some important details.

計畫的 outline 遺漏了一些重要的細節。

584 overview [ˈovɚˌvju] *n.*

例 An **overview** of our new sales strategy will be presented at the next meeting.

我們新銷售策略的 overview 將會在下次的會議中呈現。

概觀；概要

懸而未決

585 pending [ˈpɛndɪŋ] *adj.*

例 The agreement made with the company is still **pending**.

與該公司訂下的協議仍然 pending。

百分比

586 percentage [pɚˈsɛntɪdʒ] *n.*

例 The sales team was promised a **percentage** of the profits.

銷售團隊承諾得到一定 percentage 的獲利。

計畫

587 plan [plæn] *n.*

例 The sales manager said he has a new **plan** for marketing the product.

業務經理說他有個行銷此產品的新 plan。

主要的

588 primary [ˈpraɪˌmɛrɪ] *adj.*

例 The **primary** reason we haven't sold much product is poor marketing.

我們產品銷售不佳的 primary 原因是行銷不力。

印刷字體

589 print [prɪnt] *n.*

例 The **print** on the back of the product is too small to read.

產品後面的 print 太小，看不清楚。

590 **prior to** [ˈpraɪɚ tu] *prep.*

在⋯之前

☐
☐ 例 We haven't had overseas clients **prior to** this year.

Prior to 今年，我們從未有過海外客戶。

591 **progression** [prəˈɡrɛʃən] *n.*

進程

☐
☐ 例 The **progression** of the marketing campaign is slow.

行銷活動的 progression 發展緩慢。

592 **project** [ˈprɑdʒɛkt] *n.*

計畫

☐
☐ 例 The **project** is due by the end of the week.

該 project 在這星期結束前就應完成。

593 **promote** [prəˈmot] *v.*

促銷；推廣

☐
☐ 例 We need to **promote** our services in a variety of places.

我們需要在各種場合 promote 我們的服務。

594 **proposal** [prəˈpozl̩] *n.*

建議；方案

☐
☐ 例 Our boss didn't like our **proposal** for the sales strategy.

我們老闆並不喜歡我們針對銷售策略所提出的 proposal。

595 **profit** [ˈprɑfɪt] *n.*

利潤

☐
☐ 例 If we don't keep our costs down, we won't make a **profit**.

如果我們不繼續維持低成本，我們就無法創造 profit。

Chapter
04
業務行銷

有利潤的	596	**profitable** [ˈprɑfɪtabl̩] *adj.*

☐ 例 Online sales can be very **profitable**.
☐ 線上販售是很 profitable。

節目單；程序表	597	**program** [ˈprogræm] *n.*

☐ 例 Please print a lot of **programs** so we won't run out at the event.
☐ 請大量印製 programs，以免活動中會不夠用。

期望，希望	598	**prospect** [ˈprɑspɛkt] *n.*

☐ 例 The **prospect** of us making a profit on the sale of this merchandise is slim.
☐ 我們對這項商品能獲利的 prospect 是很渺茫的。

說明書，簡章	599	**prospectus** [prəˈspɛktəs] *n.*

☐ 例 It took the team over three days to prepare a **prospectus**.
☐ 團隊花了三天的時間準備一份 prospectus。

繁榮，昌盛	600	**prosper** [ˈprɑspɚ] *v.*

☐ 例 We hope that our company will continue to **prosper**, even during difficult financial times.
☐ 我們希望公司能繼續 prosper，即使在金融艱困的年代。

季度	601	**quarter** [ˈkwɔrtɚ] *n.*

☐ 例 Sales for the new product rose during the first **quarter**.
☐ 新產品的銷售在第一 quarter 上揚。

602 quarterly [ˈkwɔrtə·lɪ] *adv.*   每季

☐
☐
例 Overseas sales brings in over two million
dollars **quarterly**.

Quarterly 海外銷售賺進兩百萬元以上。

603 reach [ritʃ] *v.*   抵達；達到

☐
☐
例 If we want to **reach** a broader clientele, we need
to advertise more.

如果我們想要 reach 更廣大的客戶群，我們需要
更多的廣告宣傳。

604 remark [rɪˈmɑrk] *n.*   言論，評論

☐
☐
例 Customers have made a lot of negative **remarks**
about the quality of the product.

客戶說了許多有關產品品質方面的負面
remarks。

605 representative [ˌrɛprɪˈzɛntətɪv] *n.*   代表

☐
☐
例 We should send a senior **representative** from
the company to the meeting.

我們應該從公司派個資深 representative 去開會。

606 sale [sel] *n.*   低價拍賣

☐
☐
例 If the products are not selling, perhaps we
should have a **sale**.

假如產品不暢銷，或許我們應該辦個 sale。

607 scale [skel] *n.*   規模

☐
☐
例 We need to promote the product on a much
larger **scale**.

我們需要更大 scale 的產品促銷。

☆ 刺激，激勵

608 **stimulate** [ˋstɪmjə͵let] v.

例 The new business policy **stimulated** sales.
新的經營策略 stimulated 銷售量。

技巧，技術

609 **technique** [tɛkˋnik] n.

例 You will have to teach me your **technique** for getting what you want from the boss!
你一定要教我你從老闆那予取予求的 technique！

營業額

610 **turnover** [ˋtɝn͵ovɚ] n.

例 That store has a high **turnover** of our product.
我們產品在那家店的 turnover 很高。

☆ （有利可圖/新）風險事業

611 **venture** [ˋvɛntʃɚ] n.

例 The company's new investment is an exciting **venture** for all employees.
公司的新投資對所有的員工來說是令人興奮的 venture。

富有，有錢

612 **wealthy** [ˋwɛlθɪ] adj.

例 Online sales have made many people **wealthy**.
網路銷售讓許多人變得 wealthy。

Exercises

請從選項中，選出最適當的答案完成句子。

1. When the army landed on the beaches, they met less resistance than originally _____.

   (A) anticipated   (B) participated   (C) restricted   (D) prepared

2. There is an _____ in the paper about the popularity of Korean soap operas.

   (A) item   (B) article   (C) itinerary   (D) isolation

3. My dad told me that under no _____ should I tell lies.

   (A) elements   (B) surroundings   (C) environment   (D) circumstances

4. While a century is 100 years, a _____ is ten years.

   (A) decade   (B) decay   (C) cavity   (D) décor

5. The method is _____, as can be proven by the progress the students have made.

   (A) affective   (B) effective   (C) influential   (D) infectious

6. Larry's _____ is to be an entertainer—he loves singing, dancing and acting.

   (A) suspicion   (B) ambition   (C) retention   (D) attention

7. I don't know the theory very well; I can't _____ it to you.

   (A) reason   (B) identify   (C) explain   (D) extend

8. The new system of a 12-year compulsory education will eventually be _____ in Taiwan.

   (A) implanted   (B) substituted   (C) implemented   (D) transplanted

9. Nowadays an _____ person can live to be 70 years old.

   (A) curious   (B) common   (C) average   (D) mean

10. Ann Lee is now a _____ in the movie industry.

   (A) dispute   (B) celebrity   (C) reputation   (D) fame

11. An ad on TV or on the radio is called a _____.

    (A) commercial (B) commencement (C) graduation (D) interruption

12. Rachael _____ a scheme to promote the company's new prod-
    uct.

    (A) projected (B) devised (C) suspected (D) disguised

13. Candidates for the vacancy will be _____ for three months
    before they are officially hired.

    (A) estimated (B) predicted (C) evaluated (D) calculated

14. The club is _____ for members.

    (A) selectively (B) exclusively (C) extremely (D) intensively

15. The news that Japan was hit by both earthquakes and tsunamis
    made the _____.

    (A) markets (B) media (C) headlines (D) commerce

16. The police are _____ who committed the murder.

    (A) suspecting (B) detecting (C) surviving (D) investigating

17. Scientists have been _____ experiments to find a cure for
    cancer.

    (A) conducting (B) surveying (C) seeking (D) searching

18. As we have a very limited _____, we have to spend our mon-
    ey wisely.

    (A) economy (B) budget (C) project (D) scheme

19. Because our products are cheaper and last longer, they have an edge
    over other _____.

    (A) supervisors (B) clients (C) consumers (D) competitors

20. People who write for newspapers or magazines are called _____.

    (A) journalists (B) manufacturers (C) industrialists (D) tourists

I Photographs (33)

Look at the pictures below and listen to the statements. Then choose the statement that best describes what you see in the picture.

1. (A) (B) (C) (D)   2. (A) (B) (C) (D)

II Conversations (34)

You will hear some conversations between two people. Listen to the conversations and answer the questions below.

Questions 3-4

3. How does the woman feel about Claire?
   (A) She is kind.
   (B) She is polite.
   (C) She works very hard.
   (D) She talks too much.

4. What does the woman say she will do?
   (A) Laugh at Claire.
   (B) Apologize to the man.
   (C) Say sorry to Claire.
   (D) Try really hard.

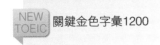

Questions 5-6

5. Why does the man look uneasy?

  (A) He has caught a cold.

  (B) He has lost his job.

  (C) He has an important presentation to make.

  (D) He has been promoted.

6. Where are the people likely to be?

  (A) In a banker's office.

  (B) At a telephone booth.

  (C) At a police station.

  (D) On a ferry.

Ⅲ Short Talks (35)

You will hear some short talks given by a single speaker. Listen to the short talks and answer the questions below.

Questions 7-8

7. What is the main cause of the problem?

  (A) The office is being repaired.

  (B) People listen to music at work.

  (C) Employees talk loudly.

  (D) The boss yells at his employees.

8. What suggestion has been made?

  (A) Keep the office tidy.

  (B) Make more phone calls.

  (C) Lower the volume on the radio.

  (D) Walk across the room to talk to people.

Questions 9-10

9. What percentage of lost customers came from the top 25 accounts?

  (A) 7.5   (B) 15   (C) 25   (D) 50

10. What will they discuss at the meeting?

    (A) A letter from a customer.

    (B) The increasing number of customers.

    (C) How to improve their customer service.

    (D) A birthday party.

IV Incomplete Sentences

A word or phrase is missing in each of the sentences below. Four answer choices are given below each sentence. Select the best answer to complete the sentence.

11. We tried every possible way to _____ you this morning.

    (A) communicate (B) generate   (C) set up   (D) contact

12. Now let's move to the next item on the _____.

    (A) agenda   (B) participant (C) outcome   (D) impact

13. The students worked together to produce a one-act play and performed before a live _____.

    (A) consumer   (B) audience   (C) assignment (D) auditorium

14. Holly is considering _____ her restaurant on the Internet.

    (A) transferring (B) generating (C) advertising (D) delivering

15. Eric _____ in Bangkok from 2003 to 2006.

    (A) lives   (B) lived   (C) living   (D) is living

16. David _____ the sales manager of Sunray Industry for three years.

    (A) is   (B) are   (C) has been   (D) have been

17. Millions of toys are _____ from China every year.

    (A) export   (B) exported   (C) exporting   (D) exports

18. "_____ do you go to the cinema?" "About twice a month."

    (A) How   (B) How many (C) How much (D) How often

V Reading Comprehension

In this part you will read a selection of texts. Each text is followed by several questions. Select the best answer for each question and circle the letter (A), (B), (C), or (D).

Questions 19-21 refer to the following email.

To:	MelissaM@hyperark.com
From:	Lewislevee@cintron.net

Dear Melissa:

To answer your questions about our cell phone service plans:

- There are no "roaming" charges. Calls made from anywhere in the country are charged at the same rate.
- There is no limit on minutes during weekends. On weekdays, the limit is 300 minutes.
- Call forwarding and voice mail are provided to all customers.

This program is available to you and all your employees when you choose Cintron as your cell phone service provider.

Thank you.

Lewis Levee

19. Where can Cintron customers make cell phone calls?

(A) Only from home.   (B) Only within the state.

(C) Anywhere nationwide.   (D) On weekdays and weekends.

21. Who can buy the service plan?

(A) Melissa and her family.   (B) All customers.

(C) Melissa and all her employees. (D) All of Melissa's employees.

20. How many minutes can a customer use on a Friday?

(A) There is no limit on Friday.

(B) Up to 300.

(C) Up to 250.

(D) It depends on where the calls are made.

Questions 22-23 refer to the following notice.

> ### What Is Happening In The IT Industry?
> #### A presentation by
> #### Tobias W. Wilson
> #### CEO of Luna Corp.
> #### December 13, 2009
> #### The Hilton Ballroom
>
> Mr. Wilson will talk about the recent developments in the IT industry. He will also discuss the future impact on investors and employees of the IT industry.
>
> The presentation will include:
> What do the recent job cuts mean for the future of the IT industry?
> How will the job cuts affect other industries?
> What are the risks for investors?
>
> We invite business people, investors, or anyone with an interest in the IT industry to attend this event.

22. What will be discussed at this event?

    (A) The risk of investing in the IT industry.

    (B) The increase in employment in the IT industry.

    (C) How to make job cuts.

    (D) The overall history of the IT industry.

23. Who should attend this event?

    (A) IT industry workers who have lost their jobs.

    (B) IT industry employers looking to hire new workers.

    (C) Anyone with an interest in the IT industry.

    (D) People who have invested more than $100,000.

VI Text Completion

Read the text that follows. A word or phrase is missing in some of the sentences. For each blank, four answer choices are given. Select the best answer to complete the text.

Cyril is nervous every time he has to give a presentation. But presentations are an important part of his job. Therefore, Cyril (24)_____ to manage his fear. He always arrives early on the day of a presentation. He checks the (25)_____ , the lights, and the (26)_____. When he is sure that everything is working, he starts to relax.

Cyril is always well prepared. He prints handouts for the audience. He also uses (27)_____ and pictures to keep his listeners' attention during his presentation. For these reasons, the audience always gives him good (28)_____. Although Cyril is still nervous before a presentation, he has learned to control his fear.

24. (A) has learned (B) have learned (C) learn (D) learns
25. (A) trust (B) tip (C) visual (D) microphone
26. (A) research (B) projector (C) competitor (D) budget
27. (A) windows (B) investment (C) graphs (D) chairperson
28. (A) divided (B) feedback (C) brochure (D) stressful

Chapter 5

Business Trip 商務旅行/出差

Companies send workers on business trips to meet with partners or clients in a different location. Planning for a business trip includes schedule arrangement and making reservations for hotel and transportation.

Business Trip
商務旅行/出差

1 Air Travel 搭飛機 ⑬

午夜至正午，上午

613 am [ˈeˈɛm] *adv.*

☐ 例 My flight leaves at 1:30 **am**.

☐ 我的班機在 am 一點半起飛。

• 為拉丁語 ante meridiem 縮寫

在國外

614 abroad [əˈbrɔd] *adv.*

☐ 例 We have many clients **abroad**.

☐ 我們 abroad 有許多客戶。

☆ 飛機票價

615 airfare [ˈɛrˌfɛr] *n.*

☐ 例 How much is the **airfare** to the conference?

☐ 參加那場研討會的 airfare 是多少呢？

航空公司

616 airline [ˈɛrˌlaɪn] *n.*

☐ 例 Which **airline** are you flying with?

☐ 你搭乘哪家 airline？

飛機

617 airplane [ˈɛrˌplen] *n.*

☐ 例 The **airplane** must be inspected before take-off.

☐ Airplane 必須在起飛前做好檢查。

機場

618 airport [ˈɛrˌport] *n.*

☐ 例 The **airport** is located about 20 minutes from the capital.

☐ 那個 airport 距離首都約二十分鐘路程。

619 **aisle seat** [ˈaɪlˌsit] *n. phr.*

□ 例 I prefer sitting in an **aisle seat**.

□ 坐飛機時，我喜歡坐在 aisle seat。

靠走道的座位

620 **alert** [əˈlɝt] *v.*

□ 例 The captain **alerted** the passengers that he must
□   make an emergency landing.

    機長 alerted 乘客，他必須迫降飛機。

提醒，警惕

621 **altitude** [ˈæltəˌtjud] *n.*

□ 例 Please leave your seat belts on until we reach
□   full **altitude**.

    在飛機上升到充分的 altitude 前，請繫好安全
    帶。

海拔高度

622 **apologize** [əˈpɑləˌdʒaɪz] *v.*

□ 例 The flight attendant **apologized** for spilling
□   coffee on the passenger's lap.

    空服員因為把咖啡濺到乘客腿上，向對方
    apologized。

道歉

623 **approximate** [əˈprɑksəmɪt] *adj.*

□ 例 The captain announced that the **approximate**
□   time to landing was one hour.

    機長廣播離降落時間 approximate 還有一小時。

大約

624 **baggage** [ˈbæɡɪdʒ] *n.*

□ 例 We need to pick up our **baggage** after we land.

□ 飛機降落後，我們得去領取 baggage。

行李

行李領取處	625	**baggage claim area** *n. phr.*
		例 I think I forgot one of my suitcases in the **baggage claim area**.
		我有個手提箱好像在 baggage claim area 忘了拿。
財產，攜帶物品	626	**belongings** [bɪˈlɔŋɪŋz] *n.*
		例 Please be sure not to leave any personal **belongings** on the plane.
		請注意別將個人的 belongings 遺留在飛機上。
上，登（船、飛機等）	627	**board** [bɔrd] *v.*
		例 The flight will start **boarding** in about ten minutes.
		飛機即將在十分鐘內開始 boarding。
登機	628	**boarding** [ˈbɔrdɪŋ] *n.*
		例 The **boarding** process for the flight is very slow.
		Boarding 的過程很緩慢。
登機證	629	**boarding pass** [ˈbɔrdɪŋ ˌpæs] *n. phr.*
		例 Please have your **boarding pass** ready to show the flight attendant.
		請將您的 boarding pass 準備好讓空服員檢查。
預約，預訂	630	**book** [bʊk] *v.*
		例 I **booked** my flight to Chicago last week.
		我上週 booked 去芝加哥的班機。

631 **broadcast** [ˋbrɔdˌkæst] *v.*

播送，廣播

☐☐ 例 Images of the airplane crash were **broadcasted** all over the world.

那場墜機空難的畫面在世界各地 broadcasted。

632 **business trip** [ˋbɪznɪsˌtrɪp] *n.*

出差

☐☐ 例 There are currently five employees away on **business trips**.

目前有五位員工在 business trips 中。

633 **captain** [ˋkæptən] *n.*

機長，船長

☐☐ 例 The **captain** asked passengers to fasten their seat belts.

Captain 要求乘客繫上安全帶。

✰ **634** **carousel** [ˌkɛrəˋsɛl] *n.*

行李轉盤，行李輸送帶

☐☐ 例 Did you see my suitcase come around on the **carousel**?

你有看見我的手提箱在 carousel 上嗎？

635 **chain** [tʃen] *n.*

鏈條

☐☐ 例 The **chain** on the carousel is broken.

行李輸送帶上的 chain 壞了。

636 **cheap** [tʃip] *adj.*

便宜的，廉價的

☐☐ 例 We were able to get **cheap** flights by booking last minute.

我們在訂票截止前訂到 cheap 機票。

結帳櫃台　637　**checkout** [ˈtʃɛkˌaʊt] *n.*

例 John was waiting at the **checkout** when he heard his flight number called.

約翰聽到他的班機號碼時，他正在 checkout 前。

淨空　638　**clearance** [ˈklɪrəns] *n.*

例 The flight cannot take off until the captain has received **clearance** from the control tower.

在機長接到塔台通知已 clearance 前，飛機無法起飛。

上升，爬升　639　**climb** [klaɪm] *v.*

例 The plane began to **climb** higher and higher.

這架飛機開始逐漸越 climb 越高。

記錄（時間）　640　**clock** [klɑk] *v.*

例 I'm going to **clock** the amount of time it takes to get from my hotel to the airport.

我要 clock 從飯店到機場要多久時間。

陰天，多雲　641　**cloudy** [ˈklaʊdɪ] *adj.*

例 The captain said that although the sky was **cloudy**, it was safe to fly.

機長說雖然天氣 cloudy，但不影響飛行安全。

轉接班機　642　**connecting flight** [kəˈnɛktɪŋ ˈflaɪt] *n. phr.*

例 Gina was able to get a good deal on her ticket, because she has two **connecting** flights.

吉娜買到便宜的機票，因為她得轉兩次 connecting flights。

643 crew [kru] *n.*

例 The flight **crew** was exhausted after the long flight.

在長途飛行之後，整個 crew 都疲憊不堪。

機組人員

644 cruise [kruz] *n.*

例 Our company will be attending a conference on a **cruise** ship.

我們公司將參加一場在 cruise 輪船上舉辦的會議。

巡遊

645 customs [ˈkʌstəmz] *n.*

例 We have to go through **customs** before we can exit the airport.

出機場前，我們需先經過 customs。

海關

646 delay [dɪˈle] *v.*

例 Heather's flight was **delayed** by three hours.

海瑟的班機 delayed 了三個多小時。

延遲，延期

647 departure [dɪˈpɑrtʃɚ] *n.*

例 What time is your **departure**?

你的 departure 是幾點？

離開，啟程

648 destination [ˌdɛstəˈneʃən] *n.*

例 We will reach our **destination** in twenty minutes.

我們將在二十分鐘內抵達 destination。

目的地；終點

國內航班   649 **domestic flight** [dəˈmɛstɪk ˌflaɪt] *n. phr.*

例 You don't need your passport for **domestic flights**.

搭乘 domestic flights 不需要護照。

經濟艙   650 **economy class** [ɪˈkɑnəmɪ ˌklæs] *n. phr.*

例 It is more affordable to go **economy class**.

搭 economy class 比較負擔得起。

引擎   651 **engine** [ˈɛndʒən] *n.*

例 When the **engine** started, I knew it wouldn't be long before take-off.

Engine 一啟動，我知道飛機很快就要起飛。

昂貴   652 **expensive** [ɪkˈspɛnsɪv] *adj.*

例 First class tickets are much more **expensive** than I thought they would be.

頭等艙機票比我想像中的還要 expensive。

班機   653 **flight** [flaɪt] *n.*

例 The **flight** will be departing in five minutes.

五分鐘內 flight 即將起飛。

空服員   654 **flight attendant** [ˈflaɪt ˌətɛndənt] *n. phr.*

例 The **flight attendant** asked passengers if they wanted chicken or beef for dinner.

Flight attendant 詢問乘客晚餐要吃雞肉餐還是牛肉餐。

655　**fuel** [ˈfjuəl] *n.*

☐
☐　例 The rising cost of **fuel** has affected the price of airplane tickets.

　　Fuel 的價格上漲已經影響了機票的價格。

燃料

656　**gate** [get] *n.*

☐
☐　例 Only passengers are allowed behind the **gate**.

　　只有旅客才能進 gate。

登機門

657　**highway** [ˈhaɪˌwe] *n.*

☐
☐　例 You have to take the **highway** to get to the airport.

　　您必須走 highway 才能到機場。

公路

658　**inexpensive** [ˌɪnɪkˈspɛnsɪv] *adj.*

☐
☐　例 Domestic flights are very **inexpensive** in this country.

　　該國的國內班機票價很 inexpensive。

便宜

659　**insurance** [ɪnˈʃurəns] *n.*

☐
☐　例 Be sure to buy **insurance** for your flight.

　　搭飛機前請務必要買 insurance。

保險

660　**landing** [ˈlændɪŋ] *n.*

☐
☐　例 Please fasten your seat belts during take-off and **landing**.

　　請在起飛與 landing 時繫緊安全帶。

降落

失物招領處 | 661 **Lost and Found** [ˈlɔst and ˈfaʊnd] *n. phr.*

例 Someone turned in my sunglasses to the **Lost and Found**.

有人把我的太陽眼鏡送到 Lost and Found。

超額預定 | 662 **overbook** [ˌovɚˈbʊk] *v.*

例 The flight was **overbooked** so we had to catch a later flight.

這班機 overbook，所以我們得搭乘之後的班機。

下午，午後 | 663 **pm** (post meridiem) [ˈpi ˈɛm] *adv.*

例 The meeting will begin at 7 **pm**.

會議將於 pm 七點開始。

乘客，旅客 | 664 **passenger** [ˈpæsn̩dʒɚ] *n.*

例 The **passengers** were asked to prepare for landing.

Passengers 被通知要準備降落。

護照 | 665 **passport** [ˈpæsˌport] *n.*

例 I missed my flight because I left my **passport** at home.

因為我把 passport 忘在家裡，所以錯過了班機。

飛行員，機師 | 666 **pilot** [ˈpaɪlət] *n.*

例 The **pilot** asked passengers to turn off all electronic devices.

Pilot 要求旅客關掉所有的電子用品。

667 **platform** [ˈplætˌfɔrm] *n.*

平臺

例 The helicopter landed on the company rooftop **platform** helipad.

直升機降落在公司屋頂上的 platform。

668 **price** [praɪs] *n.*

價格

例 International flight **prices** have gone up over the last few years.

國際機票的 prices 在最近幾年來上揚。

✓669 **procrastinate** [proˈkræstəˌnet] *v.*

延遲，拖拖拉拉

例 Please don't **procrastinate** on booking your flight, or there may not be any seats left.

請勿 procrastinate 預定您的班機，否則可能沒有機位。

670 **queue** [kju] *n.*

排隊

例 If you don't arrive at the airport early enough you will have to wait in a **queue** for a long time.

如果沒有早點到機場，您將需 queue 等很久。

671 **seat belt** [ˈsit ˌbɛlt] *n. phr.*

安全帶

例 The flight attendant informed passengers that it was okay to unfasten their **seat belts**.

空服員通知旅客可以鬆開他們的 seat belts 了。

672 **signal** [ˈsɪgnl̩] *v.*

（以動作）示意

例 The flight attendants **signaled** the way to the emergency exits.

空服員 signaled 到緊急出口的方式。

航空站

673 **terminal** [ˈtɝmən!] *n.*

例 Charlotte went to the wrong **terminal** for her flight.

夏綠蒂搭飛機時跑錯 terminal。

轉換

674 **transfer** [trænsˈfɝ] *v.*

例 I have to **transfer** airlines when I get to Chicago.

我必須 transfer 飛機到芝加哥。

運輸，運送

675 **transit** [ˈtrænsɪt] *n.*

例 The high-speed train is the most efficient means of **transit** in this country.

這國家最有效率的 transit 方法是高鐵。

亂流

676 **turbulence** [ˈtɝbjələns] *n.*

例 The captain warned the passengers that they would be experiencing some **turbulence**.

機長警告旅客將會遇到 turbulence。

---

2 Accommodation 膳宿 (14)

住宿，膳宿

677 **accommodation** [əˌkɑməˈdeʃən] *n.*

例 Does the conference fee include **accommodations**?

會務費有包含 accommodations 嗎？

指控；指責

678 **accuse** [əˈkjuz] *v.*

例 The man **accused** the airline of losing his luggage.

那位男子 accused 該家航空公司遺失他的行李。

679 arrive [əˈraɪv] *v.*　抵達，到達

例 I hope we don't **arrive** at the hotel too late.

我希望我們不會太晚 arrive 飯店。

680 ballroom [ˈbɔlˌrum] *n.*　大舞廳

例 The **ballroom** is the perfect size to host our office Christmas party.

這間 ballroom 的大小很適合用來辦公司的聖誕節派對。

681 bathroom [ˈbæθˌrum] *n.*　浴室，洗手間

例 I forgot to go to the **bathroom** before I got on the bus.

上巴士前，我忘了去 bathroom。

682 bedroom [ˈbɛdˌrum] *n.*　臥室

例 The company paid for a two-**bedroom** suite for me.

公司幫我出錢，訂了一間雙 bedroom 的套房。

683 bellhop [ˈbɛlˌhɑp] *n.*　侍者，行李員

例 The **bellhop** helped me carry my bags to my room.

飯店的 bellhop 幫我把行李提進房間。

684 booking [ˈbʊkɪŋ] *n.*　預訂

例 More and more people are using the Internet for **bookings**.

越來越多的人使用網路 bookings。

煞車，制動器

685 **brake** [brek] *n.*

☐ 例 The plane has faulty **brakes**.

☐ 這架飛機的 brakes 出了問題。

表達；傳遞

686 **convey** [kən`ve] *v.*

☐ 例 The passenger **conveyed** disappointment with the

☐ service provided by the flight attendants.

該名乘客 conveyed 不滿空服員的服務品質。

信用卡

687 **credit card** [`krɛdɪt ˌkɑrd] *n. phr.*

☐ 例 The server told me my **credit card** was declined.

☐ 服務生說我的 credit card 不能刷了。

顧客，客戶

688 **customer** [`kʌstəmɚ] *n.*

☐ 例 Many of our **customers** are overseas.

☐ 我們有許多海外 customers。

方向，方位

689 **direction** [də`rɛkʃən] *n.*

☐ 例 The taxi driver didn't understand the **directions**

☐ to my hotel.

計程車司機不清楚我下榻飯店的 directions。

距離

690 **distance** [`dɪstəns] *n.*

☐ 例 What is the **distance** from my hotel to the

☐ conference center?

從我住的飯店到會議中心的 distance 有多遠？

691 entrance [ˈɛntrəns] *n.*

門口，入口

例 The **entrance** of the hotel was blocked by two tour buses.

旅館的 entrance 被兩輛觀光巴士堵住了。

692 expense [ɪkˈspɛns] *n.*

費用，支出

例 My company told me to charge all **expenses** to my hotel room.

我的公司說所有的 expenses 都記在我旅館房間的帳上。

693 fee [fi] *n.*

費用

例 Are there any additional **fees** that I should know about before I book the flight?

在預訂機票前，有沒有什麼額外 fees 是我該知道的呢？

694 fill out [ˈfɪl ˈaʊt] *v. phr.*

填寫

例 Please **fill out** the form with your personal information.

請在這張表格 fill out 您的個人資料。

695 front desk [ˈfrʌnt ˌdɛsk] *n. phr.*

服務台

例 Jake called the **front desk** to request more towels.

傑克打電話到 front desk 要求更多的毛巾。

696 hostel [ˈhɑstl] *n.*

旅舍（尤指青年旅舍）

例 We would never arrange for overseas clients to stay at a **hostel**.

我們決不會安排海外客戶住 hostel。

旅館　　　697 **hotel** [ho`tɛl] *n.*

　　　　　例 The **hotel** is in walking distance from our office.

　　　　　從 hotel 到本公司的距離很近。

旅館大廳　698 **lobby** [`labɪ] *n.*

　　　　　例 There is information about local attractions in the **lobby**.

　　　　　Lobby 裡有當地旅遊景點的資訊。

住宿，寓所　699 **lodging** [`ladʒɪŋ] *n.*

　　　　　例 The company provided **lodging** for the entire group of guests.

　　　　　公司提供 lodging 給整團的賓客。

行李　　　700 **luggage** [`lʌgɪdʒ] *n.*

　　　　　例 I will need some assistance with my **luggage**.

　　　　　我需要人幫忙提我的 luggage。

英里，哩　701 **mile** [maɪl] *n.*

　　　　　例 The hotel is twenty **miles** from the office.

　　　　　該旅館距離本公司二十 miles 遠。

選擇　　　702 **option** [`apʃən] *n.*

　　　　　例 There aren't very many **options** on the take-out menu.

　　　　　外帶餐點的菜單上沒有太多的 options。

停放（車
輛）　　　703 **park** [park] *v.*

　　　　　例 Visitors are asked to **park** behind the building.

　　　　　遊客需將車輛 park 在建物後面。

704　parking lot [ˈpɑrkɪŋ ˌlɑt] *n. phr.*　停車場

☐　例 There are no more spots left in the **parking lot**.

☐　Parking lot 裡已經沒有停車位了。

705　reservation [ˌrɛzəˈveʃən] *n.*　預訂

☐　例 Jim made **reservations** for us at the restaurant downstairs.

☐　吉姆為我們在樓下餐廳 reservations 位子。

706　room service [ˈrumˌsɝvɪs] *n. phr.*　客房服務

☐　例 It is more expensive to order food through **room service** than it is to eat in the hotel restaurant.

☐　透過 room service 點餐比在旅館餐廳吃還要貴。

707　suitcase [ˈsutˌkes] *n.*　行李箱

☐　例 I bought a red **suitcase** so it would be easy to identify in baggage claim.

☐　我買了一個紅色的 suitcase，在領取行李時就很容易分辨出來。

708　suite [swit] *n.*　套房

☐　例 The company paid for me to stay in a **suite** during my business trip.

☐　出差時，公司會付我住 suite 的費用。

709　voucher [ˈvaʊtʃə] *n.*　抵用券，票券

☐　例 The hotel gave me a **voucher** for breakfast.

☐　飯店給了我一張早餐 voucher。

Chapter 05 商務旅行

加速，加快 | 710 **accelerate** [æk`sɛlə,ret] *v.*

例 Peter asked the taxi driver to **accelerate** so he wouldn't miss his flight.

彼得請計程車司機 accelerate，免得他錯過班機。

意外，偶然的事 | 711 **accident** [`æksədənt] *n.*

例 My meeting was delayed by the **accident**.

我因為那場 accident 而延誤會議。

抵達時間 | 712 **arrival time** [ə`raɪvḷ ,taɪm] *n. phr.*

例 What is your **arrival time**?

你的 arrival time 是幾點？

汽車 | 713 **automobile** [`ɔtəmə,bil] *n.*

例 The company I am visiting said they would lend me an **automobile** to drive while I am in town.

我將去拜訪的公司會在我停留的那段時間借我一部 automobile。

有空 | 714 **available** [ə`veləbḷ] *adj.*

例 I'm not **available** to travel during the first two weeks of June.

六月的頭兩週要出差的話，我無法 available。

取消 | 715 **cancel** [`kænsḷ] *v.*

例 We may have to **cancel** our trip in August if we do not meet the project deadline.

要是無法準時完成專案，我們可能得 cancel 八月的旅行。

716 **choice** [tʃɔɪs] *n.* 選擇，決定

☐☐ 例 I think it was a good **choice** to upgrade to first class.

我認為升等到頭等艙是個好 choice。

717 **clear** [klɪr] *adj.* 空出來的

☐☐ 例 Please keep your schedule **clear** during the first week of May.

請你將五月第一個禮拜 clear。

718 **confirm** [kənˈfɝm] *v.* 確認，證實

☐☐ 例 Jim asked his secretary to **confirm** his flight.

吉姆要他的秘書 confirm 他的班機。

719 **confirmation** [ˌkɑnfɚˈmeʃən] *n.* 確認；確實

☐☐ 例 I am waiting for **confirmation** from the travel agency that our flights have been booked.

我正等旅行社的 confirmation 以確定我們的機票已訂好。

720 **early** [ˈɝlɪ] *adv.* 早，提早

☐☐ 例 It looks like our flight will arrive **early**.

看來我們的班機將會 early 抵達。

721 **exchange rate** [ɪksˈtʃendʒ ˌret] *n. phr.* 匯率

☐☐ 例 What is the **exchange rate** for American dollars?

美元的 exchange rate 是多少？

導遊；旅遊 指南	722 **guide** [gaɪd] *n.*
	☐ 例 A **guide** will be available to show you around the city. ☐ 將會有 guide 帶您看看這個城市。
國際航班	723 **international flight** [ˌɪntɚˈnæʃənḷ ˈflaɪt] *n. phr.*
	☐ 例 You need to arrive at the airport at least two hours prior to **international flights**. ☐ 搭乘 international flights，您需提早至少兩小時到達機場。
✪ 行程，旅遊 計畫	724 **itinerary** [aɪˈtɪnəˌrɛrɪ] *n.*
	☐ 例 If you check your **itinerary**, you will see that the conference begins at 8 am. ☐ 如果您查看您的 itinerary，將會看到會議在八點鐘開始。
路程，旅程	725 **journey** [ˈdʒɝnɪ] *n.*
	☐ 例 It is a two-hour **journey** from company headquarters to the factory. ☐ 從公司總部到工廠得花兩小時的 journey。
公斤	726 **kilogram** [ˈkɪləˌgræm] *n.*
	☐ 例 The airline will not allow passengers to check luggage weighing over 20 **kilograms**. ☐ 航空公司將不會許可旅客托運超過二十 kilograms 的行李。
公里	727 **kilometer** [ˈkɪləˌmitɚ] *n.*
	☐ 例 The hotel is about ten **kilometers** from company headquarters. ☐ 從本公司總部到該旅館的距離大約是十 kilometers。

728 **late** [let] *adj.*　　　　遲到

☐
☐ 例 If we don't leave now, we are going to be **late** for the meeting.

如果我們現在不走，開會就會 late。

729 **leave for** [ˈliv ˈfɔr] *v. phr.*　　　前往

☐
☐ 例 When are you **leaving for** California?

您何時要 leave for 加州？

730 **o'clock** [əˈklɑk] *adv.*　　　…點鐘

☐
☐ 例 We need to wake up at five **o'clock** if we want to get to the airport on time.

如果我們想要準時抵達機場，就需要在五 o'clock 起床。

731 **on holiday** [ɑn ˈhɑləˌde] *adv. phr.*　　在休假中

☐
☐ 例 Our entire staff goes **on holiday** for the month of July.

七月整個月我們全部的員工都 on holiday。

732 **punctual** [ˈpʌŋktʃʊəl] *adj.*　　準時的

☐
☐ 例 It is important to be **punctual** for all your meetings.

要 punctual 出席您所有的會議是很重要的。

733 **reception** [rɪˈsɛpʃən] *n.*　　接待

☐
☐ 例 Please sign in at the **reception** desk when you arrive.

請您抵達後到 reception 處簽名。

接待員 | 734 **receptionist** [rɪˈsɛpʃənɪst] *n.*

☐
☐
例 The **receptionist** said Mr. Johnston was unavailable.

receptionist 說詹斯頓先生沒有時間見面。

路線 | 735 **route** [rut] *n.*

☐
☐
例 Can you tell me the fastest **route** to get to the airport?

你可以告訴我到機場最快的 route 嗎？

時間表；計 | 736 **schedule** [ˈskɛdʒʊl] *n.*
畫表

☐
☐
例 My **schedule** is full until next week.

我的 schedule 滿到下星期。

逗留，停留 | 737 **stay** [ste] *n.*

☐
☐
例 Wanda requested to extend her **stay** at the hotel.

汪達要求延長在旅館 stay 的時間。

時刻表 | 738 **timetable** [ˈtaɪmˌtebl̩] *n.*

☐
☐
例 My **timetable** indicates that the conference starts at nine in the morning.

我的 timetable 顯示會議在早上九點鐘舉行。

遊覽，旅行 | 739 **tour** [tʊr] *n.*

☐
☐
例 One of the employees offered to take me on a **tour** of the city after the meeting.

有個員工提議在會議後帶我 tour 城市。

740 **tourism** [ˈtʊrɪzəm] *n.*　　　　　　　　　　　觀光業

　□　例 **Tourism** is one of the biggest industries in this
　□　　city.

　　　　Tourism 是本市最重要的產業之一。

741 **tourist** [ˈtʊrɪst] *n.*　　　　　　　　　　　觀光客

　□　例 There were many **tourists** on my flight to Los
　□　　Angeles.

　　　　我這班機上有許多到洛杉磯旅遊的 tourists。

742 **transit visa** [ˈtrænsɪt ˌvizə] *n. phr.*　　　過境簽證

　□　例 I forgot to apply for a **transit visa** before I left.
　□　　出國前我忘記要申請 transit visa。

743 **travel** [ˈtrævl̩] *v.*　　　　　　　　　　　旅行

　□　例 Bob is used to **traveling** three to four months of
　□　　the year for business.

　　　　鮑伯習慣一年中總有三、四個月要商務 traveling。

744 **travel agency** [ˈtrævl̩ ˌedʒənsɪ] *n. phr.*　　旅行社

　□　例 The **travel agency** was able to get our employees
　□　　a great deal on flights to the conference in the
　　　　spring.

　　　　Travel agency 能幫我們員工拿到飛往春季會議的
　　　　優惠機票。

745 **trip** [trɪp] *n.*　　　　　　　　　　　　旅行

　□　例 I haven't taken a **trip** for pleasure in years.
　□　　我已經好幾年沒有為了消遣而 trip。

746 **visit** [ˈvɪzɪt] *v.*

例 I hope that I will be able to **visit** some historical sites on my business trip.

我希望這次出差我能夠 visit 一些歷史景點。

4 Transportation 交通運輸 ⑯

大道，大街 | 747 **avenue** [ˈævə,nu] *n.*

例 I don't even want to think about going down that **avenue** unless we are desperate.

除非真的沒辦法，不然我絕不考慮走那條 avenue。

街區 | 748 **block** [blɑk] *n.*

例 Our new office is only one **block** from the river.

我們新的辦公室離這條河只有一個 block 遠。

通勤 | 749 **commute** [kəˈmjut] *v.*

例 I wish I lived in the city so I didn't have to spend so much time **commuting** every day.

我真希望住在城裡，這樣就不用每天 commuting。

通勤者 | 750 **commuter** [kəˈmjutɚ] *n.*

例 The heavy traffic in the morning is caused by all the **commuters**.

早晨繁忙的交通是所有 commuters 造成的。

壅塞，擁擠 | 751 **congestion** [kənˈdʒɛstʃən] *n.*

例 I would prefer to stay at a hotel outside the city because there is too much **congestion** downtown.

我寧願住在城外的旅館，因為城裡實在太 congestion。

752 dangerous [ˈdendʒrəs] *adj.*

　有危險的

　☐
　☐ 例 It is much more **dangerous** to travel by car than it is by plane.

　　搭乘汽車比搭乘飛機 dangerous 多了。

753 driver [ˈdraɪvɚ] *n.*

　司機

　☐
　☐ 例 The company paid for a **driver** to pick me up at the airport.

　　公司付費讓 driver 到機場接我。

754 fare [fɛr] *n.*

　車資，票價

　☐
　☐ 例 How much is the bus **fare** in this city?

　　這城市的公車 fare 是多少？

Chapter 05 商務旅行

755 ferry [ˈfɛrɪ] *n.*

　渡輪

　☐
　☐ 例 You will have to take a **ferry** from your hotel to the office.

　　從你下榻的旅館到公司需搭乘 ferry。

756 gasoline [ˈgæslˌin] *n.*

　汽油

　☐
　☐ 例 The bus smelled like **gasoline**.

　　公車上有 gasoline 味。

757 harbor [ˈhɑrbɚ] *n.*

　港口

　☐
　☐ 例 Our main office has a view of the **harbor**.

　　我們總公司能看到 harbor 的景色。

758 minute [ˈmɪnɪt] *n.*

　分鐘

　☐
　☐ 例 The train will be arriving in five **minutes**.

　　火車將於五 minutes 內抵達。

大眾捷運系統	759 **MRT** (mass rapid transit) *n.*
	☐ 例 The **MRT** is the fastest way to travel in the city.
	☐ 在城市裡往返最快速的方式就是搭 MRT。
上船；登機	760 **on board** [ɑn ˋbɔrd] *adv. phr.*
	☐ 例 Welcome **on board**!
	☐ 歡迎 on board！
準時	761 **on time** [ɑn ˋtaɪm] *adv. phr.*
	☐ 例 The train will be arriving **on time**.
	☐ 火車將 on time 抵達。
允許，准許	762 **permit** [pɚˋmɪt] *v.*
	☐ 例 Smoking is not **permitted** on the flight.
	☐ 飛機上不 permitted 抽菸。
港口	763 **port** [pɔrt] *n.*
	☐ 例 The ferry will be arriving at the **port** in ten minutes.
	☐ 渡輪將於十分鐘內抵達 port。
鐵路	764 **railroad** [ˋrel͵rod] *n.*
	☐ 例 The **railroad** was closed after the train accident.
	☐ 在火車意外事故發生後，railroad 就關閉。
可退費的	765 **refundable** [rɪˋfʌndəbl] *adj.*
	☐ 例 Is your train ticket **refundable** if you decide to leave later?
	☐ 如果你決定晚點離開，你的火車票是 refundable 嗎？

766 **rush hour** [ˈrʌʃ ˌaʊr] *n. phr.*　　　　尖峰時間

☐
☐ 例 We should leave for the train station early if we want to avoid **rush hour**.

若要避開 rush hour，我們就應該要早點到火車站。

767 **shuttle bus** [ˈʃʌtl̩ ˌbʌs] *n. phr.*　　　　接駁車

☐
☐ 例 The **shuttle bus** leaves for the airport every half-hour.

Shuttle bus 每半小時開往機場。

768 **station** [ˈsteʃən] *n.*　　　　車站，站

☐
☐ 例 The closest bus **station** is a five-minute walk from here.

最近的公車 station 距離此處五分鐘的路程。

769 **steer** [stɪr] *v.*　　　　駕駛

☐
☐ 例 The driver **steered** the bus to the side of the road because he felt sleepy.

司機因為想睡而把公車 steered 到路邊。

770 **traffic jam** [ˈtræfɪk ˌdʒæm] *n. phr.*　　　　塞車，交通壅塞

☐
☐ 例 If this **traffic jam** doesn't clear up soon, I'm going to miss my flight.

假如 traffic jam 沒有快點清除的話，我就會錯過班機了。

771 **transportation** [ˌtrænspɚˈteʃən] *n.*　　　　交通工具

☐
☐ 例 The public **transportation** in this city is much better than I thought it would be.

這城市的公共 transportation 比我想像中的好很多。

Chapter **5**

商務旅行

隧道

772 **tunnel** [ˈtʌnl] *n.*

例 We can either take the ferry or the **tunnel** to get to the hotel.

我們可以搭渡輪或者是通過 tunnel 到旅館。

車輛

773 **vehicle** [ˈvihɪkl̩] *n.*

例 I would give your entire team a ride to the office, but my **vehicle** only seats five.

我很想載你們全體到公司，但是我的 vehicle 只有五人座。

方向盤；輪子

774 **wheel** [hwil] *n.*

例 Could you please take the **wheel** while I take off my jacket?

你可以幫我握一下 wheel 嗎？我要把夾克脫下。

Exercises *perfect!*

請從選項中，選出最適當的答案完成句子。

D 1. Airplane passengers must check in at least two hours before
 _____.

   (A) accomplishment (B) appointment (C) arrival (D) departure

B 2. Jack _____ to work every day; he takes the train.

   (A) composes (B) commutes (C) communicates (D) contends

C 3. The news that the minister resigned has been _____. A new
 minister has been appointed.

   (A) assured (B) affirmed (C) confirmed (D) decided

D 4. Life is often compared to a _____; it is the process that is important, not the destination.

   (A) flight (B) trap (C) errand (D) journey

A 5. In order to work in Taiwan, foreigners must have a work _____.

   (A) permit (B) allowance (C) agreement (D) consent

B 6. As more mainlanders are visiting Taiwan, _____ is booming.

   (A) cynicism (B) tourism (C) enthusiasm (D) criticism

B 7. If you are not satisfied with the merchandise, you can return it and
 we will _____ you.

   (A) retain (B) refund (C) repay (D) return

D 8. People are _____ outside the hall for tickets to the concert
 featuring a famous pianist.

   (A) increasing (B) adding (C) accumulating (D) queuing

A 9. Currently there are two _____ at the CKS International Airport.

   (A) terminals (B) organs (C) organisms (D) destinations

B 10. I called several hotels before I was finally able to make a _____.

   (A) determination (B) reservation (C) conservation (D) prevention

Chapter
05

測
驗
練
習

11. Passengers were asked not to leave their seats when the plane was flying through _____.

(A) nuisance (B) turbulence (C) annoyance (D) disturbance

12. Tim loves flying; he is training to be a(n) _____.

(A) aircraft (B) stewardess (C) technician (D) pilot

13. You should be _____ for your interview. You will leave a very bad impression if you are late.

(A) punctual (B) permanent (C) eternal (D) casual

14. Because of bad weather and poor visibility, there were many car _____ yesterday.

(A) bumpers (B) accidents (C) incidents (D) events

15. Jason received a full scholarship last year; it was enough to cover all his _____ at college.

(A) pills (B) expenses (C) skills (D) costs

16. Our National Health _____ is a very good welfare program admired by many other nations.

(A) Insurance (B) Assurance (C) Confidence (D) Indication

17. Carry-on _____ can be stored in the overhead compartment.

(A) luggage (B) briefcase (C) suitcase (D) staircase

18. Your _____ is your ID when you travel abroad. You should carry it with you all the time.

(A) support (B) passport (C) visa (D) signature

19. A bus is a _____ that can take you almost anywhere in the city.

(A) vehicle (B) measurement (C) instrument (D) tool

20. My cousin is visiting Taipei, so I suggested that he put the National Palace Museum on his _____.

(A) proposal (B) scheme (C) itinerary (D) project

Chapter 6
Social Events 社交活動

Social events fulfill two important purposes: networking and building relationships. They allow business people to meet potential business partners or clients, and to improve business relationships by getting to know co-workers or clients on a personal level.

Social Events
社交活動

1 Dining 用餐 ⑰

出席，參加 | 775 **attend** [əˈtɛnd] v.

☐ 例 Are you going to **attend** Bob's retirement party?
☐ 你會去 attend 鮑伯的退休派對嗎？

食慾，胃口 | 776 **appetite** [ˈæpəˌtaɪt] n.

☐ 例 Alisa hasn't had an **appetite** since she got sick.
☐ 愛莉莎自從生病之後，就一直沒有 appetite。

開胃菜 | 777 **appetizer** [ˈæpəˌtaɪzɚ] n.

☐ 例 What would you like to order as an **appetizer**?
☐ 你想點什麼 appetizer？

宴會 | 778 **banquet** [ˈbæŋkwɪt] n.

☐ 例 Gina and I went to a friend's wedding **banquet** last night.
☐ 吉娜和我昨晚參加一個朋友的結婚 banquet。

酒吧 | 779 **bar** [bɑr] n.

☐ 例 Jerry likes to hit the **bar** after a long day at work.
☐ 傑瑞喜歡在辛苦工作一天後到 bar 去。

飲料 | 780 **beverage** [ˈbɛvərɪdʒ] n.

☐ 例 This restaurant doesn't serve alcoholic **beverages**.
☐ 這家餐廳不供應含酒精的 beverages。

781 **brunch** [brʌntʃ] *n.*

早午餐

☐
☐ 例 I usually have **brunch** with my friends on Saturdays.

我通常會跟朋友在星期六的時候去吃 brunch。

782 **buffet** [bʊˈfe] *n.*

自助餐廳

☐
☐ 例 There are many dishes to choose from at all-you-can-eat **buffets**.

在吃到飽的 buffets 有很多可以選擇的菜餚。

783 **cafeteria** [ˌkæfəˈtɪrɪə] *n.*

自助餐廳

☐
☐ 例 The students don't like the food in their school **cafeteria**.

學生們不喜歡學校 cafeteria 提供的菜色。

784 **cater** [ˈketɚ] *v.*

提供飲食，
承辦宴席

☐
☐ 例 That world famous chef is going to **cater** the royal wedding.

那位世界級的主廚將為皇家婚禮 cater。

785 **check** [tʃɛk] *v.*

檢查

☐
☐ 例 Before the food was served at the annual banquet, the manager **checked** every dish himself.

尾牙的每道菜端上桌前，經理都會親自 checked。

786 **chef** [ʃɛf] *n.*

主廚

☐
☐ 例 My colleagues and I go to that restaurant so often that we have become friends with the **chef**.

我和同事太常到那家餐廳，跟 chef 都變成朋友了。

筷子　787 **chopstick** [ˈtʃɑpˌstɪk] *n.*

例 Our foreign customers are always interested in learning how to use **chopsticks**.

我們的外國客戶總是對學習使用 chopsticks 很有興趣。

雞尾酒　788 **cocktail** [ˈkɑkˌtel] *n.*

例 A bar near our office has the best **cocktails** in the world.

在我們公司附近的一間酒吧有全天下最棒的 cocktails。

甜點　789 **dessert** [dɪˈzɝt] *n.*

例 The bakery around the corner has the best **desserts** in the city.

轉角那間麵包店的 desserts 是城裡最好吃的。

消化；了解　790 **digest** [daɪˈdʒɛst] *v.*

例 The information I just got from the meeting is too much for me to **digest** right now.

剛在會議室裡的事讓我現在一時還無法 digest。

用餐　791 **dining** [ˈdaɪnɪŋ] *n.*

例 Before we get a table in the **dining** room, we have to wait at the bar.

在 dining 區有位置前，我們得在吧台等。

飲料　792 **drinks** [ˈdrɪŋks] *n.*

例 Our Japanese customers had too many **drinks** at the bar last night.

我們的日本客戶昨晚在酒吧喝了太多 drinks。

793 drunk [drʌŋk] *adj.*　　　　　　　　　　　　酒醉

例 Cocktails are easy to drink, but can also get you **drunk** very easily!

雞尾酒很容易入口卻也很容易讓你 drunk。

794 entrée [ˈɑntre] *n.*　　　　　　　　　　　　主菜

例 What would you like for your **entrée**?

你的 entrée 想點什麼？

795 etiquette [ˈɛtɪˌkɛt] *n.*　　　　　　　　　禮節，禮儀

例 According to business **etiquette**, you should present your name card when introducing yourself.

根據商業 etiquette，介紹自己的時候要遞出名片。

796 guest [gɛst] *n.*　　　　　　　　　　　　　賓客

例 Our **guests** will be arriving for dinner at 6:00.

我們晚宴的 guests 將於六點鐘抵達。

797 gourmet [ˈgʊrme] *adj.*　　　　　　　　　美味的

例 Nothing beats having a **gourmet** meal with good friends.

沒什麼比跟好友一同享受 gourmet 餐點更好的了。

798 host [host] *v.*　　　　　　　　　　　　　主辦；主持

例 Our company is **hosting** the annual business dinner for offices in our building.

我們公司為我們這棟大樓的各家公司行號 hosting 年度商業晚宴。

☆ 蕃茄醬

799 **ketchup** [ˈkɛtʃəp] *n.*

例 Could you please ask the waiter for more **ketchup**?

你可以跟服務生多要些 ketchup 嗎？

酒；烈酒

800 **liquor** [ˈlɪkɚ] *n.*

例 Lisa can really hold her **liquor**. No matter how much she drinks, she just won't get drunk.

莉莎很會喝 liquor，不管她喝多少都不會醉。

☆ 午餐會

801 **luncheon** [ˈlʌntʃən] *n.*

例 The executive manager told everyone we will be going to a fancy restaurant for the staff **luncheon**.

總經理告訴大家，我們要到一家豪華餐廳舉行員工 luncheon。

禮貌，規矩

802 **manners** [ˈmænɚz] *n.*

例 The boss's kids all have very good table **manners**.

我們老闆的小孩餐桌 manners 非常好。

（一頓）飯

803 **meal** [mil] *n.*

例 You've been working all day. When was your last **meal**?

你已經工作一整天了。你上一頓 meal 是什麼時候？

菜單

804 **menu** [ˈmɛnju] *n.*

例 May I have the **menu**, please?

請給我 menu 好嗎？

805 **preparation** [ˌprɛpəˈreʃən] *n.*　　準備

☐
☐ 例 In **preparation** for this evening's gala, we hired an event coordinator.

為了 preparation 今天的晚會，我們請了個活動企劃。

806 **sauce** [sɔs] *n.*　　醬汁

☐
☐ 例 What kind of **sauce** would you like for your steak?

你的牛排需要何種 sauce？

807 **seafood** [ˈsiˌfud] *n.*　　海鮮

☐
☐ 例 My friend is allergic to **seafood**, so please tell the kitchen.

請告訴廚房我朋友對 seafood 過敏。

808 **server** [ˈsɝvɚ] *n.*　　（餐館）服務生

☐
☐ 例 The **server** spilled coffee on my lap by accident.

這 server 不小心把咖啡灑到我的腿上。

✩ **809** **serving** [ˈsɝvɪŋ] *n.*　　一份（食物）

☐
☐ 例 The bag contains five **servings** of cookies.

這包裡頭有五 servings 餅乾。

810 **spicy** [ˈspaɪsɪ] *adj.*　　辛辣的

☐
☐ 例 Not everyone can handle **spicy** food.

不是所有人都能吃 spicy 食物。

拿走　811 **take away** [ˈtek əˈwe] *v. phr.*

☐ 例 The waiter **took away** my plate before I even
☐ finished.

我還沒吃完，服務生就把我的盤子 took away 了。

給⋯小費　812 **tip** [tɪp] *v.*

☐ 例 It is not customary to **tip** servers in Taiwan.
☐ 在台灣並沒有 tip 服務生的習慣。

紙巾　813 **tissue** [ˈtɪʃʊ] *n.*

☐ 例 I need some **tissue** to blow my nose.
☐ 我需要一些 tissue 擤鼻涕。

托盤　814 **tray** [tre] *n.*

☐ 例 Servers carry dishes on a **tray**.
☐ 服務生用 tray 端送菜餚。

2 Art & Music 藝術與音樂 ⑱

古董　815 **antique** [ænˈtik] *n.*

☐ 例 Helen loves to collect **antiques**.
☐ 海倫很愛收集 antiques。

祖先，祖宗　816 **ancestor** [ˈænsɛstɚ] *n.*

☐ 例 My **ancestors** can be traced back to the Ching
☐ Dynasty.

我的 ancestors 可以追溯到清朝年間。

166

817 **ancient** [`enʃənt] *adj.*

古老的

☐ **例** Tomb sweeping is an **ancient** custom passed on
☐ through generations.

掃墓是歷代傳承下來的 ancient 習俗。

818 **appreciation** [ˌəpriʃɪ`eʃən] *n.*

欣賞；感謝

☐ **例** The audience showed their **appreciation** for the
☐ singer by standing up and applauding.

觀眾們起立鼓掌以表達對該歌手的 appreciation。

819 **artist** [`ɑrtɪst] *n.*

藝術家；畫
家

☐ **例** Marc Chagall is one of my favorite **artists**.
☐ 馬克‧夏卡爾是我最欣賞的 artists 之一。

820 **artistic** [ɑr`tɪstɪk] *adj.*

有藝術天分
的

☐ **例** Susan is a very **artistic** person.
☐ 蘇珊很 artistic。

821 **compose** [kəm`poz] *v.*

作曲，創作

☐ **例** This song was **composed** especially for the
☐ company party.

這首歌是專為公司派對所 composed 的。

822 **concert** [`kɑnsɝt] *n.*

音樂會，演
唱會

☐ **例** That famous tenor is going to give a **concert**
☐ here next month.

這位男高音即將在下個月舉辦他的 concert。

音樂廳

823 concert hall [ˋkɑnsɝt͵hɔl] *n. phr.*

例 Enjoying a performance at a **concert hall** is such a great way to spend an evening.

到 concert hall 聆聽演奏真是消磨傍晚的最佳活動。

微妙的，敏感的

824 delicate [ˋdɛləkɪt] *n.*

例 It's important to not talk about **delicate** subjects, such as religion, with colleagues.

千萬不要跟同事談論一些像是宗教之類的 delicate 話題。

設計師

825 designer [dɪˋzaɪnɚ] *n.*

例 Tom said that if he were not a salesman, he would be a clothing **designer**.

湯姆說他要不是業務員的話，他有可能是服裝 designer。

展覽

826 exhibition [͵ɛksəˋbɪʃən] *n.*

例 The Picasso **exhibition** is something you don't want to miss.

畢卡索的 exhibition 是絕不能錯過的。

美術館；畫廊

827 gallery [ˋgælərɪ] *n.*

例 Cheryl spends a lot of time visiting **galleries** and museums.

雪柔花很多時間參觀 galleries 與博物館。

耳機，耳麥

828 headset [ˋhɛd͵sɛt] *n.*

例 A **headset** is convenient when you talk online.

用 headset 在網路上聊天很方便。

829 **historian** [hɪsˈtɔrɪən] *n.*　　　　歷史學家

例 Bob's son wants to be a **historian** when he grows up.

鮑伯的兒子長大後想當 historian。

830 **museum** [mjuˈzɪəm] *n.*　　　　博物館

例 You can spend a whole day at the Metropolitan **Museum** of Art in New York and still not see everything.

你可以在紐約的大都會藝術 Museum 逛上一整天都還看不完。

831 **musician** [mjuˈzɪʃən] *n.*　　　　音樂家

例 It takes talent and many years of training to be a good **musician**.

要成為一位傑出的 musician 得具有才華與多年的訓練。

832 **opera** [ˈɑpərə] *n.*　　　　歌劇

例 Sitting in a theater enjoying an **opera** is not something that would interest my husband.

坐在劇院裡欣賞 opera 不是我丈夫會感興趣的事。

833 **orchestra** [ˈɔrkɪstrə] *n.*　　　　管弦樂隊

例 When the **orchestra** started to play, the audience got quiet.

當 orchestra 開始演奏時，聽眾都安靜了下來。

834 **philosopher** [fəˈlɑsəfɚ] *n.*　　　　哲學家

例 He thinks like a **philosopher** because he often says things that make people think.

他思考的方式像個 philosopher，常說出讓人沈思的話。

鋼琴家 | 835 **pianist** [pɪˈænɪst] *n.*

☐ ☐ 例 James thinks he is a good **pianist** but he doesn't really play well.

詹姆士認為他是個出色的 pianist，但他其實彈得並不好。

代表 | 836 **represent** [ˌrɛprɪˈzɛnt] *v.*

☐ ☐ 例 The dove in this painting **represents** peace and love.

這幅畫裡的鴿子 represents 和平與愛。

雕像，雕刻品 | 837 **sculpture** [ˈskʌlptʃɚ] *n.*

☐ ☐ 例 The museum has both paintings and **sculptures**.

博物館裡有畫作也有 sculptures。

陳列室 | 838 **showroom** [ˈʃoˌrum] *n.*

☐ ☐ 例 All the exhibits are displayed in the **showroom**.

所有的展出品都會在 showroom 裡展示。

雕像，塑像 | 839 **statue** [ˈstætʃʊ] *n.*

☐ ☐ 例 You can see **statues** of great men in that park.

在公園裡你會看到偉人的 statues。

工作室 | 840 **studio** [ˈstjudɪˌo] *n.*

☐ ☐ 例 Amy owns a small art **studio**.

艾咪有一間小型的藝術 studio。

小提琴手 | 841 **violinist** [ˌvaɪəˈlɪnɪst] *n.*

☐ ☐ 例 Yo-Yo Ma's father was a **violinist**.

馬友友的父親曾是一位 violinist。

842 **attractive** [əˋtræktɪv] *adj.*　　　　　　　有吸引力的

☐ 例 John finds filmstars with curves more **attractive**.
☐ 約翰認為影星凹凸有致的較為 attractive。

843 **audience** [ˋɔdɪəns] *n.*　　　　　　　　　觀眾

☐ 例 The **audience** didn't really enjoy the show.
☐ 這些 audience 並不喜歡這場表演。

844 **audio** [ˋɔdɪˌo] *adj.*　　　　　　　　　　聽覺的，聲音的

☐ 例 Tim recorded himself reading and saved it as an
☐ **audio** file on his computer.
　　提姆錄下他讀書的聲音並將 audio 檔案存在電腦。

845 **audiovisual** [ˌɔdɪoˋvɪʒʊəl] *adj.*　　　　視聽的

☐ 例 Ted rents **audiovisual** equipment.
☐ 泰德專門出租 audiovisual 器材。

846 **auditorium** [ˌɔdəˋtorɪəm] *n.*　　　　　　禮堂，會堂

☐ 例 The **auditorium** was packed with people who
☐ came to enjoy the show.
　　這座 auditorium 擠滿了來看表演的群眾。

847 **drama** [ˋdrɑmə] *n.*　　　　　　　　　　戲劇

☐ 例 Nick studied **drama** in college and almost
☐ became an actor.
　　尼克在大學時修過 drama 課，還差點成為演員。

Chapter
06
社交活動

電影　848 **film** [fɪlm] *n.*

例 What **film** genre do you prefer?

你喜歡哪一種類型的 film？

導演　849 **filmmaker** [ˈfɪlmˌmekə˞] *n.*

例 Ang Lee is my favorite **filmmaker**.

李安是我最喜歡的 filmmaker。

原來的；原
創的　850 **original** [əˈrɪdʒənl] *adj.*

例 The artist's performance was very **original**.

這位藝術家的表演非常 original。

表演者　851 **performer** [pə˞ˈfɔrmə˞] *n.*

例 The **performer** fell on stage.

那位 performer 在舞台上摔倒。

攝影師　852 **photographer** [fəˈtɑgrəfə˞] *n.*

例 Jacob is an excellent **photographer** because most of his shots turn out great.

雅各是一位傑出的 photographer，他總能拍出很棒的作品。

海報　853 **poster** [ˈpostə˞] *n.*

例 A huge **poster** of the popular singer is hanging outside the building.

那受歡迎的歌手大型 poster 正掛在大樓的外面。

854 premiere [prɪˋmɪr] *n.*　首映會

例 Not everyone can be invited to a movie **premiere**.

不是任何人都能受邀參加電影 premiere。

855 present [ˋprɛznt] *adj.*　出席，在場

例 How many people will be **present** at the party?

會有多少人 present 這場派對？

856 preview [ˋpriˏvju] *n.*　預映，預告片

例 You can watch the latest movie **previews** online.

你可以在網路上看到最新的電影 previews。

857 rehearsal [rɪˋhɝsl̩] *n.*　排演，排練

例 Before officially going on the stage, all actors need to do a dress **rehearsal**.

在正式上台前，所有的演員都必需先著戲服 rehearsal。

858 theater [ˋθiətɚ] *n.*　電影院

例 Would you like to go to the **theater** with me this Sunday?

這週日你願意跟我去 theater 看電影嗎？

Chapter 06 社交活動

認識的人

859 **acquaintance** [əˈkwentəns] *n.*

☐ 例 He is just an **acquaintance** not really a friend.

☐ 他只是一個 acquaintance，不是朋友。

娛樂活動，
消遣

860 **amusement** [əˈmjuzmənt] *n.*

☐ 例 This park has many activities for **amusement**.

☐ 這個公園裡有許多 amusement 活動。

烘烤，烘焙

861 **bake** [bek] *v.*

☐ 例 **Baking** cakes is something Sara loves to do in
her spare time.

☐ Baking 蛋糕是莎拉在閒暇之餘很愛做的事。

大舞廳

862 **ballroom** [ˈbɔlˌrum] *n.*

☐ 例 A **ballroom** is a dance hall.

☐ Ballroom 就是讓人跳舞的廳堂。

炊具，烹調
器具

863 **cooker** [ˈkʊkɚ] *n.*

☐ 例 We have a rice **cooker** in the office.

☐ 我們辦公室裡有一個煮飯的 cooker。

烹飪，烹調

864 **cooking** [ˈkʊkɪŋ] *n.*

☐ 例 I like to do my own **cooking** when I get home
from work.

☐ 我喜歡下班回家後自己 cooking。

865 **ingredient** [ɪnˈgridɪənt] *n.*　　　　原料，食材

☐　例 There is a very special **ingredient** in this dish.
☐　　這道菜裡有一種很特別的 ingredient。

866 **inspire** [ɪnˈspaɪr] *v.*　　　　鼓舞，激勵

☐　例 Talking to you really **inspired** me to broaden
☐　　my horizons.
　　跟你談話 inspired 我拓廣視野。

867 **invitation** [ˌɪnvəˈteʃən] *n.*　　　　邀請

☐　例 It was a pity that Sherry turned down the
☐　　**invitation** to the company party.
　　真可惜，雪莉回絕參加公司派對的 invitation。

868 **invite** [ɪnˈvaɪt] *v.*　　　　邀請

☐　例 Thanks for **inviting** me for a drink, but I think I
☐　　am going to head home.
　　謝謝你 inviting 我去喝一杯，但我還是想先回家
　　了。

869 **juicy** [ˈdʒusɪ] *adj.*　　　　多汁

☐　例 The steak we had yesterday was tender and
☐　　**juicy**.
　　我們昨天吃的牛排真是又嫩又 juicy。

870 **leisure** [ˈliʒɚ] *adj.*　　　　閒暇的

☐　例 Michelle loves to read during her **leisure** time.
☐　　蜜雪兒喜歡在 leisure 時看書。

麥克風　871 **microphone** [ˈmaɪkrəˌfon] *n.*

☐
☐ 例 When some people sing karaoke, they just won't let go of the **microphone**!

有些人一唱卡拉 OK 就無法放下 microphone！

表演　872 **perform** [pɚˈfɔrm] *v.*

☐
☐ 例 There will be a belly dancer **performing** tonight at the restaurant.

這家餐廳今晚將會有肚皮舞孃 perform。

照片　873 **photo** (photograph) [ˈfoto] *n.*

☐
☐ 例 Taking **photos** of wild birds is one of her hobbies.

拍攝野鳥的 photos 是她的嗜好之一。

食譜　874 **recipe** [ˈrɛsəpɪ] *n.*

☐
☐ 例 Can you share your pasta **recipe**? It is so delicious!

你可以給我你的義大利麵 recipe 嗎？這實在太好吃了！

☆ 娛樂，消遣　875 **recreation** [ˌrɛkrɪˈeʃən] *n.*

☐
☐ 例 Dancing is a form of **recreation** for Mary.

舞蹈對瑪麗來說是一種 recreation。

放鬆，休息　876 **relax** [rɪˈlæks] *v.*

☐
☐ 例 You always work so hard. You really need to **relax** more.

你老是拼命工作，你需要多 relax。

877 **release** [rɪˈlis] *v.*　　　　　　　　　　　釋放

例 Massages can help **release** the tension in your body.

按摩可以幫你 release 身體的緊繃。

878 **roast** [rost] *v.*　　　　　　　　　　　　烘，烤

例 At Chris's barbeque, he **roasted** a big chunk of beef.

在克里斯的烤肉會上，他 roasted 一大塊的牛肉。

✦ 879 **rotten** [ˈrɑtn̩] *adj.*　　　　　　　　　　腐敗的

例 You should throw out the **rotten** food in your refrigerator.

你該把你冰箱裡那些 rotten 食物丟掉。

✦ 880 **stadium** [ˈstedɪəm] *n.*　　　　　　　　運動場

例 Yankee **Stadium** has a long history.

洋基 Stadium 具有悠久的歷史。

881 **tablecloth** [ˈtebl̩ˌklɔθ] *n.*　　　　　　桌布

例 I can't believe you made this **tablecloth**. It is so beautiful.

我真不敢相信你做了這件 tablecloth。它好漂亮。

882 **tasty** [ˈtestɪ] *adj.*　　　　　　　　　　美味，可口

例 Whatever you are cooking, it must be **tasty**; it smells so good!

不管你在煮什麼一定很 tasty，因為聞起來好香啊！

用具

883 **utensils** [juˈtɛnsl̩z] *n.*

例 Helen bought her parents a set of stainless steel cooking **utensils**.

海倫買了一組不銹鋼的烹飪 utensils 給她父母。

素食者

884 **vegetarian** [ˌvɛdʒəˈtɛrɪən] *n.*

例 More and more people are becoming **vegetarians** for the sake of the environment.

為了地球環境，越來越多人成為 vegetarians。

Exercises

請從選項中，選出最適當的答案完成句子。

1. Jenny doesn't eat meat; she is a _____.
   (A) librarian (B) historian (C) vegetarian (D) politician

2. When Lily was told that snake meat was being served, she lost her _____ and left the table.
   (A) etiquette (B) stomach (C) appetite (D) attitude

3. A famous chef, Sam, will _____ my sister's wedding feast.
   (A) cook (B) attend (C) carter (D) prepare

4. They prepared _____ to entertain their guest, including a concert.
   (A) amusements (B) apartments (C) compartments (D) developments

5. Topics concerning religion and politics should be avoided because they are _____.
   (A) weak (B) delicate (C) tender (D) fragile

6. The _____ were amazed when the magician mysteriously made the elephant disappear.
   (A) congress (B) audience (C) congregation (D) assembly

7. Nick _____ a love song for his girlfriend, which she liked.
   (A) compiled (B) condensed (C) composed (D) adopted

8. The anniversary _____ was a success; many friends came and the food was good.
   (A) banquet (B) bouquet (C) bunch (D) handkerchief

9. Lily found Roy _____; he had a kind heart and was knowledgeable.
   (A) constructive (B) inactive (C) attractive (D) distractive

10. The twin brothers look so much alike that I often fail to _____ one from the other.
    (A) recognize (B) identify (C) extinguish (D) distinguish

11. Don't buy _____ CDs; it is against the law and it hurts the entertainment industry.

(A) duplicated (B) imported (C) exported (D) pirated

12. The dance will be held at the school _____, the only place large enough for 500 students.

(A) conference (B) library (C) laboratory (D) auditorium

13. I intend to sell my car, so I put an _____ in the paper.

(A) suggestion(B) advertisement (C) commercial (D) advice

14. I like gardening; I weed the flower beds and water the plants in my _____ time.

(A) leisure (B) lifetime (C) hobby (D) boredom

15. I've seen the _____, so I am not going to your performance tomorrow.

(A) operation (B) exercise (C) rehearsal (D) drill

16. Social _____ requires that men wear a tie on formal occasions.

(A) etiquette (B) cigarette (C) eaglet (D) regulation

17. The elderly lady hugged the young man to show her _____ for his kindness in taking her across the busy street.

(A) suspension (B) comprehension (C) apprehension (D) appreciation

18. After dinner, they had apple pie for _____.

(A) assertion (B) concert (C) dessert (D) desert

19. Two presidential candidates attended the _____ of the movie.

(A) prevention (B) premiere (C) primary (D) primitive

20. Many filmmakers were _____ by the writer; they based their stories on her novels.

(A) inflicted (B) spurred (C) stimulated (D) inspired

I Photographs (36)

Look at the pictures below and listen to the statements. Then choose the statement that best describes what you see in the picture.

1. (A) (B) (C) (D)   2. (A) (B) (C) (D)

II Conversations (37)

測
驗
練
習

You will hear some conversations between two people. Listen to the conversations and answer the questions below.

Questions 3-4

3. Which location will the man choose?
   (A) Near the city center.
   (B) Near the airport.
   (C) By the beach.
   (D) He hasn't decided yet.

4. What does the woman say about the traffic?
   (A) It is bad downtown all day.
   (B) It is bad downtown early in the morning.
   (C) It is bad near the airport in the evening.
   (D) It is bad near the airport early in the morning.

Questions 5-6

5. What does the woman think about trains?

    (A) The price is reasonable.

    (B) It is a very fast method of travel.

    (C) The man has too many bags for a train.

    (D) The beautiful scenery is worthwhile.

6. What is the man's main reason for taking the train?

    (A) It is cheaper.

    (B) The scenery is beautiful.

    (C) He can take more luggage.

    (D) It helps protect the environment.

Ⅲ Short Talks (38)

You will hear some short talks given by a single speaker. Listen to the short talks and answer the questions below.

Questions 7-8

7. What time is this information being given?

    (A) 7:15 am   (B) 8:00 am

    (C) 1:01 pm   (D) 7:45 pm

8. Who is this announcement for?

    (A) Truck drivers.   (B) Traffic policemen.

    (C) People driving to work.   (D) Cleaning staff.

Questions 9-10

9. What does the speaker say about St. Monique?

    (A) There used to be more painters working there.

    (B) It is a business district.

    (C) It is famous for its cafés.

    (D) Many famous people live there.

10. Where are they going next?

    (A) To see a studio.   (B) To visit an art gallery.

    (C) To have a drink.   (D) To exchange money.

IV Incomplete Sentences

A word or phrase is missing in each of the sentences below. Four answer choices are given below each sentence. Select the best answer to complete the sentence.

11. I hope _____ you again soon.

    (A) see   (B) to see   (C) seeing   (D) will see

12. Steven is planning _____ a long vacation at the end of this year.

    (A) to take   (B) taking   (C) take   (D) took

13. I'm thinking of _____ a day off on Monday.

    (A) to take   (B) taking   (C) take   (D) will take

14. The driver asked me how _____ to the airport.

    (A) getting   (B) he gets   (C) can get   (D) to get

15. I'm sorry, but I'm too busy _____ you right now.

    (A) seeing   (B) to see   (C) not see you   (D) see

16. Ben suggested _____ the event until after the national holiday.

    (A) postpone   (B) to postpone (C) postponing (D) to postponing

17. I remember nothing about the day of the accident, except _____ the house in the morning.

    (A) I left   (B) to leave   (C) leaving   (D) leave

18. We booked a _____ car when we traveled by overnight train to Madrid.

    (A) sleep   (B) slept   (C) to sleep   (D) sleeping

Review
3

測
驗
練
習

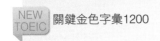
V Reading Comprehension

In this part you will read a text. The text is followed by several questions. Select the best answer for each question and mark the letter (A), (B), (C), or (D).

Questions 19-20 refer to the following review.

Stepping into Yanyan's cozy little restaurant, one first notices the pleasantly strong presence of authentic aromas. You will be greeted by Yanyan's wife as the two do all of the work at the restaurant themselves – Yanyan cooking and his wife taking care of the customers. Anything you order off the menu will be authentic and delicious, but most famous are Yanyan's large prawn spring rolls and Shanghai style noodles in sesame seed soup. Don't let the inexpensive prices fool you – everything on the menu tastes so good that you'd be willing to pay three times as much. So, for those of you who are big fans of good Chinese food, no place in the area could be more highly recommended than Yanyan's.

Yanyan's is open every night except Tuesdays from 5 until midnight.

19. What might a customer at the restaurant think?

   (A) That the food is overpriced.

   (B) That Yanyan uses a microwave oven.

   (C) That the food is poor quality because of the low prices.

   (D) That Yanyan does not pay his employees well.

20. What does the author recommend?

   (A) Leaving a tip.

   (B) Arriving early.

   (C) Looking for a different restaurant in the area.

   (D) Trying the prawn spring rolls.

VI Text Completion

Read the text that follows. A word or phrase is missing in some of the sentences. For each blank, four answer choices are given below. Select the best answer to complete the text.

Dear Clifford Hotel (21)_____,
(22)_____ is your hotel room card key. To use this card, simply slide the card into the slot on the door handle. Then (23)_____ the card. The red light will turn green and you just turn the handle to (24)_____ the room. If you lose this card key, please (25)_____ the front desk (26)_____; your old card will be (27)_____ and a new card will be issued to you. We thank you for your (28)_____ and wish you a very pleasant stay.
Yours sincerely,
Ronald Diego
Front Desk (29)_____

Review 03 測驗練習

21. (A) customer   (B) consumer   (C) guest   (D) staff
22. (A) Enclosed   (B) Recommended (C) Targeted   (D) Scheduled
23. (A) recommend (B) remove   (C) arrange   (D) slide
24. (A) enter   (B) entered   (C) entering   (D) have entered
25. (A) assume   (B) inform   (C) approve   (D) recognize
26. (A) immediate (B) immediately (C) convenient (D) conveniently
27. (A) canceled   (B) reduced   (C) removed   (D) contributed
28. (A) cooperation (B) information (C) resignation (D) arrangement
29. (A) Member   (B) Employer   (C) Supervisor (D) Boss

Chapter 7
Finance 財務

A company's accounting department keeps records of all financial transactions that take place. Company managers refer to the accounting department's financial reports when making business decisions. The reports also provide information to investors who are considering investing in a business.

Finance
財務

1 Accounting 會計 (21)

會計；會計
師

885 **accountant** [əˈkaʊntənt] *n.*

例 You need to be thorough to be a good
accountant.

你需要非常仔細才能當一個好 accountant。

會計，會計
學

886 **accounting** [əˈkaʊntɪŋ] *n.*

例 The company just decided to switch to a new
accounting system.

我們公司剛決定更換新的 accounting 系統。

分析

887 **analysis** [əˈnæləsɪs] *n.*

例 After more **analysis**, Peter has decided the only
way to reduce costs is to lay off two employees.

彼得在經過諸多 analysis 後，決定解雇兩名員工以
降低成本。

申請；申請
書

888 **application** [ˌæpləˈkeʃən] *n.*

例 John's **application** for a bank loan was denied.

約翰向銀行貸款的 application 遭到拒絕。

債券，公債

889 **bond** [band] *n.*

例 During the economic recession, many people
sold their **bonds**.

在經濟衰退時，許多人都將他們的 bonds 賣了。

890 **broker** [ˈbrokɚ] *n.*

例 Many people want to work on Wall Street as stock **brokers**.

有很多人想到華爾街當股票 brokers。

（股票或證券）經紀人

891 **check** [tʃɛk] *n.*

例 The **check** you gave me bounced.

你給我的 check 跳票了。

支票

892 **checkbook** [ˈtʃɛk͵bʊk] *n.*

例 A **checkbook** comes in handy when you don't have cash.

手邊沒現金的時候，checkbook 就很方便了。

支票簿

893 **controller** [kənˈtrolɚ] *n.*

例 The accounting department error must be discussed with the financial **controller**.

會計部出的錯要會同財務 controller 一起討論。

主計員，查帳員

894 **conversion** [kənˈvɝʃən] *n.*

例 What's the currency **conversion** between the US dollar and Euro today?

今天美元對歐元的貨幣 conversion 是多少？

折合，換算

895 **currency** [ˈkɝənsɪ] *n.*

例 Most countries have their own **currencies**.

大部分的國家都有自己的 currencies。

貨幣，通貨

削減，減少　896 **cut down** [ˋkʌt ˋdaʊn] *v. phr.*

例 Our company wants us to **cut down** on the amount of paper we use.

公司希望大家 cut down 用紙量。

借款，債務　897 **debt** [dɛt] *n.*

例 The company went out of business because it ran up huge **debts**.

這家公司因為巨額 debts 而關門大吉了。

減少，降低　898 **decrease** [dɪˋkris] *v.*

例 In order to make more profit, the company has to **decrease** costs.

為了要增加利潤，公司必須要 decrease 成本。

資產，財產　899 **estate** [əˋstet] *n.*

例 The family **estate** was worth over five million dollars.

這家人的 estate 價值五百萬美元以上。

位數　900 **figure** [ˋfɪgjɚ] *n.*

例 If we can pull off the deal, there will be at least a seven **figure** profit for the company.

如果我們能談成這個案子，公司將至少會有位七 figure 的進帳。

財務狀況，資金　901 **finances** [ˋfaɪnænsɪz] *n.*

例 Before going to the bank for a loan, make sure your **finances** are in order.

去銀行貸款前，請確定您的 finances 無虞。

902 fluctuate [ˈflʌktʃʊˌet] *v.*　波動，變動

例 The stock market has **fluctuated** due to the recent earthquakes in Japan.

日本近日發生的地震造成股市 fluctuated。

903 inflation [ɪnˈfleʃən] *n.*　通貨膨脹

例 The **increase** in the cost of the product takes inflation rates into account.

產品成本的增加考慮到了 inflation 率。

904 investor [ɪnˈvɛstɚ] *n.*　投資者

例 The country tried to attract foreign **investors** by offering low interest rates.

這個國家希望藉由提供低率優惠吸引外來 investors。

905 loan [lon] *n.*　貸款

例 Lisa still owes the bank a hundred thousand dollars on her student **loan**.

莉莎還欠銀行十萬美元的學生 loan。

906 maximum [ˈmæksəməm] *n.*　最大值

例 Ten thousand NT dollars is the **maximum** we can spend on the company dinner.

公司晚上聚餐的預算 maximum 到一萬元。

907 mean [min] *n.*　平均值

例 Could you get me the sales totals for each day of the month so I can calculate the daily **mean**?

可以給我當月每日的銷售金額，我好計算每日的 mean 嗎？

Chapter 7 財務

191

最小值；最
低的，最少
的

908 **minimum** [ˈmɪnəməm] *adj.*

例 The **minimum** wage is 95 NT per hour.

Minimum 時薪為 95 元。

欠

909 **owe** [o] *v.*

例 The company still **owes** the supplier two thousand dollars.

我們公司還 owes 供應商兩千元。

預測，預言

910 **predict** [prɪˈdɪkt] *v.*

例 Some financial experts **predict** the economy will stay the same as last year.

有些金融專家 predict 經濟情況將和去年一樣。

壓力

911 **pressure** [ˈprɛʃɚ] *n.*

例 Many households are feeling financial **pressure** due to the rise of living costs.

許多家庭都因為物價上漲而有經濟 pressure。

不動產

912 **real estate** [ˈril əˌstet] *n.*

例 **Real estate** in Shanghai is constantly going up.

上海的 real estate 不斷地飆漲。

（經濟）衰
退

913 **recession** [rɪˈsɛʃən] *n.*

例 Everyone tightened their belts during the economic **recession**.

經濟 recession 時，大家都會節省開銷。

914 report [rɪˋpɔrt] *n.*

報告

☐
☐ 例 The annual fiscal **report** will be presented during the shareholders meeting.

年度會計 report 將會在股東大會上提出。

915 risk [rɪsk] *n.*

危險，風險

☐
☐ 例 Your are taking a **risk** when you invest money in the stock market.

投資股市是有 risk 的。

916 savings [ˋsevɪŋz] *n.*

積蓄，存款

☐
☐ 例 Danny has enough **savings** to put a down payment on a new home.

丹尼有足夠的 savings 來付新房子的頭期款。

917 settlement [ˋsɛtḷmənt] *n.*

結算，（欠款的）償付

☐
☐ 例 Your job is to handle the **settlement** of customer accounts.

你的工作是要處理顧客帳戶的 settlement。

918 shares [ʃɛrz] *n.*

股份，股票

☐
☐ 例 He holds half of the **shares** in this company.

他擁有那間公司一半的 shares。

919 slump [slʌmp] *n.*

暴跌，衰退

☐
☐ 例 There was a big **slump** in third-quarter revenues.

第三季的盈收慘遭重大 slump。

☆ 推測

920 **speculate** [ˋspɛkjəˌlet] *v.*

例 Lola **speculates** there will be a drop in stock values.

蘿拉 speculates 股市將會大跌。

穩定的

921 **stable** [ˋstebl̩] *adj.*

例 We should make sure our finances are **stable** before we invest in that new idea.

在投資那個新構想前，我們應該確保我們的財務是 stable。

統計的，統計學的

922 **statistical** [stəˋtɪstɪkl̩] *adj.*

例 Accounting is a **statistical** method of calculating numbers.

會計是一種計算數字的 statistical 方法。

股票市場

923 **stock market** [ˋstak ˌmarkɪt] *n.*

例 The **stock market** in that country crashed during the war.

在戰爭爆發期間，該國家的 stock market 崩盤了。

股東

924 **shareholder** [ˋʃɛrˌholdɚ] *n.*

例 There are many **shareholders** involved in the project.

有許多 shareholders 參與這項計畫。

小計

925 **subtotal** [ˋsʌbˌtotl̩] *n.*

例 The **subtotal** for your purchase is twelve thousand NT (dollars).

你所購物品的 subtotal 為一萬兩千元。

926 **transaction** [trænz`ækʃən] *n.*　　　交易

☐☐ 例 How many **transactions** do you have with clients each day?

你每天與客戶有多少 transactions？

927 **valuate** [`væljʊˌet] *v.*　　　估計

☐☐ 例 The merchandise in stock was **valuated** at over one hundred thousand dollars.

商品存貨 valuated 有十萬美元以上的價值。

928 **yearly** [`jɪrlɪ] *adj.*　　　年度的

☐☐ 例 The **yearly** accounting report is confidential.

這份 yearly 會計報告屬機密文件。

2 Assets 資產 (22)

929 **afford** [ə`fɔrd] *v.*　　　負擔得起

☐☐ 例 The company can't **afford** to lose profit on the sale of their downtown office building.

公司無法 afford 賣掉市區辦公大樓所造成的虧損。

930 **apartment** [ə`pɑrtmənt] *n.*　　　公寓

☐☐ 例 The **apartment** is only available to purchase as a residence, not as office space.

這 apartment 只能買來作為住家，不能作為辦公室。

931 **appraisal** [əˈprezl̩] *n.*

例 Jack had someone do an **appraisal** on the house he inherited.

傑克請人將他繼承的房子作個 appraisal。

932 **asset** [ˈæsɛt] *n.*

例 Patricia's downtown property is one of her more valuable **assets**.

派翠西亞位於市區的房地產是她較有價值的 asset 之一。

933 **auction** [ˈɔkʃən] *n.*

例 The company is up for **auction**.

那家公司將付之 auction。

934 **certificate** [səˈtɪfəkɪt] *n.*

例 All employees were given a **certificate** that details their investment in company stocks.

所有的員工都會有一份 certificate，詳註投資公司股票的細目。

935 **drain** [dren] *v.*

例 Mark and Judy **drained** their savings to purchase the small office space.

馬克和茱蒂 drain 他們的積蓄，買了那間小小的辦公室。

936 **estimate** [ˈɛstəmet] *n.*

例 Frank asked for an **estimate** on the cost of the repairs needed in the foyer.

法蘭克要求知道維修玄關所需的費用 estimate。

937 **facilitate** [fəˈsɪləˌtet] v.　　協助

　例 Maria **facilitates** at least two open houses every weekend.

　瑪麗亞每個週末至少 facilitates 兩件以上的房屋物件。

938 **housing** [ˈhaʊzɪŋ] n.　　（總稱）房屋，住宅

　例 **Housing** downtown can be very expensive.

　市區的 housing 可能非常昂貴。

939 **landmark** [ˈlændˌmɑrk] n.　　地標

　例 The property is located next to one of the city's most famous **landmarks**.

　物件就座落在該市最富盛名的 landmark 旁。

940 **lend** [lɛnd] v.　　出借

　例 Jake's parents offered to **lend** him enough money for a down payment on the property.

　傑克的父母 lend 給他買房子的頭期款。

941 **ownership** [ˈonɚˌʃɪp] n.　　所有權

　例 Please sign this agreement to indicate the date **ownership** takes effect.

　請簽同意書以表建物 ownership 移轉生效日期。

942 **period** [ˈpɪrɪəd] n.　　一段時間，時期

　例 The property was on the market for a long **period** before any offers were made.

　這房子公開銷售很長的 period 後才有人出價。

財產

943 **possession** [pə`zɛʃən] n.

例 They lost all of their **possessions**, including their house.

他們已經喪失全部的 possessions，包括他們的房子。

重建

944 **rebuild** [ri`bɪld] v.

例 It is going to take at least three months to **rebuild** the house that burned down.

Rebuild 這間燒毀的房子少說也要三個月。

遷徙，重新安置

945 **relocate** [ri`loket] v.

例 If we are going to **relocate** the business by the end of the month, we'd better start packing now!

如果我們要在月底前 relocate 公司，那麼我們最好現在開始打包。

修繕，整修

946 **renovation** [ˌrɛnə`veʃən] n.

例 The estimated **renovation** cost exceeds our budget.

預估的 renovation 費用超過我們的預算。

租

947 **rent** [rɛnt] v.

例 It might be a good idea to **rent** a small retail space before purchasing one.

在買之前先 rent 個小店面或許是個不錯的主意。

租賃的

948 **rental** [`rɛntḷ] adj.

例 **Rental** spaces in this neighborhood are quite affordable.

這附近 rental 物件價錢合適，租得起。

949 residence [ˈrɛzədəns] *n.* 住家

☐ 例 This office space used to be a **residence**.

☐ 這辦公室曾經是 residence。

950 restructuring [riˈstrʌktʃərɪŋ] *n.* 重組

☐ 例 The company is currently undergoing a troubled
☐ debt **restructuring**.

公司正在進行債務 restructuring。

951 sale [sel] *n.* 買賣交易

☐ 例 The **sale** of the property was in the news.

☐ 該房產的 sale 上了新聞。

⭐ **952 tenant** [ˈtɛnənt] *n.* 房客

☐ 例 Rent from all **tenants** is due on the first of each
☐ month.

所有 tenants 的租金都是在每月的第一天到期。

Exercises

請從選項中，選出最適當的答案完成句子。

A 1. The _____ received a three-day notice from his landlord. If he didn't pay his rent then, he would have to move out.

   (A) tenant   (B) client   (C) guest   (D) customer

D 2. The ability to speak a foreign language is a great personal _____.

   (A) property   (B) asset   (C) belonging   (D) estate

C 3. Your _____ of US$500 has been received; the balance of US$1500 is due in two months.

   (A) consumption   (B) investment   (C) deposit   (D) composite

C 4. The builder designer _____ that the remodeling cost would be around one hundred thousand.

   (A) investigated   (B) commented   (C) estimated   (D) surveyed

A 5. The government is issuing _____ to raise funds for the housing project.

   (A) bonds   (B) tickets   (C) coupons   (D) checks

A 6. Jane needs a _____ to expand her company.

   (A) loan   (B) load   (C) ladder   (D) lantern

A 7. Having made substantial profits, the investors had a difficult time trying to decide who should get the lion's _____.

   (A) share   (B) sector   (C) part   (D) section

A 8. What is the _____ of 30 and 50?

   (A) mean   (B) addition   (C) division   (D) result

B 9. There is a certain _____ in going out with someone you don't know very well.

   (A) embarrassment   (B) risk   (C) reason   (D) anxiety

D 10. The _____ of your purchase is NT$ 3458.

   (A) title   (B) subtotal   (C) measure   (D) amount

11. The dollar has been a strong _____ for quite some time, but the Euro seems to be catching up.

    (A) efficiency (B) currency (C) tendency (D) fluency

12. We benefit from the _____ wisdom of our elders, if we listen to them.

    (A) concerned (B) related (C) assembled (D) accumulated

13. The _____ said she could advance my payment if necessary.

    (A) salesman (B) attendant (C) waiter (D) accountant

14. The country is gradually recovering from a _____. The unemployment rate is dropping.

    (A) recession (B) detention (C) frustration (D) discussion

15. Because competition is intense, children are under a lot of _____ to do well in school.

    (A) pressure (B) treasure (C) leisure (D) pleasure

16. I'd rather not invest my money on the stock market; it _____ and makes me full of uncertainty.

    (A) violates (B) vibrates (C) fluctuates (D) drops

17. The company has gone bankrupt; it is up for _____.

    (A) auction (B) action (C) reduction (D) induction

18. I prefer to pay by _____ rather than by credit card.

    (A) note (B) cash (C) sum (D) unit

19. The _____ discount we can offer is 20 percent.

    (A) highest (B) minimum (C) maximum (D) largest

20. The figure doesn't look right. Please do the _____ again.

    (A) speculation (B) calculation (C) circulation (D) ventilation

Chapter
07
測
驗
練
習

Chapter 8
Purchasing & Logistics 採購與後勤

Logistics is the flow of transporting goods to customers or the places where they are bought. Usually logistics activities include storage, delivery of goods and supply chain.

8 Purchasing & Logistics
採購與後勤

1 Purchasing 採購 ㉓

贊成；同意 953 **approve** [əˈpruv] v.

☐ 例 The accounting department doesn't **approve** of
☐ the stationery purchase.

會計部不 approve 購買文具。

討價還價 954 **bargain** [ˈbɑrgɪn] v.

☐ 例 Always **bargain** before you agree to the final
☐ price.

在同意最後的價錢之前一定要 bargain。

出價；喊價 955 **bid** [bɪd] v.

☐ 例 The two companies are **bidding** to be the sole
☐ agent for a famous brand.

這兩家公司在競爭 bidding 知名品牌的獨家代理
權。

提貨單 956 **bill of lading** [ˈbɪl əv ˈledɪŋ] n.

☐ 例 A **bill of lading** usually contains the shipping
☐ company name, shipper's name and description
of goods.

Bill of landing 上通常會有海運公司的名稱、托運
人的名字以及商品名稱。

957 **brand-new** [ˋbrænd ˋnju] *adj.*　　　　全新的，嶄新的

例 A **brand-new** machine has been set up in the factory.

工廠裡裝設了一架 brand-new 機器。

958 **buyer** [ˋbaɪɚ] *n.*　　　　採購員；買主

例 Tom works at that company as a **buyer**.

湯姆在該公司擔任 buyer 的職位。

959 **carriage** [ˋkærɪdʒ] *n.*　　　　運輸；運費

例 That airline charges a lot for **carriage**.

這家航空公司收取高額 carriage 費用。

960 **cash** [kæʃ] *n.*　　　　現金

例 If you pay the bill in **cash**, the owner might not charge you tax.

如果你以 cash 交易，賣家可能不會加收稅金。

961 **catalog** [ˋkætl̩͵ɔg] *n.*　　　　目錄

例 **Catalogs** were mailed to customers in the mail.

Catalogs 以郵寄的方式送達客戶。

962 **charge** [tʃɑrdʒ] *v.*　　　　要價

例 That company is **charging** way too much for photocopy paper.

那家公司的影印紙 charging 太高了。

商品；貨物	963	**commodity** [kə`madətɪ] *n.*
		☐ 例 Coffee is one of South America's biggest **commodities**.
		☐ 咖啡是南非最大宗的 commodities。

優惠券	964	**coupon** [`kjupɑn] *n.*
		☐ 例 If you have a **coupon**, you can save ten percent on your purchase.
		☐ 如果你有 coupon 的話，購買的商品可以打九折。

貿易商	965	**dealer** [`dilɚ] *n.*
		☐ 例 The computer **dealer** visits the office once a year to sell us updates.
		☐ 電腦 dealer 每年都會來我們公司拜訪，兜售最新的產品。

折扣	966	**discount** [`dɪskaʊnt] *n.*
		☐ 例 We received a **discount** on the office furniture.
		☐ 我們收到採買辦公室家具的 discount。

免（稅）	967	**exemption** [ɪg`zɛmpʃən] *n.*
		☐ 例 The government offered a tax **exemption** on the purchase of wheelchair ramps for businesses.
		☐ 政府提供企業 exemption 的條件設置無障礙坡道。

出口產品，輸出品	968	**export** [`ɛkspɔrt] *n.*
		☐ 例 Sugar cane is one of the major **exports** of the Philippines.
		☐ 甘蔗是菲律賓主要 exports 之一。

969 **import** [ɪmˋpɔrt] *v.*　　　　進口

☐
☐　　**例** The coffee in Canada is **imported** from
　　　　 countries with warmer climates.

　　　　 加拿大的咖啡是從較暖和氣候的國家 imported 而
　　　　 來的。

970 **invoice** [ˋɪnvɔɪs] *n.*　　　　發票

☐
☐　　**例** The shipping department forgot to put the
　　　　 invoice in the box.

　　　　 船運部忘記將 invoice 入箱。

971 **negotiate** [nɪˋgoʃɪ,et] *v.*　　　　談判；商議

☐
☐　　**例** We will need to **negotiate** the price when
　　　　 purchasing new computers for the office.

　　　　 我們為公司購買新電腦時將需要 negotiate 價格。

972 **on sale** [ɑn ˋsel] *phr.*　　　　（廉價）出
　　　　　　　　　　　　　　　　售，特價

☐
☐　　**例** The secretary said there are desks **on sale** at the
　　　　 furniture store down the street.

　　　　 秘書說這條街下去有間家具行，他們的書桌正在
　　　　 on sale。

973 **order** [ˋɔrdɚ] *v.*　　　　訂購

☐
☐　　**例** We usually **order** enough pens and pencils to
　　　　 last an entire year.

　　　　 我們平常會 order 足夠一年份使用的筆和鉛筆。

974 **payable** [ˋpeəbl̩] *adj.*　　　　支付給…

☐
☐　　**例** Please make your check **payable** to the owner.

　　　　 請您開支票，payable 給業主。

付款

975 **payment** [ˈpemənt] *n.*

☐ 例 **Payment** is due upon arrival of the order.

☐ 所訂購的貨物到達後即應 payment。

預付

976 **prepay** [priˈpe] *v.*

☐ 例 We prefer for our customers to **prepay**, but you can also wait until delivery.

☐ 我們比較希望客戶能夠 prepay，但是您也可以等貨到了再付款。

價格

977 **price** [praɪs] *n.*

☐ 例 The **price** of mailing labels has gone up.

☐ 地址標籤的 price 已經上揚。

（尤指為政府或機構）採購；收購

978 **procurement** [proˈkjʊrmənt] *n.*

☐ 例 When purchasing the company, the organization used a number of **procurement** strategies to lower costs and risks.

該機構採用一些 procurement 策略，就為了在收購該公司時能降低成本與風險。

採購；購買

979 **purchase** [ˈpɝtʃəs] *v.*

☐ 例 We have **purchased** enough staples for the entire year.

☐ 我們已經 purchased 一整年用量的釘書針。

折抵

980 **rebate** [ˈribet] *n.*

☐ 例 If we purchase five laptops for the office, we can receive a two-hundred dollar **rebate**.

☐ 如果我們辦公室買五部筆電，我們就能得到兩百元的 rebate。

208

981 receipt [rɪˋsit] *n.*   收據

☐ 例 I can't find the **receipt** for the new fax machine.

☐ 我找不到新傳真機的 receipt。

982 refuse [rɪˋfjuz] *v.*   拒絕

☐ 例 The salesperson **refused** to give us a lower price.

☐ 銷售員 refused 降價賣我們。

983 reimbursement [ˌriɪmˋbɝsmənt] *n.*   償還；退款

☐ 例 If this coffee maker doesn't work, I will want a full **reimbursement**.

☐ 如果咖啡機無法運作，我要求全額 reimbursement。

984 second-hand [ˋsɛkəndˋhænd] *adj.*   二手的

☐ 例 If we cannot afford new office furniture, we may be able to find some **second-hand** furniture in good condition.

☐ 如果我們買不起新的辦公家具，也許可以買一些狀況不錯的 second-hand 家具。

985 secure [sɪˋkjʊr] *adj.*   安全的

☐ 例 Don't pay with a credit card online unless you are sure it is **secure**.

☐ 別使用線上信用卡付款，除非你確信它很 secure。

986 seller [ˋsɛlɚ] *n.*   賣方

☐ 例 The **seller** requested that payment be made up front.

☐ Seller 要求當面付款。

買東西，購物

987 **shop** [ʃɑp] *v.*

☐ 例 The only way we can compare prices is if we
☐ **shop** around.

我們唯一可以比價的方式就是到處去 shop。

商人

988 **trader** [ˈtredɚ] *n.*

☐ 例 Mark has been a **trader** in the industry for over
☐ ten years.

馬克在業界當 trader 已超過十年了。

緊急的

989 **urgent** [ˈɝdʒənt] *adj.*

☐ 例 The manager of the purchasing department has
☐ an **urgent** call on line one.

採購經理在一線有一通 urgent 電話。

多樣化；種類

990 **variety** [vəˈraɪətɪ] *n.*

☐ 例 When selecting the products for the spring line,
☐ make sure there is a lot of **variety**.

在選擇春季產品時，要確定有許多 variety。

販賣

991 **vend** [vɛnd] *v.*

☐ 例 Before becoming a salesperson in the company,
☐ Maria used to **vend** clothing at night markets.

瑪麗亞在成為公司的業務員之前，她曾經在夜市
vend 衣服。

992 **airmail** [ˈɛrˌmel] *n.* 航空郵件

☐ **例** Please send the invoice by **airmail**.
☐ 請將發票以 airmail 寄出。

993 **by sea** [baɪ ˈsi] *adv. phr.* 經由海運地

☐ **例** Sending products **by sea** takes a long time.
☐ 以 by sea 寄送貨物需要很長的時間。

994 **cargo** [ˈkɑrgo] *n.* 船貨，貨物

☐ **例** The **cargo** was delivered to the warehouse in poor condition.
☐ Cargo 送到倉庫時已經破損。

995 **courier** [ˈkʊrɪɚ] *n.* 快遞員

☐ **例** The **courier** was supposed to drop off the package before noon.
☐ Courier 應該在中午之前將包裹送達。

996 **coverage** [ˈkʌvərɪdʒ] *n.* 保固，擔保

☐ **例** The warranty for the fax machine gives us **coverage**.
☐ 這張保證書給予這台傳真機 coverage。

997 **damage** [ˈdæmɪdʒ] *v.* 損害

☐ **例** The gifts I packed were **damaged** during the flight.
☐ 我包好的禮物在飛機運送過程中 damaged 了。

Chapter
8
採購與後勤

遞送

998 **deliver** [dɪˈlɪvɚ] *v.*

☐ 例 If the package isn't **delivered** on time, it will
☐ delay our work.

如果那件包裹沒有準時 delivered，那將會延宕我
們的工作。

☆ 經銷

999 **distribution** [ˌdɪstrəˈbjuʃən] *n.*

☐ 例 **Distribution** of the product across the country is
☐ our number one goal.

我們的首要目標是將產品 distribution 到全國各地。

快捷

1000 **express** [ɪkˈsprɛs] *adj.*

☐ 例 It costs extra to ship the product via **express** mail.
☐ 用 express 郵件寄出這產品得支付額外的費用。

☆ 運輸的貨物

1001 **freight** [fret] *n.*

☐ 例 The **freight** was damaged in the accident.
☐ Freight 不小心損毀了。

☆ 檢查，檢驗

1002 **inspection** [ɪnˈspɛkʃən] *n.*

☐ 例 All merchandise must go through a careful
☐ **inspection** process before being shipped to
buyers.

所有的商品在出貨給買方之前，必須經過仔細
inspection 的過程。

有存貨／庫
存

1003 **in stock** [ɪnˈstɑk] *phr.*

☐ 例 Unfortunately, we don't have any more colored
☐ paper **in stock**.

很遺憾，我們並沒有任何的色紙 in stock。

1004 **merchandise** [ˈmɝtʃənˌdaɪz] *n.*　　　　商品；貨物

　例 All **merchandise** must be inspected when it
　　　arrives.

　　所有的 merchandise 到貨時皆須經過檢驗。

1005 **origin** [ˈɔrədʒɪn] *n.*　　　　由來；起源

　例 Does anyone know the **origin** of this coffee?

　　有人知道這咖啡的 origin 嗎？

1006 **out of stock** [ˈaʊt əv ˈstɑk] *phr.*　　　　售完，沒有
　　　　　　　　　　　　　　　　　　　　庫存

　例 When I called to place an order, the supplier
　　　said they were currently **out of stock**.

　　我打電話給供應商下訂單時，他們說現已 out of
　　stock。

1007 **overweight** [ˈovɚˈwet] *adj.*　　　　超重

　例 You are going to have to remove some
　　　merchandise from the box because it is
　　　overweight.

　　因為箱子 overweight，你必須把一些貨物移出
　　來。

1008 **package** [ˈpækɪdʒ] *n.*　　　　包裝

　例 The **package** got wet during shipment.

　　在運送過程中，外 package 潮濕了。

1009 **parcel** [ˈpɑrsl̩] *n.*　　　　包裹

　例 Jane sent the **parcel** by airmail.

　　珍以航空郵件寄這 parcel。

郵資　　　　1010 **postage** [ˈpostɪdʒ] *n.*

☐　例 How much is the **postage** for an over-sized
☐　　 envelope?

　　　　　　特大信封的 postage 是多少錢？

郵務的，郵　1011 **postal** [ˈpostl̩] *adj.*
遞的
☐　例 The **postal** service is expensive in this country.
☐　　 該國的 postal 服務是昂貴的。

郵政的　　　1012 **postal** [ˈpostl̩] *n.*

☐　例 The **postal** service isn't as effective as it used to
☐　　 be.

　　　　　　Postal 服務的效率不若以往的好。

郵戳　　　　1013 **postmark** [ˈpost,mɑrk] *n.*

☐　例 The **postmark** indicates the package was sent
☐　　 last Monday.

　　　　　　Postmark 顯示，這包裹是上星期一寄出的。

收件者　　　1014 **recipient** [rɪˈsɪpiənt] *n.*

☐　例 The **recipient** should check the contents of the
☐　　 package carefully.

　　　　　　Recipient 應該小心檢查包裹的內容物。

零售　　　　1015 **retail** [ˈritel] *n.*

☐　例 Most **retail** stores are open from 9 am to 9 pm.
☐　　 大多數的 retail 商店營業時間為早上九點到晚上九
　　　　　　點。

1016 retailer [ˈritelɚ] *n.* 零售商

☐
☐ 例 Bob Hendry is one of the biggest **retailers** in the city.

鮑伯・亨德利是本市最大的 retailers 之一。

1017 return [rɪˈtɜn] *n.* 退貨

☐ 例 We only accept **returns** up to thirty days after purchase.
☐
我們只接受購買後三十天內的 returns。

1018 review [rɪˈvju] *n.* 檢查，複查

☐ 例 The packaging process is under **review**.
☐
包裝過程正在 review 中。

1019 ship [ʃɪp] *v.* 運送

☐ 例 Your products will be **shipped** within the next two weeks.
☐
您的產品將於兩星期內 shipped。

1020 shipment [ˈʃɪpmənt] *n.* （裝運的）貨物；貨運

☐ 例 Your **shipment** has been delayed due to availability issues.
☐
您的 shipment 因產品缺貨而延遲出貨。

Chapter
08
採購與後勤

1021 shipper [ˈʃɪpɚ] *n.* 承運商，運貨商

☐ 例 The **shipper** misplaced your package.
☐
Shipper 出錯貨了。

商店經理；店主	1022 **shopkeeper** [ˈʃɑpˌkipɚ] *n.*
	例 If the **shopkeeper** is not in, ask to speak to the assistant manager.
	如果 shopkeeper 不在，那就找副理。

存貨；庫存品	1023 **stock** [stɑk] *n.*
	例 We need to place a new order because our **stock** is getting low.
	我們需要下新的訂單，因為我們的 stock 快沒了。

貯藏；倉庫	1024 **storage** [ˈstorɪdʒ] *n.*
	例 The **storage** shelves are full of office supplies.
	Storage 架上放滿了辦公用品。

供應商	1025 **supplier** [səˈplaɪɚ] *n.*
	例 Our **supplier** contacts us regularly to see if we need to place an order.
	我們的 supplier 固定與我們聯絡，察看我們是否有下單的需求。

庫存；供應	1026 **supply** [səˈplaɪ] *n.*
	例 The **supply** closet is too small for all our supplies.
	Supply 櫃太小了，放不下我們所有的存貨。

（貨運）追蹤編號	1027 **tracking number** [ˈtrækɪŋ ˌnʌmbɚ] *n. phr.*
	例 Make sure you keep the **tracking number**, just in case the parcel goes missing.
	一定要保留貨運的 tracking number，以防包裹遺失。

1028 transport [træns`pɔrt] *v.* 運送，運輸

☐ ☐ 例 How will the product be **transported**?

產品將要怎麼 transported 呢？

1029 trunk [trʌŋk] *n.* 汽車車尾的行李箱

☐ ☐ 例 You will have to ship the order to my office because it won't fit in my **trunk**.

因為訂貨無法放進我車子的 trunk，你必須要用貨運寄出。

1030 unload [ʌn`lod] *v.* 卸貨

☐ ☐ 例 I will need some help to **unload** the product from my car.

我需要人幫忙從我的車子 unload 產品。

1031 unpack [ʌn`pæk] *v.* 打開包裹

☐ ☐ 例 Employees in the shipping and receiving department are asked to **unpack** merchandise carefully.

貨物收發部門的職員須要小心翼翼地 unpack 商品。

1032 unsecured [ˌʌnsɪ`kjʊrd] *adj.* 無擔保的

☐ ☐ 例 The boxes were **unsecured** during shipment.

貨箱在托運過程中是 unsecured。

1033 via [`vaɪə] *prep.* 經由

☐ ☐ 例 Your package will be shipped **via** express mail.

你的包裹將會 via 快捷郵遞運送。

Chapter 8
☐ 採購與後勤

倉庫　1034 **warehouse** [ˈwɛr,haʊs] *n.*

例 Please drop off the merchandise at the **warehouse**, not our office.

請到 warehouse 卸貨，而不是在我們的辦公室。

在世界各地　1035 **worldwide** [ˈwɝˈlˈwaɪd] *adv.*

例 The cost of shipping product **worldwide** is very high.

運送貨物的費用 worldwide 都很高。

包裹　1036 **wrap** [ræp] *v.*

例 Be sure to **wrap** the breakable items with newspaper to prevent damage.

要用報紙 wrap 易碎的物品來避免毀壞。

X光，X射線　1037 **X-ray** [ˈɛksˈre] *n.*

例 Products that are shipped by air will need to go through **X-ray**.

用空運寄送的貨品需要通過 X-ray 檢查。

Exercises −2

請從選項中，選出最適當的答案完成句子。

1. There was a communication _____ when the customer ordered a snake instead of a snack.

   (A) breakdown (B) shutdown (C) breakup (D) destruction

2. You need a birth _____ to provide information regarding
   your birthplace.

   (A) declaration (B) degree (C) certificate (D) diploma

3. A(n) _____ of food can be found at the night market.

   (A) odd (B) variety (C) obstacle (D) structure

4. The manager told the secretary to order more _____ for the
   office.

   (A) resources (B) supplies (C) services (D) attendants

5. Jack has a part time job _____ pizza.

   (A) providing (B) delivering (C) offering (D) sending

6. The man is very sick; it is _____ that he be sent to a hospital.

   (A) desirable (B) urgent (C) unavoidable (D) inevitable

7. Some parents don't _____ of their children staying overnight
   at a friend's place.

   (A) approve (B) agree (C) consent (D) allow

8. The _____ of the word datum is Latin, while the _____
   of kung fu is Chinese.

   (A) benchmark (B) milestone (C) origin (D) source

9. Bicycles are one of the products that are _____ from Taiwan.

   (A) extended (B) exposed (C) escorted (D) exported

10. We put all the fishing gear in the _____ of the car and head-
    ed for the sea.

    (A) cabinet (B) trunk (C) closet (D) case

11. You can return any defected _____ and we will refund your money or give you a replacement.

(A) commodity (B) supply (C) amount (D) catalog

12. My dealer said I could delay the _____ until I was satisfied with his product.

(A) total (B) payment (C) debt (D) sum

13. I think you are being unreasonably _____—this used car isn't worth that much.

(A) confined (B) chained (C) charged (D) changed

14. When you buy anything, be sure to keep the _____; you might win some big prize money.

(A) attention (B) reception (C) receipt (D) deception

15. The _____ let me test drive the new car, and I bought it as a result.

(A) leader (B) dealer (C) healer (D) jumper

16. Remember you have the right to _____ to be questioned by the police without the presence of your lawyer.

(A) cancel (B) refuse (C) deject (D) project

17. I was hesitant about the party, but my sister _____ me to go and I had a good time.

(A) pretended (B) intended (C) dissuaded (D) persuaded

18. The kidnappers didn't want to_____; the only thing they would accept was the full ransom, not a penny less.

(A) communicate (B) negotiate (C) associate (D) depreciate

19. A(n) _____ is a very useful guide when you go shopping.

(A) catalog (B) index (C) appendix (D) summary

20. Troops were _____ to the battlefield by plane and ship.

(A) delivered (B) mailed (C) assigned (D) transported

REVIEW 4

I Photographs

Look at the pictures below and listen to the statements. Then choose the statement that best describes what you see in the picture.

1. (A) (B) (C) (D) 2. (A) (B) (C) (D)

II Conversations

You will hear some conversations between two people. Listen to the conversations and answer the questions below.

Questions 3-4

3. What is the problem?
   (A) A customer made a complaint.
   (B) The phone isn't working.
   (C) A client hasn't paid his bill.
   (D) The notice didn't arrive.

4. What does the man suggest?
   (A) Calling the customer.
   (B) Notifying the police.
   (C) Sending a notice.
   (D) Paying the bill.

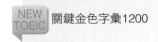

Questions 5-6

5. Which statement is true?

    (A) They made fewer long-distance phone calls this month.

    (B) Their phone bill is less expensive than last month's.

    (C) The company informed them in advance.

    (D) They recently found a new provider.

6. What does the woman suggest?

    (A) Informing the bank.

    (B) Complaining about the fees.

    (C) Making fewer phone calls.

    (D) Changing to a different company.

III Short Talks (41)

You will hear a short talk given by a single speaker. Listen to the short talk and answer the questions below.

Questions 7-8

7. What is the purpose of this meeting?

    (A) To discuss last year's financial statement.

    (B) To talk about the economic crisis.

    (C) To collect suggestions for cutting expenses.

    (D) To propose ideas for a new product.

8. What does the financial statement show?

    (A) The accounting department did a good job.

    (B) The company is in a state of emergency.

    (C) The economy is finally picking up again.

    (D) The company's revenue has gone down.

IV Incomplete Sentences

A word or phrase is missing in each of the sentences below. Four answer choices are given below each sentence. Select the best answer to complete the sentence.

9. I'm very _____ about my job interview tomorrow.
   (A) excite   (B) excited   (C) exciting   (D) excitement

10. The manager's office is _____ on the second floor.
   (A) locate   (B) located   (C) locating   (D) location

11. I will collect all the suggestions _____ in today's meeting.
   (A) make   (B) made   (C) were made   (D) making

12. The _____ team will receive $1000 in cash.
   (A) win   (B) won   (C) winning   (D) winner

13. To get to the marketing department, go _____ those stairs and turn right.
   (A) along   (B) down   (C) over   (D) through

14. She left school and started working _____ the age of sixteen.
   (A) at   (B) when   (C) on   (D) in

15. Emily is the girl standing _____ the man in the blue suit.
   (A) at   (B) around   (C) besides   (D) next to

16. I'll grab some lunch _____ two meetings.
   (A) in between   (B) out of   (C) during   (D) over

Review
4

測
驗
練
習

223

V Reading Comprehension

In this part you will read a selection of texts. Each text is followed by several questions. Select the best answer for each question and mark the letter (A), (B), (C), or (D).

Questions 17-19 refer to the following notice.

Wiring money overseas is not a difficult thing. In fact, it can be quite easy if we have the correct information. First, we will need the bank's name, branch, address, telephone number, and bank code. We also need the recipient's account name and number. And finally, we will need your signature on the wire registration form. After all of this has been completed, you will be able to request a wire transfer of funds via our 24-hour customer service line.

17. What is being discussed?
    (A) Opening a bank account.
    (B) Applying for a credit card.
    (C) Sending money.
    (D) Finding a good bank.

18. What is needed for this process?
    (A) A deposit.
    (B) A check.
    (C) A signature.
    (D) An email address.

19. What is an advantage of this process?
    (A) You can do it by phone.
    (B) You can get a gift.
    (C) You can travel overseas.
    (D) You don't have to sign anything.

Questions 20-21 refer to the following letter.

June 4, 2010

Ms. Isabel Tan

3419 Green Street

Singapore

Dear Ms. Tan,

Our accounting department has noted a serious error in the billing of your recent order for carpeting. In computing the total amount, Sales Representative Alan Lim failed to include the estimates given to you for two of the bedrooms. The true cost of the carpeting is in fact SGD 3,605, not SGD 2,495. A new invoice is attached.

We sincerely regret any inconvenience our error has caused you.

We appreciate your down payment of SGD 1,500 and request that the new balance due of SGD 2,105 be paid within thirty days. Again, we apologize for the confusion and appreciate your business.

Sincerely,

Mark Chua

Owner

Carpets Plus

20. What did the Carpets Plus sales representative do wrong?

(A) He undercharged a customer.

(B) He told the customer that the carpet would cost SGD 2,105.

(C) He did not apologize for raising the price of the carpet.

(D) He forgot to send the bill.

21. How much does Ms. Tan still owe?

(A) SGD 1,500.

(B) SGD 2,105.

(C) SGD 2,495.

(D) SGD 3,605.

Ⅵ Text Completion

Read the text that follows. A word or phrase is missing in some of the sentences. For each blank, four answer choices are given below. Select the best answer to complete the text.

Dear New Subscriber,

We thank you for your (22)_____ order for Sport Times Magazine – the best, most exciting magazine in sports. We would like to (23)_____ you that your subscription (24)_____ is overdue. If you would like to continue (25)_____ issues, please send in your payment no later than January 10.

If you have already (26)_____ your payment, kindly disregard this letter and we thank you in (27)_____. If you have any questions or comments, please call our tollfree (28)_____ service center at 1-800-788-4637.

Thank you very much.
ALF Distribution Services

22. (A) payment   (B) questionnaire (C) invoice   (D) subscription
23. (A) maintain   (B) remind   (C) appreciate   (D) ship
24. (A) purchase   (B) payment   (C) survey   (D) package
25. (A) receive   (B) received   (C) receiving   (D) will receive
26. (A) make   (B) made   (C) have made   (D) had made
27. (A) exchange   (B) purchase   (C) refund   (D) advance
28. (A) employee   (B) consumer   (C) customer   (D) staff

Chapter 9
Production 生產

Production refers to the process of making goods in large numbers in a factory or on a farm.

1 Equipment 設備 (25)

先進的，進
階的

1038 **advanced** [əd`vænst] *adj.*

☐☐ 例 Our company has an **advanced** assembly line to reduce the number of defects in our products.

本公司有 advanced 生產線可減少產品的不良數。

器具，器械

1039 **appliance** [ə`plaɪəns] *n.*

☐☐ 例 The **appliances** made at our factory are energy efficient.

本工廠所製造的 appliances 都是節能的。

自動的

1040 **automatic** [ˌɔtə`mætɪk] *adj.*

☐☐ 例 Jim created an **automatic** machine that replaces the need for employees to seal packages manually.

吉姆製造出一台 automatic 機器，可取代以人工封袋的人員需求。

停電

1041 **blackout** [`blæk͵aʊt] *n.*

☐☐ 例 The factory is equipped with emergency lights in case of a **blackout**.

工廠裝置了緊急照明燈，以防萬一發生 blackout。

攪拌，混合

1042 **blend** [blɛnd] *v.*

☐☐ 例 It is important to **blend** the mixture thoroughly before putting it in the machine.

把混合物投入機器前，徹底 blend 是至關重要的。

1043 bulb [bʌlb] *n.* 　　　　　　電燈泡

☐ 例 The headlights in the new car model have faulty
☐ **bulbs**.

新車款的前大燈 bulbs 有瑕疵。

1044 chip [tʃɪp] *v.* 　　　　　　碰出缺口

☐ 例 We can't sell any merchandise that has been
☐ **chipped**.

我們不能將已經 chipped 的商品賣出去。

1045 device [dɪˋvaɪs] *n.* 　　　　　　裝置

☐ 例 The company is designing a new **device** that
☐ will decrease the number of people needed on
the assembly line.

公司正在研發一款新 device，能減少生產線上所
需的人力。

1046 electric [ɪˋlɛktrɪk] *adj.* 　　　　　　電動的，電
的

☐ 例 Due to the poor economy, production of the
☐ newest model of **electric** cars has slowed down.

由於經濟不景氣，最新款 electric 車的生產已趨
減緩。

1047 factory [ˋfæktərɪ] *n.* 　　　　　　工廠

☐ 例 Production was delayed because of a fire at the
☐ **factory**.

因 factory 發生火災造成生產的延誤。

Chapter 9
生產

1048 fridge [frɪdʒ] *n.* 　　　　　　電冰箱

☐ 例 If you are looking for a new **fridge**, be sure to
☐ purchase one that is energy efficient.

假如我們要買新的 fridge，一定要買節能的。

運轉，作用 | 1049 **function** [ˈfʌŋkʃən] v.

☐ 例 The machine isn't **functioning** properly today.

☐ 今天機器有些 functioning 不良。

齒輪組 | 1050 **gear** [gɪr] n.

☐ 例 The **gears** in the machine are jammed.

☐ 機器的 gears 卡住了。

失準，錯誤 | 1051 **inaccuracy** [ɪnˈækjərəsɪ] n.

☐ 例 The **inaccuracy** of the new machine has created many production errors.

☐ 新機器的 inaccuracy 造成諸多生產錯誤。

結合，合併 | 1052 **incorporation** [ɪnˌkɔrpəˈreʃən] n.

☐ 例 The **incorporation** of this new technology will help us work faster.

☐ 這項新科技的 incorporation 將有助我們加速作業。

器具，儀器 | 1053 **instrument** [ˈɪnstrəmənt] n.

☐ 例 All **instruments** used in the manufacturing process need to be inspected on a daily basis.

☐ 製造過程中所使用的一切 instrument，每天都要檢測。

介紹 | 1054 **introduce** [ˌɪntrəˈdjus] v.

☐ 例 The new equipment will be **introduced** to the staff at the next meeting.

☐ 下次會議將會把新設備 introduce 給員工。

1055 **laboratory** [ˈlæbrəˌtɔrɪ] *n.* 　　　　　實驗室

　　例 The chemists are testing the quality of the new product in the **laboratory**.

　　化學家正在 laboratory 裡測試新產品的品質。

1056 **machine** [məˈʃin] *n.* 　　　　　機器，機械

　　例 The **machines** in the factory often break down.

　　工廠裡的 machines 時常故障。

1057 **machinery** [məˈʃinərɪ] *n.* 　　　　　（總稱）機器，機械

　　例 Jacob's company is purchasing new **machinery** for the factory.

　　雅各的公司將買進新 machinery。

1058 **maintenance** [ˈmentənəns] *n.* 　　　　　保養，維修

　　例 It is important that regular **maintenance** is performed on the assembly line equipment.

　　生產設備的定期 maintenance 是很重要的。

1059 **malfunction** [mælˈfʌŋkʃən] *v.* 　　　　　故障，失靈

　　例 When the equipment **malfunctions**, production (of the product) slows down.

　　當設備 malfunctions 時，產品製造的速度就會減慢。

1060 **mechanic** [məˈkænɪk] *n.* 　　　　　機械工，修理工

　　例 The **mechanic** said he wouldn't be able to fix the machine until tomorrow afternoon.

　　Mechanic 說他沒辦法在明天下午前修好這台機器。

★ 機械的 | 1061 **mechanical** [mə`kænɪkl̩] *adj.*

☐
☐ 例 There is no one on staff that knows how to fix the **mechanical** issues with the photocopier.

員工裡無人知曉如何修理影印機 mechanical 方面的問題。

操作 | 1062 **operate** [`ɑpə‚ret] *v.*

☐
☐ 例 Frank is training new employees on how to **operate** the machinery.

法蘭克正訓練新員工如何 operate 機器。

操作人員 | 1063 **operator** [`ɑpə‚retɚ] *n.*

☐
☐ 例 The **operator** reported a problem with the old equipment in the factory.

Operator 報告工廠的老舊設備所衍生出的問題。

復原，恢復 | 1064 **recovery** [rɪ`kʌvərɪ] *n.*

☐
☐ 例 The computer has gone into **recovery** mode because it was not shut down properly.

由於未正常關機， 電腦進入了 recovery 模式。

★ 調整，校準 | 1065 **regulate** [`rɛgjə‚let] *v.*

☐
☐ 例 Michael **regulated** the machinery so it would work properly again.

麥可 regulated 機器，以便能再度正常運轉。

★ 調整，校準 | 1066 **regulation** [‚rɛgjə`leʃən] *n.*

☐
☐ 例 It is important to ensure machine **regulation** at all times.

隨時確保機器 regulation 是很重要的。

1067 repair [rɪˋpɛr] *v.*　　　　　　　　修理，修補

例 If we aren't able to **repair** the equipment by this afternoon, we won't be able to meet our daily quota.

如果我們在今天下午前沒辦法 repair 設備，我們將無法達到每日分配額。

1068 revolution [ˌrɛvəˋluʃən] *n.*　　　變革，革命

例 This equipment is the latest **revolution** in the manufacturing industry.

這個設備可說是製造業最新的 revolution。

1069 software [ˋsɔftˌwɛr] *n.*　　　　　　軟體

例 Could you help me install this **software** on my computer?

能麻煩您幫我把這 software 安裝到我的電腦嗎？

1070 standard [ˋstændəd] *n.*　　　　　　標準

例 The equipment in the factory does not meet industry **standards**.

工廠設備無法達到產業 standards。

1071 steel [stil] *n.*　　　　　　　　　　鋼鐵

例 The support beams in the warehouse are **steel**.

倉庫裡的支撐梁是 steel 做的。

Chapter 9
生產

1072 tool [tul] *n.*　　　　　　　　　　　工具

例 This software program is an excellent **tool** for employees.

這套軟體程式對員工來說是很棒的 tool。

關閉

1073 **turn off** [ˈtɜ˞n ˈɔf] *v. phr.*

☐
☐ 例 Employees are asked to **turn off** all equipment before leaving the office.

員工要在離開辦公室時 turn off 所有的設備。

開啟

1074 **turn on** [ˈtɜ˞n ˈɑn] *v. phr.*

☐
☐ 例 The machine must be **turned on** at least one hour before production begins.

至少在開始製造前一小時先 turn on 機器。

升級

1075 **upgrade** [ˈʌpˈgred] *v.*

☐
☐ 例 The boss is paying for all the computers in the office to be **upgraded**.

我們老闆付錢讓公司裡所有的電腦都能 upgraded。

保固

1076 **warranty** [ˈwɔrəntɪ] *n.*

☐
☐ 例 The photocopier came with a five year **warranty**.

影印機有五年的 warranty。

線路

1077 **wire** [waɪr] *n.*

☐
☐ 例 If the **wires** are not connected properly, the machine won't work.

如果 wire 沒有接對，機器就無法運轉。

standred.

2 Production 生產 (26)

1078 amazing [ə`mezɪŋ] *adj.*　　　　　　令人驚訝的

例 Jane has an **amazing** idea to reduce production costs.

珍有個降低生產成本的 amazing 構想。

1079 analyze [`ænḷ͵aɪz] *v.*　　　　　　分析

例 The accountants **analyzed** the sales data from last year to estimate this year's production costs.

會計師 analyzed 去年的銷貨數據來預估今年的生產成本。

1080 approach [ə`protʃ] *n.*　　　　　　方法，方式

例 We need to take a creative **approach** in promoting our new software.

我們需採取創意的 approach 來推廣新軟體。

1081 artificial [͵ɑrtə`fɪʃəl] *adj.*　　　　　　人工的

例 None of the products made in our factory contain **artificial** ingredients.

本工廠生產製造的產品都不含 artificial 成分。

1082 assemble [ə`sɛmbḷ] *v.*　　　　　　裝配，組裝

例 All of our office furniture comes with instructions on how to **assemble** the pieces.

本公司所有的辦公家具皆附上如何 assemble 的說明書。

生產線　1083 **assembly line** [əˈsɛmblɪ,laɪn] *n. phr.*

☐ 例 It is important that employees working on the **assembly line** wear a hair net.

☐ Assembly line 上的作業員戴髮網這件事很重要。

滲開，散開　1084 **bleed** [blid] *v.*

☐ 例 The dye used on this garment **bleeds** when wet.

☐ 染在這衣服上的顏色一碰到水就 bleeds 了。

品種　1085 **breed** [brid] *n.*

☐ 例 In our body lotions we use extracts from rare plant **breeds** found only in the Amazon.

☐ 我們在身體乳液產品中所使用的濃縮精華，來自亞馬遜河地區才有的稀有植物 breeds。

分門別類　1086 **categorize** [ˈkætəgə,raɪz] *v.*

☐ 例 They should **categorize** the products by weight, not size.

☐ 他們應以產品的重量，而非大小來 categorize。

化學物質　1087 **chemical** [ˈkɛmɪkl̩] *n.*

☐ 例 All factory employees must wear protective goggles when handling **chemicals**.

☐ 工廠所有的員工在處理 chemicals 時，皆需戴上護目鏡。

化學家；藥劑師　1088 **chemist** [ˈkɛmɪst] *n.*

☐ 例 The **chemist** will be sharing the results from the product trials at the meeting this morning.

☐ Chemist 將在今早的會議上告訴大家產品測試的結果。

1089 **chemistry** [ˈkɛmɪstrɪ] n.

化學

☐
☐

例 We will need to hire someone with qualifications in **chemistry** for the design of the new dish washing liquid.

我們需要聘雇具 chemistry 專長的人研發新洗碗精。

1090 **competitive** [kəmˈpɛtətɪv] adj.

有競爭力的

☐
☐

例 Even though our sales are up, we have to remain **competitive** by trying to speed up production.

儘管我們的銷售量成長，仍須設法加速生產以維持 competitive。

1091 **consist** [kənˈsɪst] v.

組成，構成

☐
☐

例 Our factory staff **consists** of twenty full-time and ten part-time workers.

本工廠的員工是由二十名全職與十名兼職員工所 consists。

1092 **convenient** [kənˈvinjənt] adj.

便利，方便

☐
☐

例 It would be more **convenient** if the warehouse was closer to the factory.

如果倉庫能更靠近工廠，那就會更加 convenient。

1093 **discover** [dɪˈskʌvɚ] v.

發現

☐
☐

例 It is important for us to **discover** a better way to package our product to ensure it is not damaged.

對我們來說，discover 更有效率的方式包裝商品，確保商品完好無缺是至關重要的。

Chapter
9

生產

劑量

1094 **dose** [dos] *n.*

例 The instructions included on the back of the vitamin bottle indicate the recommended **dose** for adults.

維他命瓶身上的使用說明指示了成人建議攝取的 dose。

電氣技師，
電氣工

1095 **electrician** [ɪˌlɛkˈtrɪʃən] *n.*

例 We have to wait until the **electrician** inspects the building before we can continue working safely.

我們得等到 electrician 檢驗過大樓後才能繼續安全地施工。

發現，調查
結果

1096 **finding** [ˈfaɪndɪŋ] *n.*

例 The research conducted by the production team made some very important **findings**.

生產團隊所進行的研究有非常重要的 findings。

指導原則，
準則

1097 **guideline** [ˈgaɪdˌlaɪn] *n.*

例 There are many safety **guidelines** to follow when working in a factory.

在工廠工作有許多安全 guidelines 需要遵循。

產業

1098 **industry** [ˈɪndəstrɪ] *n.*

例 The automotive **industry** is on a decline.

汽車 industry 在衰退中。

產業的；工
業的

1099 **industrial** [ɪnˈdʌstrɪəl] *adj.*

例 Our office is located in an **industrial** area of the city.

我們公司位於本市的 industrial 區。

1100 **invention** [ɪnˈvɛnʃən] *n.* 發明

例 One of our employees came up with an **invention** to save time and money on the production of our best selling product.

有個職員提出一項 invention，能讓公司的暢銷產品製程省時又省錢。

1101 **journal** [ˈdʒɝ-n̩l] *n.* 日誌

例 Employees are asked to keep a **journal** of the number of product defects found each day.

員工必需寫 journal 以記錄每日發現的產品瑕疵數量。

1102 **manufacture** [ˌmænjəˈfæktʃɚ] *v.* 生產，製造

例 The factory **manufactures** affordable vehicles.

這家工廠 manufactures 價格實惠的車輛。

1103 **measure** [ˈmɛʒɚ] *v.* 估量，斟酌

例 To avoid problems it is important to carefully **measure** the amount of material put into the machine.

為避免任何問題發生，精細 measure 放進機器裡的原料量是很重要的。

1104 **organic** [ɔrˈgænɪk] *adj.* 有機的

例 Mary's company only uses **organic** ingredients in their food products.

瑪莉的公司的食品只使用 organic 食材。

Chapter 9 生產

組織；規劃 | 1105 **organize** [ˈɔrgənˌaɪz] *v.*

☐ 例 This software program allows managers to easily
☐ **organize** deadlines and delivery dates.

軟體程式可讓經理人員輕而易舉 organize 完工日
與出貨日。

產量；輸出 | 1106 **output** [ˈaʊtˌpʊt] *n.*

☐ 例 If we don't increase the amount of product
☐ **output**, we will not be able to keep up with
demand.

假如我們不增加產品的 output，將無法趕上需求。

全面的，全 | 1107 **overall** [ˈovɚˌɔl] *adj.*
體的
☐ 例 Our newest mini-van has the best **overall** rating
☐ in the industry.

在業界，我們最新款迷你廂型車的 overall 評比都
是最佳的。

（製造）工 | 1108 **plant** [plænt] *n.*
廠
☐ 例 The **plant** was closed for two weeks after the
☐ explosion.

Plant 在爆炸事件後二個星期關廠。

移動式的 | 1109 **portable** [ˈpɔrtəbl] *adj.*

☐ 例 Staff members had to use **portable** toilets while
☐ the bathrooms were undergoing maintenance.

工作人員在洗手間進行維修期間必須使用 portable
廁所。

1110 power failure [ˈpaʊɚ ˌfeljɚ] *n. phr.*

例 Production stopped for two days when the city experienced a **power failure** last year.

去年該市歷經 power failure，工廠還因此停工了二天。

1111 power plant [ˈpaʊɚ ˌplænt] *n. phr.*

例 Many people protested against the construction of a **power plant** so close to a residential neighborhood.

許多人示威抗議緊鄰住宅區旁興建 power plant。

1112 practical [ˈpræktɪkl̩] *adj.*

例 At present, hybrid electric vehicles seem to be a more **practical** solution to the problem of greenhouse gas emissions.

目前油電混合車似乎是減少溫室氣體排放問題較 practical 解決辦法。

1113 prevent [prɪˈvɛnt] *v.*

例 To **prevent** injury, please tie long hair back when using machinery.

為了 prevent 受傷，操作器械時長髮請束起。

1114 prevention [prɪˈvɛnʃən] *n.*

例 Employees wear goggles while operating the equipment as an injury **prevention** measure.

工作人員在操作設備時戴護目鏡是為了避免受傷而採取的 prevention。

繼續進行	1115 **proceed** [prə`sid] *v.*

例 The workers were told to **proceed** with production of the new product.

告知工人 proceed 生產新產品。

程序，步驟	1116 **procedure** [prə`sidʒɚ] *n.*

例 Please follow the **procedure** accurately.

請精確無誤地遵守 procedure。

過程，程序	1117 **process** [`prɑsɛs] *n.*

例 This **process** is very similar to the one at my previous company.

這 process 與我先前待過的公司很類似。

生產，製造	1118 **produce** [prə`djus] *v.*

例 Our company has been **producing** high quality products for the past thirty years.

本公司三十年來都 producing 高品質的產品。

有生產力的	1119 **productive** [prə`dʌktɪv] *adj.*

例 The manager said that the assembly line workers were not **productive** enough.

經理說生產線上的工人不夠 productive。

職業的	1120 **professional** [prə`fɛʃən!] *adj.*

例 Employees have to dress appropriately in a **professional** environment.

員工在 professional 的場所必須穿戴合宜。

1121 prohibit [proˋhɪbɪt] *v.*　　禁止

　例 Jewelry is **prohibited** in the factory.

　　在廠內 prohibit 戴珠寶飾物。

1122 proof [pruf] *n.*　　證明，證據

　例 Our research demonstrates **proof** of the quality
　　of the product.

　　我們的研究結果提供了本產品品質的 proof。

1123 quality control [ˋkwɑlətɪ ͵kəntrol] *n. phr.*　　品管

　例 The company has an excellent reputation for
　　quality control.

　　該公司享有優良 quality control 的聲譽。

1124 quantity [ˋkwɑntətɪ] *n.*　　數量

　例 Employees in the packaging department are
　　asked to indicate the **quantity** of products in
　　each box.

　　要求包裝部門的員工標示出每箱產品的 quantity。

1125 quota [ˋkwotə] *n.*　　配額

　例 It is only Thursday and we have already met our
　　weekly **quota**.

　　今天才星期四，我們就已經達到每週的 quota。

1126 rapidly [ˋræpɪdlɪ] *adv.*　　迅速地，很
　　　　　　　　　　　　　　　　　快地

　例 If we cannot manufacture the product **rapidly**,
　　our boss will be disappointed.

　　如果我們無法 rapidly 生產，我們老闆將會失望。

改良，改革

1127 **reform** [rɪˋfɔrm] v.

☐
☐ 例 We need to **reform** the manufacturing process to improve the quality of the product.

為改善產品的品質，我們需要 reform 製程。

補救（辦法）

1128 **remedy** [ˋrɛmədɪ] n.

☐
☐ 例 Trina found a **remedy** for the issue with the computer system.

崔娜找到電腦系統問題的 remedy。

更新

1129 **renewal** [rɪˋnjuəl] n.

☐
☐ 例 The clients asked for a **renewal** of the contract.

客戶要求合約的 renewal。

整頓，重組

1130 **reorganization** [ˌriɔrgənaɪˋzeʃən] n.

☐
☐ 例 The entire company is undergoing **reorganization** under new management.

整個公司在新管理團隊下接受 reorganization。

重複，一成不變

1131 **repetition** [ˌrɛpɪˋtɪʃən] n.

☐
☐ 例 Assembly line workers must get used to the **repetition** involved in their position.

生產線上的員工必須習慣工作上的 repetition。

要求

1132 **request** [rɪˋkwɛst] v.

☐
☐ 例 The clients **requested** that one of their staff members be at the factory during production.

客戶 requested 讓他們的一名員工在產品生產時留在工廠。

1133 research [rɪˈsɝtʃ] *n.*　　　研究

☐ 例 A lot of **research** went into the development of
☐ the product.

許多 research 進入了產品的研發。

1134 researcher [rɪˈsɝtʃɚ] *n.*　　　研究員

☐ 例 We need to hire a team of **researchers** to
☐ investigate the problem.

我們需聘雇一團隊的 researchers 來調查問題。

1135 resolution [ˌrɛzəˈluʃən] *n.*　　　解決，解答

☐ 例 The production team is meeting to find a
☐ **resolution** to the problems in the factory.

為了找出問題的 resolution，廠方的工作人員正在
開會。

1136 routine [ruˈtin] *adj.*　　　常規的，例
　　　　　　　　　　　　　　　　　　　行公事的

☐ 例 Daily inspection of the machinery is a **routine**
☐ procedure.

每日檢驗機器是 routine 程序。

1137 safety [ˈseftɪ] *n.*　　　安全

☐ 例 **Safety** in the factory is a very important issue.
☐ 工廠裡 safety 是非常重要的議題。

1138 scheme [skim] *n.*　　　計畫，方案

☐ 例 Our manager is working on a new **scheme** for
☐ the maintenance of machinery.

本公司經理正在研究有關機器維修的新 scheme。

科學家　　1139 **scientist** [ˈsaɪəntɪst] *n.*

囗 **例** Our research team consists of five **scientists**.

囗 　 本公司的研究團隊是由五名 scientist 組成的。

篩選　　　1140 **screening** [ˈskrinɪŋ] *n.*

囗 **例** All products made in the factory go through
囗 　 careful **screening** before being sent to clients.

　　　工廠生產的所有產品在送到客戶手上前，都會經
　　　過仔細的 screening。

簡化　　　1141 **simplify** [ˈsɪmpləˌfaɪ] *v.*

囗 **例** The assembly process must be **simplified** to save
囗 　 time.

　　　裝配程序必須 simplified，以節省時間。

步驟　　　1142 **step** [stɛp] *n.*

囗 **例** Please follow all the **steps** carefully.

囗 　 請小心遵循所有的 step。

監督，管理　1143 **supervise** [ˈsupɚˌvaɪz] *v.*

囗 **例** There must be someone in the factory at all times
囗 　 to **supervise** production.

　　　工廠裡必定有人隨時 supervise 產品的生產。

有系統的，　1144 **systematic** [ˌsɪstəˈmætɪk] *adj.*
有條理的
囗 **例** Manufacturing follows a very **systematic**
囗 　 process.

　　　生產製造依循非常 systematic 流程。

1145 **target** [ˈtɑrgɪt] *v.*

例 The computer technician **targeted** the problem.

電腦維修技術員 targeted 問題。

挑出

1146 **technical** [ˈtɛknɪkl] *adj.*

例 We are experiencing **technical** difficulties with our equipment.

我們的設備現正遭遇 technical 的困難。

技術上的

1147 **technician** [tɛkˈnɪʃən] *n.*

例 The **technician** isn't able to repair the machine.

Technician 無法維修這台機器。

技師，技術員

Exercises

請從選項中，選出最適當的答案完成句子。

1. The cell phone is an ingenious _____ that has made a great difference in our everyday life.

   (A) trap   (B) deceit   (C) device   (D) gadget

2. It is _____ to keep my hair short; I don't have a lot of time taking care of it.

   (A) amazing   (B) convenient   (C) satisfying   (D) exciting

3. All sports are _____; runners, for example, try to improve their skill by tenths of a second.

   (A) competitive   (B) reluctant   (C) memorable   (D) indecisive

4. The guitar and the harp are both string _____.

   (A) movements   (B) actions   (C) instruments   (D) organs

5. Students need to learn how to _____ their thoughts.

   (A) organize   (B) dispute   (C) rationalize   (D) realize

6. As an old saying goes, _____ is better than cure.

   (A) intervention   (B) industrialization   (C) automation   (D) prevention

7. The author made a detailed _____ regarding the cause and effect of the event.

   (A) conviction   (B) persuasion   (C) analysis   (D) narration

8. Although I am independent now, my parents' views still _____ mine.

   (A) contain   (B) contact   (C) affect   (D) infect

9. The bicycle can easily be _____ if you follow the instructions.

   (A) assembled   (B) organized   (C) departed   (D) assured

10. Automatic cars are the _____, but I prefer a manual.

    (A) trend   (B) fashion   (C) tendency   (D) indication

11. A _____ once widely used to kill insects, DDT is now banned in many countries.

(A) chemical (B) chemistry (C) drug chemist (D) medicine

12. Car owners today enjoy a five year _____ over the life of the car engine.

(A) promise (B) warranty (C) authority (D) security

13. The student's presentation was _____; he had everything well organized.

(A) realistic (B) strategic (C) systematic (D) automatic

14. Recent _____ show that there is an increase in the number of cars sold.

(A) statistics (B) tactics (C) techniques (D) strategies

15. Your theory is too complicated. Can you _____ it?

(A) signify (B) indentify (C) simplify (D) intensify

16. The invention of the computer was a _____ in many ways, especially in creating documents.

(A) rotation (B) revelation (C) evolution (D) revolution

17. As Christmas approaches, many people begin to make their New Year _____.

(A) isolations (B) resolutions (C) solutions (D) pollutions

18. The popularity of laptop computers is increasing _____; more and more people are carrying them wherever they go.

(A) hardly (B) rapidly (C) sensibly (D) agreeably

19. The _____ of the suspect has begun; he has been identified by security cameras as a tall man wearing dark glasses.

(A) pursuit (B) invitation (C) investment (D) transaction

20. _____, that is, saying the same thing over and over again, is necessary in language learning.

(A) Association (B) Repetition (C) Assertion (D) Competition

Legal Affairs & Tax 法務與稅務

When business partners decide to cooperate for mutual benefit, they sign a contract listing the terms and conditions of the cooperation.

1 Contract 合約 (27)

| 協議 | 1148 **agreement** [əˈgrimənt] *n.* |

☐ 例 The two clients reached an **agreement**.

☐ 這兩家公司達成了 agreement。

| 條款；條件 | 1149 **condition** [kənˈdɪʃən] *n.* |

☐ 例 Please read the **conditions** in the contract
carefully.

請仔細閱讀合約裡的 conditions。

| 內容 | 1150 **content** [ˈkɑntɛnt] *n.* |

☐ 例 My client did not agree with the **content** of the
agreement.

我的客戶不同意協議書裡的 content。

| 合約 | 1151 **contract** [ˈkɑntrækt] *n.* |

☐ 例 We need to meet the lawyers at 4 pm to sign the
contract.

我們下午四點要跟律師碰面簽 contract。

| 配合，合作 | 1152 **cooperate** [koˈɑpəˌret] *v.* |

☐ 例 If we don't **cooperate** according to the agreement,
they could take us to court.

如果我們不 cooperate 協議，他們可能會訴諸法
庭。

1153 **copy** [ˈkɑpɪ] *n.*　　副本，影本

例 Make sure you keep a **copy** of all your important documents.

要確定你所有的重要文件都保留 copy。

1154 **correction** [kəˈrɛkʃən] *n.*　　修正

例 There are several **corrections** that need to be made to the agreement.

協議書中有幾個地方需要做些 corrections。

1155 **counselor** [ˈkaʊnslɚ] *n.*　　律師；法律顧問

例 As a **counselor**, he is able to practice law in this state.

身為 counselor，他可以在本州執業。

1156 **counterpart** [ˈkaʊntɚˌpɑrt] *n.*　　對等者，雙方

例 Both business **counterparts** need to sign the contract.

交易 counterparts 皆需在合約上簽名。

1157 **countersignature** [ˌkaʊntɚˈsɪɡnətʃɚ] *n.*　　會簽

例 The document requires a **countersignature**.

文件需經 countersignature。

1158 **date** [det] *v.*　　註明日期

例 Don't forget to **date** the contract.

別忘了在合約上 date。

Chapter 10 法務與稅務

細節　　　　1159 **detail** [dɪˋtel] *n.*

☐ 例 Please meet me at my office so we can discuss
☐ 　　the **details** of the contract.
　　請到我辦公室來，我們好討論合約的 details。

文件　　　　1160 **document** [ˋdɑkjəmənt] *n.*

☐ 例 Don't forget to bring enough copies of the
☐ 　　**document** with you to the meeting.
　　開會時別忘了帶足夠的 document 副本。

草案；草稿　1161 **draft** [dræft] *n.*

☐ 例 This is only the first **draft** contract.
☐ 　　這是第一份合約 draft。

缺點　　　　1162 **drawback** [ˋdrɔ,bæk] *n.*

☐ 例 There are many **drawbacks** when proceeding
☐ 　　with a business deal without a contract.
　　進行一場沒有合約的商業交易是有許多的
　　drawback。

副本　　　　1163 **duplicate** [ˋdjupləkɪt] *n.*

☐ 例 Please make a **duplicate** of the contract for my
☐ 　　client.
　　請給我的客戶一份合約 duplicate。

持續期間　　1164 **duration** [djʊˋreʃən] *n.*

☐ 例 The **duration** of the contract is three months.
☐ 　　合約的 duration 是三個月。

1165 **expire** [ɪkˋspaɪr] *v.*

☐
☐ 例 The contract will **expire** before the work has been completed.

合約在工作結束前就會 expire。

屆期，滿期

1166 **negotiate** [nɪˋgoʃɪˏet] *v.*

☐
☐ 例 We should **negotiate** the terms of the contractual before we sign.

在簽約前，我們應該 negotiate 合約的條款。

談判，協商

1167 **obligation** [ˏɑbləˋgeʃən] *n.*

☐
☐ 例 You are under **obligation** of the contract to work for two more months.

合約顯示你有 obligation 多工作兩個月。

義務

1168 **offer** [ˋɔfɚ] *n.*

☐
☐ 例 She was disappointed with the **offer**.

她對這 offer 感到失望。

報價；提議

1169 **on behalf of** [an bɪˋhæf əv] *phr.*

☐
☐ 例 I gave my lawyer the authority to sign **on** my **behalf**.

我授權給我的律師 on behalf of 我簽名。

代表

1170 **partner** [ˋpɑrtnɚ] *n.*

☐
☐ 例 My business **partner** is not able to sign contracts without my approval.

我的 partner 沒有我的同意不能簽任何合約。

合夥人

合夥關係 1171 **partnership** [ˈpɑrtnəˌʃɪp] *n.*

例 They have had a business **partnership** for years.
他們曾經在生意上有多年的 partnership。

延續 1172 **renew** [rɪˈnju] *v.*

例 My boss offered to **renew** my contract.
我老闆表示願意 renew 我的合約。

修正 1173 **revise** [rɪˈvaɪz] *v.*

例 Please **revise** the contract.
請 revise 合約。

簽名 1174 **sign** [saɪn] *v.*

例 Please **sign** your name on the line.
請在線上 sign 您的大名。

簽名 1175 **signature** [ˈsɪgnətʃə] *n.*

例 The contract requires your **signature**.
這合約需要你的 signature。

條款 1176 **term** [tɝm] *n.*

例 If you signed the contract, you are obligated to fulfill the **terms**.
如果你簽下合約，你就有義務履行 terms。

1177 **accumulate** [əˋkjumjəˏlet] v.　　累積，積聚

□□ 例 The law firm has **accumulated** a fortune from winning so many court cases.

這間律師事務所因打贏不少官司而 accumulated 很多錢。

1178 **attorney** [əˋtɝnɪ] n.　　律師

□□ 例 My **attorney** said he would contact me with the court date.

我的 attorney 說他會聯絡我開庭的日期。

1179 **commitment** [kəˋmɪtmənt] n.　　承諾，保證

□□ 例 The company is being sued because they backed out of a **commitment**.

該公司因沒有履行 commitment 而被告。

1180 **case** [kes] n.　　案例，事例

□□ 例 In this **case**, I think you might be right.

我想你在這 case 上也許是對的。

1181 **confidential** [ˏkɑnfəˋdɛnʃəl] adj.　　機密的

□□ 例 The company lawyer keeps all information **confidential**.

公司的法務專員對所有資訊都保持 confidential。

1182 **consent** [kənˋsɛnt] n.　　同意，贊成

□□ 例 We need your **consent** before we proceed.

在著手進行前，我們需要你的 consent。

Chapter 10
法務與稅務

257

削減，減少

☆

1183 **curtail** [kɜˈtel] v.

例 The lawyer told his client to **curtail** his public appearances during the trial.

律師告訴他的客戶在審理期間 curtail 公開露面。

協議

1184 **deal** [dil] n.

例 Let's try to make a **deal** without getting lawyers involved.

我們試看看在沒有律師涉入的情況下進行 deal。

決定

1185 **decide** [dɪˈsaɪd] v.

例 If you **decide** to plead not guilty, you'd better be prepared for a long trial.

如果你們 decide 不承認有罪，最好要有心理準備接下來的長期審理。

宣告

1186 **declare** [dɪˈklɛr] v.

例 After James was **declared** innocent, he took a long vacation.

在詹姆士被 declared 無罪後，他放了個長假。

討論

1187 **discussion** [dɪˈskʌʃən] n.

例 The attorneys are having a serious **discussion** in the office.

律師們正在辦公室裡嚴肅地進行 discussion。

額外的

1188 **extra** [ˈɛkstrə] adj.

例 We may need some **extra** time to prepare for your court appearance.

我們需要 extra 時間準備你的出庭。

1189 **lawyer** [ˈlɔjɚ] *n.*　　　　　　　　　　　律師

例 If you are looking for an attorney, I can give you my **lawyer**'s contact information.

如果你要找律師，我可以給你我 lawyer's 連絡方式。

1190 **legal** [ˈligl] *adj.*　　　　　　　　　　法律上的

例 I need to talk to my lawyer to get some **legal** advice.

我需要跟我的律師談談，尋求他的 legal 建議。

1191 **pirate** [ˈpaɪrət] *v.*　　　　　　　　　非法複製

例 You can be put in jail for **pirating** CDs.

你要是 pirating 音樂光碟是會坐牢的。

1192 **priority** [praɪˈɔrətɪ] *n.*　　　　　　　優先（權）

例 Please make this client's case a **priority**.

請將這位客戶的案子列為 priority。

1193 **privacy** [ˈpraɪvəsɪ] *n.*　　　　　　　　隱私

例 Employees don't have much **privacy** because the offices have glass walls.

因為辦公室有玻璃牆，所以員工沒有什麼 privacy 可言。

1194 **promise** [ˈprɑmɪs] *v.*　　　　　　　承諾，保證

例 I **promised** my client I would meet him in the morning.

我向客戶 promised 我早上會跟他碰面。

Chapter 10
法務與稅務

重新考慮　　1195 **reconsider** [ˌrikənˈsɪdə˞] *v.*

☐ 例 I hope you will **reconsider** our offer.

☐ 　我希望你能 reconsider 我們的提議。

代表　　　1196 **represent** [ˌrɛprɪˈzɛnt] *v.*

☐ 例 It isn't a good idea to **represent** yourself in court.

☐ 　在法庭上 represent 你自己並不是個好主意。

壓力　　　1197 **stress** [strɛs] *n.*

☐ 例 Court battles can cause a lot of **stress**.

☐ 　法庭上的攻防戰會帶來很大的 stress。

緊張　　　1198 **stressful** [ˈstrɛsfəl] *adj.*

☐ 例 The situation was **stressful** for all involved.

☐ 　對所有關係人來說，情況令人 stressful。

3 Tax 稅務 ㉙

優勢　　　1199 **advantage** [ədˈvæntɪdʒ] *n.*

☐ 例 The luxury tax provides an apparent **advantage**
☐ 　 to self-occupancy in the real estate market.

　奢侈稅提供房地產市場中的自住客表面上的
　advantage。

總額　　　1200 **amount** [əˈmaʊnt] *n.*

☐ 例 What **amount** do I owe the government?

☐ 　我欠政府多少 amount？

☆ 1201 **audit** [ˈɔdɪt] *v.*　　査帳，查核

　　例 The company will be **audited** at the end of the month.

　　公司月底要 audited。

1202 **authority** [əˈθɔrətɪ] *n.*　　權，職權

　　例 The judge has the **authority** to decide on the penalty.

　　法官有 authority 決定罰款的金額。

1203 **authorize** [ˈɔθəˌraɪz] *v.*　　授權

　　例 I did not **authorize** these charges on my credit card.

　　我沒有 authorize 用信用卡支付這些費用。

1204 **calculate** [ˈkælkjəˌlet] *v.*　　計算

　　例 My accountant made a mistake when **calculating** my taxes.

　　我的會計師在 calculating 我的稅金時弄錯了。

1205 **citizen** [ˈsɪtəzn̩] *n.*　　公民

　　例 All **citizens** must pay tax.

　　所有的 citizens 皆需納稅。

1206 **claim** [klem] *v.*　　申報

　　例 You must **claim** the amount of money you made when you file your income tax.

　　在申報所得稅時，你必須 claim 所得總額。

Chapter 10
法務與稅務

客戶

1207 **client** [ˈklaɪənt] *n.*

☐ 例 The accountant does taxes for all of his **clients**.
☐ 會計師替他所有的 clients 處理稅務。

佣金

1208 **commission** [kəˈmɪʃən] *n.*

☐ 例 People who work in sales must claim the money
☐ they make on **commissions**.
業務從業人員必須申報 commissions 所得。

扣減

1209 **deduct** [dɪˈdʌkt] *v.*

☐ 例 The company **deducted** too much tax from my
☐ pay.
公司從我的收入中 deducted 了太多的稅。

到期

1210 **due** [dju] *adj.*

☐ 例 Tax returns are **due** at the end of the month.
☐ 退稅這個月底 due。

經濟的

1211 **economic** [ˌikəˈnɑmɪk] *adj.*

☐ 例 The entire country is going through tough
☐ **economic** times.
整個國家正經歷 economic 艱困時期。

經濟

1212 **economy** [ɪˈkɑnəmɪ] *n.*

☐ 例 The bad **economy** is causing stress for lot of
☐ people.
economy 不振讓許多人感到壓力。

1213 financial [faɪˋnænʃəl] *adj.*

例 The company's **financial** security depends on the success of this product.

公司的 financial 安全取決於產品的成功。

財務的；金融的

1214 government [ˋgʌvɚmənt] *n.*

例 The **government** audits people at random.

Government 隨機查帳。

政府

1215 impose [ɪmˋpoz] *v.*

例 Higher taxes are **imposed** on people who have high incomes.

高所得者要 imposed 較高的稅。

課徵

1216 insurance [ɪnˋʃʊrəns] *n.*

例 It is important to purchase home **insurance**.

買房屋 insurance 是很重要的。

保險

1217 penalty [ˋpɛnḷtɪ] *n.*

例 You will have to pay a **penalty** if you file your taxes late.

如果太晚報稅，你得付 penalty。

罰金

1218 property [ˋprɑpɚtɪ] *n.*

例 **Property** taxes downtown are really high.

市區的 property 稅真的很高。

房地產

Chapter 10

法務與稅務

☆ 代扣，代繳 | 1219 **remit** [rɪˋmɪt] *v.*

　　□ 例 Employers must **remit** income taxes from their
　　□ 　　 employees' income.
　　　　 雇主必須從員工的收入中 remit 所得稅。

增加，提高 | 1220 **rise** [raɪz] *v.*

　　□ 例 Income taxes are expected to **rise** this year.
　　□ 　　 今年的所得稅預期會 rise。

提交，呈遞 | 1221 **submit** [səbˋmɪt] *v.*

　　□ 例 Don't forget to **submit** your taxes by the
　　□ 　　 deadline.
　　　　 別忘了在截止日前 submit 報稅。

☆ 關稅 | 1222 **tariff** [ˋtærɪf] *n.*

　　□ 例 We need to pay a **tariff** on all imported
　　□ 　　 merchandise.
　　　　 所有進口的商品都必須付 tariff。

稅 | 1223 **tax** [tæks] *n.*

　　□ 例 There is no sales **tax** on clothing in that country.
　　□ 　　 該國不課徵衣服的銷售 tax。

稅捐機關 | 1224 **tax authority** [ˋtæks əˏθɔrətɪ] *n. phr.*

　　□ 例 The **tax authority** is investigating our company
　　□ 　　 finances.
　　　　 Tax authority 正在調查我們公司的財務。

1225 **tax revenue** [ˈtæks ˌrɛvənju] *n. phr.*　　　税收

　　例 A lot of the country's **tax revenue** goes to
　　　 health care.

　　　國家的 tax revenue 很多用於醫療保健。

1226 **tendency** [ˈtɛndənsɪ] *n.*　　　傾向，習慣

　　例 I have a **tendency** to wait until the last minute
　　　 to file my taxes.

　　　我有等到最後一刻才要報稅的 tendency。

1227 **violation** [ˌvaɪəˈleʃən] *n.*　　　違法行為

　　例 The company is being charged with several tax
　　　 violations.

　　　該公司因數件稅務 violations 遭起訴。

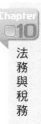

Chapter
10
法
務
與
稅
務

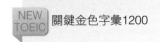
Exercises

請從選項中，選出最適當的答案完成句子。

B 1. The words lawyer and _____ are synonyms; they mean roughly the same.

(A) practitioner (B) attorney (C) layman (D) intern

A 2. The police found the stolen car abandoned by a river, and called the owner to _____ it.

(A) claim (B) pronounce (C) compliment (D) raise

A 3. The _____ told his lawyer that he wanted an end to the lawsuit.

(A) client (B) agent (C) informer (D) obsessed

C 4. After Pearl Harbor, the US _____ war on Japan.

(A) claimed (B) announced (C) declared (D) determined

D 5. My parents told me not to make _____ that I can't keep.

(A) comments (B) judgments (C) decisions (D) promises

A 6. Being the best salesperson, Jessie will _____ the company at the national conference.

(A) represent (B) suppress (C) introduce (D) inform

B 7. If you do something wrong such as breaking the law, you will have to pay a _____.

(A) ticket (B) penalty (C) punishment (D) payment

AC 8. I am under no _____ to help you, but for old time's sake, I will help you one last time.

(A) obligation (B) duty (C) responsibility (D) entertainment

D 9. My driver's license _____ on my birthday; I have to renew it.

(A) provokes (B) despises (C) inspires (D) expires

A 10. People are more or less under _____; it is important that we learn how to deal with it so that it won't cause much harm.

(A) stress (B) frustration (C) setback (D) inflation

11. I have worked out a solution to the company's financial problems. I
    will _____ the solution to the president tomorrow.

    (A) submit   (B) yield   (C) postpone   (D) tease

12. If you are married, you have a _____ to your spouse; faithful-
    ness, that is.

    (A) restoration   (B) commitment   (C) conservation   (D) reservation

13. After I brainstormed, I was able to write a _____, which later
    became a full essay.

    (A) abstract   (B) briefing   (C) scribble   (D) draft

14. There is a _____ for dogs to have their own way; it is essen-
    tial that the owner demonstrate leadership so their pets know what
    to follow.

    (A) certainty   (B) continuity   (C) tendency   (D) responsibility

15. Without the applicant's _____, the application is not valid.

    (A) signature   (B) symbol   (C) metaphor   (D) significance

16. My teacher said I had to _____ my composition because it
    was poorly organized.

    (A) resume   (B) revise   (C) contain   (D) constrain

17. The owners of the company decided to continue their _____
    by signing a contract.

    (A) scholarship   (B) citizenship   (C) censorship   (D) partnership

18. Since the new law took effect, there have been very few _____.
    People must like it or else they are naturally law-abiding.

    (A) violations   (B) intentions   (C) indications   (D) implications

19. My lease is due next week, so I have to _____ it in order to
    continue living in this nice apartment.

    (A) return   (B) reverse   (C) revise   (D) renew

20. It's hard trying to take advantage of Jim; he is a _____ busi-
    nessman.

    (A) inspecting   (B) calculating   (C) circulating   (D) transp

Chapter
10
測
驗
練
習

267

REVIEW 5

I Photographs (42)

Look at the pictures below and listen to the statements. Then choose the statement that best describes what you see in the picture.

1. (A) (B) (C) (D)   2. (A) (B) (C) (D)

II Conversations (43)

You will hear a conversation between two people. Listen to the conversation and answer the questions below.

Questions 3-5

3. What are the people talking about?
   (A) Product prices.   (B) Delivery options and fees.
   (C) A customer complaint.   (D) Ordering online.

4. When will a product be delivered that was ordered at 2 pm?

  (A) Within 15 minutes.

  (B) By 5 pm the same day.

  (C) Between 5 and 6 pm the same day.

  (D) The next day.

5. What does the company charge for regular delivery if the order is more than $100?

  (A) No charge.

  (B) $5

  (C) $10

  (D) It depends on the exact price of the order.

III Short Talks (44)

You will hear two short talks given by a single speaker. Listen to the short talks and answer the questions below.

Questions 6-8

6. Who is the speaker talking to?

  (A) The board of directors.   (B) Laboratory workers.

  (C) Company employees.   (D) His boss.

7. What is said about the new badges?

  (A) They must be worn at all times.

  (B) They only need to be worn in the laboratory.

  (C) In order to receive a badge, employees need to submit a request.

  (D) The loss of a badge must be reported to the Research and Development Department.

8. What is said about the laboratory?

  (A) It is accessible to all employees.

  (B) You need your badge with a magnetic strip to open the door to the laboratory.

  (C) You need written authorization to use the lab.

  (D) You need to make a request 90 minutes before entering the lab.

Questions 9-11

9. What type of announcement is this?
    (A) A safety warning.   (B) An advertisement.
    (C) A press release.   (D) A lab report.

10. How does the sunscreen work?
    (A) By getting under the skin. (B) By having a strong effect on skin.
    (C) By combining chemicals.   (D) By covering the skin's cells.

11. Why is it safer than other sunscreens?
    (A) It is made of non-allergenic ingredients.
    (B) It has been tested on lab animals.
    (C) It is made of new chemicals.
    (D) It is convenient to apply.

IV Reading Comprehension

You will read a text followed by several questions. Select the best answer for each question and circle the letter (A), (B), (C), or (D).

Questions 12-14 refer to the following email.

Mr. Kimura:

I am writing this to ask you a favor. Remember those designs you began last year and then gave to me to work on?

Well, I decided that I like them just as they are, so I plan to use them in the upcoming fashion show, giving you full credit. I know you told me I could use them however I want, but the lawyers at my company want me to get a signed statement from you.

I am sorry for any trouble this may cause you. Lawyers always want everything to be so official. In order to save you time and energy, I have written a first draft of the short document and attached it to this email. The show is next week, so could you sign it and send it back to me as soon as possible?

As always, thanks for everything.

Samantha Bird

Review
05

測
驗
練
習

12. What does Samantha want Mr. Kimura to do?

(A) Give her some fashion designs.

(B) Confirm that she has permission to use his designs.

(C) Send her designs back to her.

(D) Call her company lawyer.

13. Why does Samantha need him to hurry with the request?

(A) Because the lawyers insist on getting it immediately.

(B) Because they need it before the show.

(C) Because it has to be official.

(D) Because last time, his response was too slow.

14. What is attached to the email?

(A) A document written by Samantha.

(B) A letter from the lawyers.

(C) A picture of the designs.

(D) A signed statement.

V Text Completion

Read the text that follows. A word or phrase is missing in some of the sentences. For each blank, four answer choices are given. Select the best answer to complete the text.

Stanford University, the University of California in Berkeley, and the University of Michigan have all signed (15)_____ authorizing Google to scan books from their libraries.
The librarians say the initiative can give new life to books that have been forgotten.

However, there is some (16)_____ surrounding Google's project. Digitizing current books whose (17)_____ holders are known is not in dispute. Neither is digitizing older books whose copyrights have expired. Problems arise over digitizing books that are out of print and still under copyright, but the current holder of that copyright is unknown. Selling digital copies of those books could become (18)_____, and there are questions over who will get those profits.

Google (19)_____ the project is about more than money. A spokesperson said the greatest (20)_____ for Google and for all Internet users would come from improving its search system.

15. (A) lawsuits   (B) inspections   (C) damages   (D) agreements
16. (A) controversy (B) prosperity   (C) motive   (D) regulation
17. (A) design   (B) infringement (C) patent   (D) copyright
18. (A) profitable   (B) accessible   (C) debatable   (D) gratifying
19. (A) claims   (B) denies   (C) enforces   (D) provokes
20. (A) revenue   (B) benefit   (C) damages   (D) innovation

Answer Key

Chapter 1

Exercises (p.28)

1. D	2. D	3. A	4. A	5. C
6. C	7. C	8. B	9. B	10. A
11. B	12. C	13. D	14. D	15. A
16. C	17. B	18. D	19. A	20. C

Chapter 2

Exercises (p.46)

1. executive	2. advice
3. position	4. staff
5. founder	6. branch
7. secretary	8. division

Chapter 3

Exercises (p.95)

1. D	2. B	3. C	4. C	5. B
6. A	7. D	8. C	9. A	10. D
11. B	12. A	13. B	14. C	15. B
16. D	17. A	18. B	19. C	20. B

Chapter 4

Exercises (p.121)

1. A	2. B	3. D	4. A	5. B
6. B	7. C	8. C	9. C	10. B
11. A	12. B	13. C	14. B	15. C
16. D	17. A	18. B	19. D	20. A

Chapter 5

Exercises (p.157)

1. D	2. B	3. C	4. D	5. A
6. B	7. B	8. D	9. A	10. B
11. B	12. D	13. A	14. B	15. B
16. A	17. A	18. B	19. A	20. C

Chapter 6

Exercises (p.179)

1. C	2. C	3. C	4. A	5. B
6. B	7. C	8. A	9. C	10. D
11. D	12. D	13. B	14. A	15. C
16. A	17. D	18. C	19. B	20. D

Chapter 7

Exercises (p.200)

1. A	2. D	3. C	4. C	5. A
6. A	7. A	8. A	9. B	10. B
11. B	12. D	13. D	14. A	15. A
16. C	17. A	18. B	19. C	20. B

Chapter 8

Exercises (p.219)

1. A	2. C	3. B	4. B	5. B
6. B	7. A	8. C	9. D	10. B
11. A	12. B	13. C	14. C	15. B
16. B	17. D	18. B	19. A	20. D

Chapter 9

Exercises (p.248)

1. C	2. B	3. A	4. C	5. A
6. D	7. C	8. C	9. A	10. A
11. A	12. B	13. C	14. A	15. C
16. D	17. B	18. B	19. A	20. B

Chapter 10

Exercises (p.266)

1. B	2. A	3. A	4. C	5. D
6. A	7. B	8. A	9. D	10. A
11. A	12. B	13. D	14. C	15. A
16. B	17. D	18. A	19. D	20. C

Answer key

測
驗
解
答

Review 1

I. Photographs (p.47)

Picture 1

(A) People are giving away free food.

(B) People are asking about job opportunities.

(C) The woman on the right is wearing a mini skirt.

(D) They are at a fancy dress party.

Picture 2

(A) A ship is picking up passengers.

(B) There is a beach volleyball competition going on.

(C) A man is flying a kite on the beach.

(D) Many people are sunbathing on the beach.

II. Conversations (p.47)

Questions 3-5

(Man)	So according to your résumé, you worked at Sunray Industries for two and a half years. Can you tell me about your work there?
(Woman)	Yes, I was a manager for new projects.
(Man)	Tell me about that. What kinds of things did you do?
(Woman)	Well, I made contact with our target company and discussed business opportunities with them. Then, after

	I had learned more about their abilities, I prepared and suggested new project plans.

Questions 6-7

(Woman)	I'm afraid we'll be late for the concert on Friday evening. The traffic in town is always heavy on Friday nights.
(Man)	Can you take this Friday off? Then we can leave early and avoid the traffic jam.
(Woman)	That might be hard. My boss is really strict. If we want to take leave, we have to give notice at least two weeks in advance.
(Man)	Well, see if you can just take the afternoon off.

III. Short Talks (p.48)

Questions 8-9

You sent in your résumé and you got a job interview. Now you have to make sure that you get what you want from the interview. Many people say it is best to tell the interviewer what he or she wants to hear. However, this is not good advice. You might get a job that is not suitable for you. Your answers at an interview should always be truthful. By showing respect and selfconfidence, you will make the employer believe that you are the best person for the job.

Questions 10-11

Good morning, everyone. As you know, our baseball club has interviewed several candidates to be our next manager. Today, I am pleased to announce that Michael Hunter is the new manager of the Johnstown Bears. Michael was a player for the Bears and has been our coach for the last two years. Michael is well-liked by the organization and brings a lot of experience. Ladies and gentlemen, please welcome Michael Hunter.

Answer keys

1. B	2. D	3. A	4. B	5. C
6. D	7. C	8. B	9. A	10. A
11. B	12. D	13. B	14. A	15. B
16. C	17. D	18. A	19. B	20. C
21. B	22. D	23. B	24. C	25. A
26. B	27. D	28. B		

Review 2

I. Photographs (p.123)

Picture 1

(A) The men are playing chess.

(B) The men are having a meeting.

(C) The man on the left is reading through his glasses.

(D) The men are in the middle of a presentation.

Picture 2

(A) People are boarding the train.

(B) A woman is getting off the train.

(C) This is an underground platform.

(D) There are advertisements on the side of the train.

II. Conversations (p.123)

Questions 3-4

(Man)	I know you aren't getting along with Claire, but please don't be so obvious about it.
(Woman)	It's really hard to be polite. She's so talkative. She distracts me from my work.
(Man)	I understand. But she looked really sad this morning. Just try to be nice.
(Woman)	Alright. I'll go apologize to her later.

Questions 5-6

(Woman)	You look a bit uneasy today. Is anything wrong?
(Man)	The managers from the head office will arrive in one hour, and I have to make an important presentation in the meeting.
(Woman)	Is there anything I can do for you?
(Man)	Could you listen to my presentation now and tell me what you think of it?

Answer key

測
驗
解
答

277

III. Short Talks (p.124)

Questions 7-8

We have had a lot of complaints about noise in the office. The main causes of this problem are people talking loudly on the phone or shouting to others to get their attention. Sometimes the sound on people's computers is also too loud. To create a better working environment for everybody, please try to be thoughtful of others. If you need to talk to someone, go over to their desk, instead of yelling across the room.

Questions 9-10

Thank you all for coming to this department meeting. In the last year and a half, we have seen the number of our customers decrease by 15 percent. Of that 15 percent, half came from our 25 biggest customers. We're here today to discuss what we can do to make sure that we are keeping our customers happy.

Answer keys

1. B	2. D	3. D	4. C	5. C
6. A	7. C	8. D	9. D	10. C
11. D	12. A	13. B	14. C	15. B
16. C	17. B	18. D	19. C	20. B
21. C	22. A	23. C	24. A	25. D
26. B	27. C	28. B		

Review 3

I. Photographs (p.181)

Picture 1

(A) People are waiting on the platform.

(B) The bus is departing.

(C) The train has arrived at the station.

(D) The man is carrying a suitcase.

Picture 2

(A) The people are having a picnic.

(B) The award ceremony has started.

(C) The man is proposing a toast.

(D) They are sitting outdoors.

II. Conversations (p.181)

Questions 3-4

(Woman)	Would you like a hotel room near the airport or would you prefer one downtown?
(Man)	What do you suggest?
(Woman)	You're leaving on an early morning flight and downtown traffic can be really bad at that time.
(Man)	OK, I'll follow your recommendation then.

Questions 5-6

(Woman)	How are you going to take all that luggage on an airplane?
(Man)	I'm not flying. I'm taking a train.

(Woman)	What a good idea! Sure, it takes longer, but the scenery should be worth it.
(Man)	Yes. I always take the train because it's better for the environment.

III. Short Talks (p.182)

Questions 7-8

Those of you on your morning drive to work need to be aware that a section of Route 101 has been closed. It seems that a truck carrying chemicals overturned about 15 minutes ago. Police are directing traffic away from the scene. At this time, we don't know what caused the accident, but it looks as if it will take some time to clean up. If that is your normal route, we suggest you make a detour via Andersen Parkway. We'll let you know when the situation has cleared up. And now we'll go over to Dave in the studio for the 8:00 am weather report.

Questions 9-10

To your left, we are passing the St. Monique district. This is a famous artists' community. As you can see, there are many painters still at work in some studios along this street. Even so, many of these former studios have now been converted into small art galleries. Now, follow me as we are going to stop and have some coffee at one of the cafés that many famous artists frequented to exchange ideas and recite poetry.

Answer keys

1. C	2. D	3. B	4. B	5. D
6. D	7. B	8. C	9. A	10. C
11. B	12. A	13. B	14. D	15. B
16. C	17. C	18. D	19. C	20. D
21. C	22. A	23. B	24. A	25. B
26. B	27. A	28. A	29. C	

Review 4

I. Photographs (p.221)

Picture 1

(A) The woman is holding a receipt.

(B) The woman is waiting to be served.

(C) The man is standing in line.

(D) The man is carrying a box.

Picture 2

(A) The women are in a restaurant.

(B) The shop is full of customers.

(C) The woman is at the checkout.

(D) The boy is buying candy.

II. Conversations (p.221)

Questions 3-4

(Woman)	This client's bill is overdue. The payment was due a month ago.
(Man)	Have you sent him a notice?
(Woman)	I've already sent him two.
(Man)	This is a frequent customer. We've never had problems before. Try calling him to find out what's going on.

Answer key

測
驗
解
答

Questions 5-6

(Woman)	This phone bill is much more expensive than last month's, yet we actually made fewer longdistance phone calls.
(Man)	I know. If you look at the bill, they added some new fees they never told us about.
(Woman)	This is ridiculous. They could have at least informed us in advance. I think we should start looking for a new provider.

III. Short Talks (p.222)

Questions 7-8

Three days ago, the accounting department released the financial statement for last year. As expected, the numbers reflect a serious downturn. The economic crisis is affecting each region of the country. We have no way of knowing when the economy will begin picking up again. Therefore, the president has called this emergency meeting in order to come up with some ideas on how to cut back on spending. We're open to any suggestions.

Answer keys

1. A	2. C	3. C	4. A	5. A
6. D	7. C	8. D	9. B	10. B
11. B	12. C	13. B	14. A	15. D
16. A	17. C	18. C	19. A	20. A
21. B	22. D	23. B	24. B	25. C
26. B	27. D	28. C		

Review 5

I. Photographs (p.269)

Picture 1

(A) She is pushing a shopping cart.

(B) She is using a hand-held device to take inventory.

(C) She is moving boxes in the warehouse.

(D) She is distributing products.

Picture 2

(A) They are leaving the premises.

(B) They are investigating a patent infringement.

(C) They are wearing hairnets.

(D) The man on the right is interfering with their work.

II. Conversations (p.269)

Questions 3-5

(Woman)	Hello, I'm calling to ask whether your company provides same-day delivery.
(Man)	Yes, we do. We provide same-day delivery for all products that we have in stock. Products ordered before noon can be received by 5:00 pm.
(Woman)	I see. Is there an additional fee for same-day delivery?
(Man)	We deliver your order to you at no cost if the total value of your order exceeds $100. For all other orders, we

charge $5 for regular delivery and $10 for same-day delivery.

III. Short Talks (p.270)

Questions 6-8

Good morning, and thank you for coming today. I have some important announcements to make. Starting next month, new photo identification badges with a magnetic strip on them will be distributed to all employees. This badge must be visible at all times while you are on company property. Lost or misplaced badges must be reported immediately to the Personnel Department.

In addition, the entire Research and Development section of the main building will be accessible only to authorized laboratory employees. Should you be required to enter that area, a request must be made to division staff at least 90 minutes prior to your desired entry time. Thank you for your cooperation.

Questions 9-11

Now that summer is finally here, we are proud to announce the launch of a new sunscreen that will make your time out in the sun safer than ever before.
Some sunscreens contain chemicals, which may have an effect on more sensitive skin, but our sunscreen is made of safe ingredients. Lab tests have shown that it does not cause allergic reactions.

Major active ingredients include natural plant extracts and anti-oxidants ground so fine that these ingredients actually cover your skin at a microscopic level, not letting the sun's rays come in contact with your skin cells. No other sunscreen will keep your skin healthier and younger-looking.

Answer keys

1. B	2. C	3. B	4. D	5. A
6. C	7. A	8. D	9. B	10. D
11. A	12. B	13. B	14. A	15. D
16. A	17. D	18. A	19. A	20. B

Answer key
測
驗
解
答